A Forest of Fear

Ken Palmrose

A Forest of Fear

Crossroads Publishing, LLC—620-204-1710

ISBN: 979-8-9926485-1-5

Author Ken Palmrose

Cover Design Ken Palmrose

Edited by Elizabeth Morquecho

Preface

This is Ben's story. Drafted into the Vietnam War, he fought for his country with determination and pride. Returning home as a Vietnam Veteran, Ben was sure the exciting chapters in his life were behind him, but he was wrong. Years after his homecoming, Ben would be drafted a second time. This time, by a unique team bent on fighting urban criminals encroaching upon rural America. From the jungle palms to the western pines, Ben finds himself on a lonely bus to Oregon where he embarks upon an exciting and dangerous 25-year outdoor adventure that will change his life forever.

Dedication

This book is dedicated to the hard-working men and women who help manage and protect America's public lands, parks, and forests. It is also dedicated to those Vietnam Veterans whose stories are seldom heard.

Crossroads Publishing, LLC
Thankful For
Those Who Have Served in the
Military and Their Sacrifices Made

The Early Years

Chapter 1

Ben Hautenan's gaze roamed the dark, half-empty bus heading east. *What am I doing?* The thought slammed him, but he knew the answer. He was leaving home on a gray dog going nowhere.

His homecoming from Vietnam hung like a warm memory in his soul—he could still feel the arms of his family wrapped tight around him as they welcomed him back to American soil. Despite this, he knew it was time. At the end of this journey, a job awaited him which most could only dream of. Sure, there were more glamorous paths he could have chosen, but Forest Management was somewhere he could make a difference in the world—as he had in Vietnam. His hopes were set on making a career of it. This would be his first full-time, paying job outside his military service. Thanks to his veteran status, he had a higher chance of becoming a permanent employee than a temporary one.

As the bus headed away from Sisu Bay, Ben stretched across an empty row of seats in the back. *I hope this is all worth it.* The bus ride was proving to be boring and uncomfortable. He shifted, but the hard-worn leather seats were nothing compared to his bed. The bus was hot and clammy. Telling himself to suck it up since the trip would take all night, he adjusted his hat and thought about the town where he was headed. A town smaller than his neighborhood. He looked forward to working in the Blue Hills National Forest. It would sure beat working in the woods as a logger like most of his family did. Yeah, things were finally looking up. His forestry degree had taken two years to complete, and he'd spent fourteen months in Nam. It was time to reap the benefits of all that hard work.

Giving up on sleep, Ben sat up and stared at the passengers traveling with him. *What a group of characters.* He snorted. *Check out that old guy up front…*He stared harder at the man and guessed him to be in his late 70's or early 80's. Sporting a scraggly beard, his stringy, white hair peeked out from beneath a well-worn, dirty-brown baseball cap. It was obvious Arthritis had seized the old, bony hands clutching a brown paper bag. Ben smirked at the sight of the booze bottle peeking out. When the man unscrewed the top and the bus began to reek of cheap wine, Ben scrunched up his nose as he attempted to guess which horrible brand he was drinking. Super chicken? Mad Dog? Whatever it was, had heads turning every time the old boy took a hit.

Reminding himself he would change buses in Centerville in about three hours, Ben continued his perusal of his fellow occupants. *Geez, he thought, could the guy behind me snore any louder? And what are they doing? They could get arrested for that!* He couldn't tear his eyes from the couple two rows ahead of him. A young hippie-looking guy with long, black hair and a short beard was nuzzled next to a beautiful, young redhead who appeared a lot younger. *Is she even of legal age? I am not a prude,* Ben continued his musings, *but crap! They both need to take a cold shower.*

Ben watched in horror as the guy snaked his hand up the girl's skirt. Snorting, he rolled his eyes. *This young redhead is practically holding her skirt open like my old Grandma's front gate in an invitation!*

When the couple began making out like they were at home, Ben started to squirm. Anyone within eyesight of the two could see them touching parts of each other that usually never see the light of day.

"Okay," Ben said aloud, raking a hand down his face. *Let's get this bus moving a little faster so I can transfer to the Trailways and escape this freak show!*

"Look at those two," the guy behind him whispered. "If he undresses her any further, I'm heading up front."

Unable to take any more, Ben pulled his hat low over his face and shut his eyes, crossing his arms in front of him. *How did I get stuck with this group?* he grumbled to himself. *I have no desire to know those two hippies on an intimate level. The slogan 'Leave the Driving to Us' is a joke. With the smell of wine mixing with those two sweating all over each other, the miles are longer—not shorter.*

However, Ben smiled, *I will say they are definitely a lot more athletic between the seats than anyone else on the bus.*

Raising his hat above his eyes, Ben glanced at the older gentleman driving the bus and was reminded of the first time he saw someone who looked like him—a Negro, or a Black man as some liked to be called. Ben had grown up in the essentially all-white, coastal resort of Sisu Bay. But, getting drafted changed all that. This bus driver reminded him of another bus driver. The one who had taken the newly sworn-in draftees to the old North Fort section of Fort Clark. He, too, was a Negro and always had a big smile and a friendly hello.

In a flash, Ben was back in basic training. The stern, athletic-looking, black drill instructor went by the name of Sgt. Wiford.

4

Despite being only five-foot-seven, this man could yell a dozen consecutive orders without ever taking a breath. He'd had everyone lined up, gear in hand, marching off to their barracks in a matter of seconds after disembarking from the bus. Every one of them was scared to death of Wilford, and he knew it.

Although Ben remembered everything about his eight weeks of basic training, one specific day was burned into his memory more than the others. He could still hear Sgt. Wilford yelling:

"Listen up, you whiney cry-babies, and pay attention to what I'm about to tell you! From now on no one—I repeat no one—is to go past those red posts halfway down the parade grounds. You are not going anywhere but your barracks and dayroom without my permission. Is that understood?"

The warning had been firmer than usual, eliciting a somber chorus of "Sir, yes, sir!" from the group, though no one understood his warning until two nights later when a recruit blurted, "Look at the barracks across the grounds! What's going on?"

Everyone had scrambled to the window of the dayroom to watch as several men, dressed in strange military gear, stacked bedding, mattresses, and other items onto a huge pile that must have been 50

5

mattresses high. The spectators' eyes had been huge when one of the officers poured gas onto the pile and set the mountain on fire. Ben had guessed the flames were at least 50 feet high and, by that time, everyone in the barracks was glued to the windows to watch the show

"What's going on? Anyone have a clue?" one of the recruits asked.

Sgt. Wilford crossed his arms and leaned against the doorjam, his eyes surveying his crew. "I may as well tell you. The news will be broadcasting it tonight anyway." His voice was quiet and contemplative, drawing the attention of the men. "We're confined to this side of the grounds because of a serious disease outbreak. Several cases of spinal meningitis were confirmed in those barracks. Everything must be decontaminated, cleansed, or burned to make the barracks and grounds safe for training again. Five members of one training platoon were taken to the hospital two weeks ago." Wilford dropped his gaze. "They didn't make it. This disease is devastating and deadly. You girls had better remember your order is to stay away."
****

The bus hit a pothole, startling Ben from his dreams. Rubbing the sleep from his eyes, he stretched as much as the seating allowed,

6

irritated when his legs hit the seat in front of him. He'd been having more dreams and flashbacks of service years and found himself plagued by some of the memories. Back in boot camp, it had been a roll of the dice whether he'd even make it through. Some hadn't and had been forced to return home.

A half hour and a Charlie-Horse later, relief washed through Ben as the lights of Centerville shone through the windshield. It was finally time to switch buses and get the last leg of this trip over with. Yawning, he glanced at his watch and sighed. One A.M. He was exhausted and looking forward to stretching out on a bed.

"Holy crap, look at that dump we are stopping at! That's the worst-looking cafe I've ever seen," a passenger up front exclaimed as the driver parked the bus. "Damned if I am going to eat anything they're serving!"

A lone light flickered outside the run-down café—the only light working in the village. From the looks of the bug carnage clinging to it, Ben assumed it drew every moth within a hundred miles. Centerville wasn't just dead center in the state, it was also deader than a doornail. As he stepped out of the bus and glanced at his surroundings, he raised a brow. It seemed Centerville had been abandoned, aside from the café, gas station, a run-down, motor hotel, and a few ramshackle houses.

As the old driver unloaded the suitcases for those transferring buses, fifteen passengers stumbled sleepily off the bus for their middle-of-the-night rest-stop. The next leg of their journey east would last another four or five hours.

Ben bemoaned the fact that, in a car, the remaining trip would take only two, maybe two-and-a-half hours. But the bus was obligated to slow down for a thousand curves and stop at every village and gas station as its route wound through hills and mountains for the remaining hours.

Ben followed the crowd, noticing that the old geezer had ditched his brown paper bag somewhere along the way and had joined the young couple who had managed to untangle themselves long enough to step off the bus.

The café housed two rows of three hand-made, picnic tables complete with wooden benches on each side. They were draped with tablecloths, except they weren't *really* tablecloths at all, but rather some kind of fancy-grade, off-white, butcher paper tacked down. The "fancy" tablecloths looked like they'd been there for more than one sloppy meal. The discolored paper sported ketchup stains and brown coffee cup rings, joined by a dead bug or two.

Abruptly, the owner appeared from the tiny kitchen and approached his guests. He flipped several one-page menus on each table like a card shark dealing bad poker hands. Ben took one look at this 'cook' and marveled. This guy could be the cook in Chaucer's Canterbury Tales, one of his favorite classics from high school English. With matted, brown hair all crumpled in a greasy mess, Ben had no doubt he had probably just rolled out of bed, or off a cot from somewhere in the back room. This fat, old guy, with his dirty apron barely covering his oversized gut could have been right out of the novel, large face—sores and all.

The menu had a few sandwiches, hamburgers, and fries. There were also a couple of choices of soft drinks and shakes.

Ben watched as the hippie-looking dude leaned close and whispered to his young girlfriend, "I am not eating anything that greasy-looking, fat slob touches."

She looked at him and whispered back, "Shh, he might hear you. I don't think he'd like you calling him those names."

He ended up ordering her a bag of chips and a coke, and a 7-Up for himself.

Everyone sighed with relief when the pops were delivered in cans rather than out of the filthy, stained soda fountain.

Nobody ate much. Most ordered ham and cheese sandwiches with way-too-warm mayonnaise and mustard. Several commented about the possibility of food poisoning, while others were too tired and hungry to care. Ben settled on chips and a drink, not excited at the possibility of getting sick on a bus as it wound its way through the mountains. One glance at his fellow, eastbound travel companions told him they had entertained the same thought.

****

An hour later, Ben climbed aboard the Trailways for the last part of the trip, fighting exhaustion as it weighed down his steps. Only a few passengers were boarded with him, and he was grateful the bus would be less crowded. This bus smelled better than the last, and it rode ten times smoother. Without a word, the passengers stretched out in their rows of seats, settling in for a short snooze.

Much better, Ben thought as his eyes began to droop. As the bus jolted down the highway, however, Ben quickly realized sleep was not in his near future. Finally, after fitful attempts to doze, Ben saw the sun peeking over a jagged mountaintop. Sitting up straight and leaning against his window, his breath caught in his lungs as he stared out over the most beautiful river canyons he'd ever seen. This last canyon bottom, surrounded by steep, rocky walls on both sides, reached up to higher peaks and seemed to stretch forever.

As the sun continued to rise, its bright, narrow, golden rays breaking across the sky as it rose over the top of a nearby mountain range, Ben began to think. *Man, I've seen a lot of sunsets over the ocean back home, but nothing like this sunrise.* He watched in awe as the bright colors hit the canyon walls and changed the rock formation hues from dark to light brown, at times appearing golden as the sun rose higher.

Up ahead, he caught the first glimpse of barns and rooftops. In the distance, a row of streetlights was beginning to shut off as the sun shone brighter. *Not many lights,* Ben thought. Back home in Sisu Bay, the town lit up like a carnival. But in this small, sleepy town resembling something out of a John Wayne movie, the streetlights were few and far between.

The canyon bottom widened as the bus approached Riverton, and the walls gave way to wide green fields divided by barbed-wire fences. The green, fertile valley seemed to stretch for miles, and all the pastures were full of horses, cattle, sheep, deer, and antelope. He had never seen so many antelopes scurrying through the fields in the midst of herds of cattle.

Chapter 2

Riverton, at last. Ben surveyed the town as the bus entered its city limits. To the left was the local drive-in theater, followed by a couple of sawmills, one with a huge millpond giving way to small pastures around the houses. He stretched his aching muscles and yawned. He'd endured twelve hours, two buses, 11 towns, and a ton of weird people to travel 350 miles to a strange, new town. Though it beat putting miles on his truck and spending his hard-earned money on gas, the trip had been hard on his butt, and he'd hardly gotten any sleep.

When the bus stopped in front of the local drug store, which doubled as the bus station, Ben searched for the District Timber forester who'd promised to pick him up between 6 and 7 AM and take him to the workstation.

Amongst the three people waiting in front of the bus stop, Ben spotted a guy in his 30s. Scrutinizing his appearance, he dismissed the possibility of him being any woodsman. *This guy can't be more than 5 foot 8,* he thought. *I'm skinny, but man, this guy is the slimmest.*

Stepping off the bus, Ben was surprised when the man walked toward him and extended his hand.

13

"Well, you're the only one under 25 on this bus, so I'm guessing you're Ben, my newest crew member—am I right?"

Ben stared at this strange man whose protruding eyeballs guarded an uncommonly large, hook nose. He was sporting a weird stare through what looked like his grandpa's gold, horned-rim glasses, and that skinny build.

"Yeah, that's me," Ben said. "Thanks for picking me up. There's no way I could afford to drive clear across the state and keep my truck with me during this summer's field season. I need to save all I can for the winter."

"John Parsons," the man said, shoving a hand toward Ben. "We're going to stop by the house first. Jeane is expecting us. She's got to head into her teaching job but wanted to make us a quick breakfast before she leaves."

"Great," Ben said. He hadn't been able to eat anything during the bus change in Centerville. A passenger had yelled at the fat cook and waitress about his can of Coke being flat and about too many flies fighting for their share of his sandwich and fries. After that, Ben abandoned his order on the table and got out of there. He was starving.

Once they'd grabbed Ben's military duffel bag—packed with almost everything he owned in this world—they headed over to John's place. It was located behind the local food market in a nice-sized, two-story frame, clapboard-sided house.

John tipped his head up, peering through his glasses at Ben over his large nose. "Not bad for only $65 per month, eh? I think we got a good deal. Most likely, it's because my wife teaches third grade, and I'm a Fed with a guaranteed paycheck. In this county, they don't much care for us Forest Resource managers and newcomers or, as the locals refer to us, 'untrustworthy transients.' They don't see us as capable of managing THEIR local forest. But" John added, "we earn good pay, and they know we won't skip out on paying our bills. Heck, if you aren't born and raised here, the locals think you have no business messing with their public lands." Glancing at Ben's tight features, he laughed. "It's not so bad once they get to know you, though. Usually, you won't have any problems. They just don't seem to like me for some reason."

He's a little strange, Ben thought to himself, *but I don't see a reason for the locals to dislike him...*

Little did he know, this was a question that would be answered before the end of the summer's field season.

Jeane welcomed them into the front room as they walked inside the sparsely furnished home. The room reminded Ben of a trailer house with cheap, grooved, imitation wood paneling. The paneling in the front room had been painted over, and every dent and crack showed through the rushed paint job. The furniture consisted of plain, worn, tan-colored material unfamiliar to Ben. The floor, covered in wall-to-wall, light brown, thick shag carpet, showed traffic paths like a trail cutting through the forest. A few lamps were scattered around the room, providing a minimal amount of light to brighten the place up and, in his opinion, it needed it.

In the corner, Ben spotted boxes of empty pop bottles, with other jars, bottles, and numerous small boxes full of random items.

John noticed Ben's puzzled look and grinned. "I turn everything into money. I grab and save anything I find that has value or a deposit. If it has value and I find it, it's more money in our bank account."

Chapter 3

After a nice breakfast and lots of good, strong coffee, John looked at Ben. "Let's head up the mountain. We need to be at the work center by 9:00AM to meet up with some of your new crew members and, of course, you gotta meet Randy, the camp boss up there. He's been there ever since he started college four years ago. The station is pretty much his domain. Just a word to the wise, he can be very ornery and doesn't take any crap from anyone."

****

The scenery along State Highway 39 held Ben captive. The mountain road ran alongside Mineral Creek, winding past old, abandoned mining claims with tailing piles everywhere. Shacks and a few isolated ranch houses had been strategically built high enough to avoid flooding at the bottom of the narrow canyon. A canyon that supposedly held more gold than anywhere else in the State.

The road abruptly curved around a sharp bend and started up a new canyon that was steeper and more winding than the last. Ben gaped at the switchback curves, one right after another, winding like a ribbon looped on top of a gift box for the next 10 miles. Speed limit signs shouted their warning not to drive faster than 15 MPH, and

Ben's stomach dropped at the realization that there were no barriers on the canyon-side of the highway with drop-offs as much as 1,000 feet straight down to the creek bottom below.

When they topped out at the summit, Ben was amazed by how fast the topography flattened out as they entered a beautiful, high-elevation valley. There were miles and miles of fertile rangeland surrounded by vast expanses of ponderosa pine forest. *What an outstanding piece of country,* Ben thought as he stared out the window. Across these high plains, grassy mountain meadows interrupted small streams and creeks and were ringed by dense stands of pine trees as far as the eye could see.

They turned off the highway and onto a county road, and within minutes arrived at the workstation. The truck turned sharply off the county road and into a driveway, crossing Mineral Creek and over a cattleguard into a large parking area in front of what used to be the District Ranger's house some ten to twenty years ago. Now it housed the thinning crew Ben would be joining.

When Ben stepped out of John's old, beat-up pickup, he had a new respect for this part of the state. The warm, late-morning sun burst through the tall Ponderosa pines, bathing him in a flood of light. He squinted against the beams, taking in the majestic pine trees surrounding the homestead. There was no describing the smell of fresh pine and the feel of the needles underfoot—a stark contrast to the coastal surroundings he'd grown up in. His gaze traveled higher, his mouth falling open in amazement at the deep blue sky and clouds so white and puffy he was sure he could reach out and touch them. *What a change from the rainy and windy coast!*

He looked at the house that would be his home. *What an impressive old house,* Ben thought. Standing proud with its tall, steep-pitched roof and massive, stone front porch with hand-laid stone steps, the house rested on a foundation constructed with the same hand-cut, hand-laid, quarry stones. The entire design displayed typical features of the homes built by the Civilian Conservation Corps during the 1930s. The cedar plank siding surrounded the whole house was interrupted by massive windows. Small, pine tree cut-outs were at each end of the house beneath the eaves near the roof peak and in the shutters on each side of the larger windows.

Behind the crew quarters were several small cabins. Further up the driveway, Ben noticed a small warehouse and gas shack. Around the other side of the compound stood a curious, white, wooden cage on four legs.

Ben turned to John. "What is that, a chicken coop on stilts?"

John chuckled. "It's a weather station. Part of your crew's duties is to take weather readings twice a day—more often, during fire season. The good news is that we pay you an extra 50 cents a day for the readings. The bad news is that someone has to stay here and take the readings on weekends."

This is quite the compound, Ben thought, impressed. *All built in the middle of the forest and miles from everything else in the world.*

A hand-hewn post and pole fence surrounded the front yard. Further out, a barbed wire fence around the compound perimeter kept neighboring ranchers' cattle out.

The small cabins were particularly nice, and Ben soon learned that those were reserved for married crew members or employees doing summer fieldwork. Besides his crew, there were crews of fire guards, engineers, and other summer employees stationed at the work center. Some engineering crew members lived in trailer houses at the upper end of the driveway. The center, named 'The Mineral Creek

Work Center,' had received its name from the creek flowing about 50 feet away, crossing the front entrance.

As John led Ben into the crew house, Ben's gaze wandered the plain living room. It was decorated with an old, brown Herculin couch and chair, and several vinyl aluminum chairs lined up against the walls.

"So, another new girl, huh?"

Ben's eyes snapped to the man entering the room, shuddering as he took in his appearance. *What did I get myself into?*

"Ben, this is Randy Thompson, your new boss," John grinned.

Towering over him at six-foot-five inches, Randy was a hulk of a young man—at least 230 lbs. of pure muscle rolling beneath his t-shirt. The Norwegian stared at Ben with an evil look in his menacing, blue eyes. A mop of blond hair blanketed his rather large head, and his deep-sunken, blank-looking eyes were framed by a bulging, wide forehead with bones that protruded like a pigeon chest. He looked like a beat-up pro from Friday Night Wrestling, when, in fact, he was just a college kid in his last year of school—a starting forward on their basketball team who sometimes played backup center.

21

He could play basketball, Ben thought. *He must be damned tough under the basket.*

"Come on, I'll show you where you're bunking and where you can put your stuff," John said.

Ben followed him down a short hall to a bedroom with walls of knotty pine tongue and grooved planks. Inside the bedroom, an army-style bunk was situated on each side of the room. A small wood table stood by each bed, with a small lamp. Outside the bedroom door were two vertical rows of wooden drawers, four high, built into the wall.

"You get the top three drawers on the left," Randy grunted. "The bottom one is mine, so stay out of it! Your roommate got the same damn message. Unpack your crap and come over to the kitchen. I'll show you some chores you and the other girls will do this summer."

Ben grabbed his Army duffel bag and emptied its contents on the bed. Loading the drawers with his sparse belongings, he reached for his McDonald Safety-T hard hat—one that resembled the one his dad had worn when falling timber—and his beat-up leather gloves.

After he settled in, Ben wandered into the kitchen. *Wow,* he thought, *this looks like the kitchen in the restaurant back home. Sure, was a good summer, working there during college.* He admired the large gas range with a huge grill over the ovens. The kitchen also contained a huge restaurant-sized fridge, across from two large sinks next to a pantry. *That could hold enough food for six months.* On the other side of the oven was a gray, fifty-gallon, government-issue garbage can near the back wall.

His attention was drawn to a hand-crank, old-fashioned wall phone, powered by two large, dry-cell batteries. The black metal housing was impressive for such a simple, old phone. Ben could not believe anyone still used those old antiques.

"You ever seen one of those before?" Thompson asked, catching Ben staring. "We still have number 9 wire on insulators on trees and poles running throughout the Forest, and along the roads to all the neighboring ranches. It's the only way to talk to the guard stations, lookouts, and the Forest Supervisor's office. There are no phone numbers here. Our code is two longs, a short, and a long. It's like Morse code—you hand-crank them out!

"I'll tell you the same thing I told the other summer camp girls: stay away from the phone during lightning storms. It's metal, and if lightning is near the area, it'll travel down the lines and ground out through the phone and, quite possibly, through you! If you even hear distant thunder, stay off the damn thing!"

"Hey, dude, you must be my roommate," a voice blared from the living room.

Ben and Randy's eyes flew to the man entering the kitchen. Randy looked like he might explode from the interruption, but Ben only frowned. The man looked like a war-protesting draft dodger with a full head of long, straight black hair, a peace symbol on his t-shirt, and a headband with 'Make Love Not War' written across it and bordered by white doves.

"Wes Jackson," the man said, shoving a hand toward him.

I still haven't figured out how I let myself get drafted into the Army, and here this Hippie escaped the draft. Where was he when he got his notice from the President—in Canada? Little did Ben know, the two would become good friends over the summer. For now, he was left to wonder what kind of anti-war mess he'd have to endure from his new roommate.

"Listen, girls, here's the deal. This my camp, you do what I say," Randy interrupted. "You can socialize later. Can either of you cook? Oh, forget it. Probably not. Every day, you make your own lunches. I

24

cook all the dinners, you girls clear the table, wipe everything down, do the dishes, and dry and put them away, understood? Now once again, can either of you cook?"

"I cooked breakfasts at a restaurant I worked at during summers in college," Ben offered. "Mainly for the five to ten night-shift workers—not the general public."

"Did any of them ever get sick—or die?" Randy sneered. "No? Alright then. Ben, you and Wes will be cooking breakfasts the entire first week starting the day after tomorrow—that's everyone's first Monday morning workday."

Chapter 4

Monday morning came quickly. Ben and Wes learned there would be at least two more men on their crew. One of them lived 10 miles from the camp on a 10-acre homestead west of Riverton with his wife and four kids. William Eller, the oldest crewmember, had made a point of telling everyone to call him Bill.

"You'll be meeting another crewmember named Chris Clifton— the self-proclaimed 'greatest crew leader in the world.' He's from a farming community in Beeton, about 135 miles east of here near the border. He's driving up now and shares the bedroom across the hall from you two," Randy said, pointing at Ben and Wes.

When Chris Clifton walked into the crew house, Ben's eyes were glued to him. *I've never seen anyone walk with a swagger like that.* Ben watched with curiosity as Chris walked across the room. His posture was so straight it was almost backward, causing him to sway from side to side from the waist up, and he looked down his nose at anyone who entered his comfort zone. *Geez,* Ben thought, *he reminds me of one of my teachers in high school. I remember thinking she had a stick of dynamite up her butt by the way she walked so stiff and straight.*

"Hey, newbies!" Chris bellowed. "You guys are gonna be counting your blessings after working with someone as experienced as me. You college boys will learn a lot from me. I became crew boss after learning all this forestry stuff here on the job after leaving high school five years ago. You'll get a lot more from me than them books you were cheating out of—this job is more than some damned, old, sullencutchure, college textbook."

"What the heck is he talking about?" Ben whispered, turning to Wes.

"I think he means 'silviculture,' but who knows? Can't expect much sense from someone who's worked five years in a dead-end crew boss job. Man, this is going to be an interesting year!"

Ben's only interest was to save money to bring his truck cross-state. He would find a place to stay after this year's field season ended. He intended to learn all he could from the crew and to stay out of trouble. From the looks of things, he was the only person here who wanted to make a career out of this job. He knew he had to keep his nose clean since he'd been promised a permanent position if things went well during the summer field season.

The first week on the job was routine. The crew learned how to determine different areas of the forest needing to be thinned, then they had to measure the distances around them and calculate the acres. Each unit would end up in a contract with either a company or an individual hired to thin the forested area so that only a specified number of trees remained on each acre.

At the end of the week, Bill pulled Ben aside to talk. "Don't worry about Chris. He means well, even though he's in way over his head. One good thing about him is that he'll stand up for his crew."

Bill was an interesting individual. He came from ranching stock and lived within 20 miles of the family ranch where he grew up. His parents still ran several hundred head of cattle and raised Quarter Horses and Tennessee Walkers for extra cash.

Beautiful horses, Ben had thought when Bill told him. The two got along very well and exchanged stories of Bill's local ranching experiences and Ben's growing up on the coast, along with his recent tour in Vietnam.

Bill looked the part of a western cowboy. He was five or six years older than most of the crewmembers and had a sun-weathered face that stretched in an easy smile. He was never without a solid, silver and gold, oversized, rodeo, belt buckle holding up his well-warn jeans. He always wore an old pair of *Levis* covering the tops of his *Tony Lama* cowboy boots. On his head, was a sweat-stained, old Stetson that Bill wore every day. He went home for the weekends but usually stayed at the work center during the week.

Out of all the crewman, Bill liked Wes the least, despite the first week getting off to a great start. There was just something about the two men that didn't mix.

****

Friday afternoon, the crew drove through Riverton to drop Bill off west of town before heading to the work center. The men rode in a '65 Dodge 'six pack,' a crew rig meant to hold six people, with four doors and a short pickup bed for equipment.

As they stopped in the middle of town, the engine began to grind loudly beneath the hood and the motor died, though the grinding continued, with a sickening "metal-on-metal" sound. They were stuck. Right in the middle of town at the only four-way stop for fifty miles.

Chris cursed into the air. "Come on, Bill. Let's show them how it's done. You new guys pay attention. Ben, get up here and take the

29

driver's seat. Grab hold of the key and start 'er up when I yell to do so."

Like a well-oiled machine, Bill and Chris jumped out and Ben quickly jumped into the driver's seat.

Ben watched as Bill grabbed a Sandvik from the back of the truck. He'd already learned the usefulness of this tool—a two-foot-long brush axe with a four-inch blade at the end protected by a curved piece of steel.

In one smooth motion, Chris popped and propped the hood while Bill jumped on the bumper and swung the Sandvik at the left side of the engine compartment.

These two really are a well-oiled machine, thought Ben as he watched them work.

The grinding noise continued as Bill swung and struck the inside of the hood, whacking the curved metal end of the Sandvik against the Dodge's starter motor. Bill continued swinging as though the Sandvik was a sledgehammer, pounding the starter motor into submission until somewhere inside its housing something broke loose.

"Hit the starter, Ben, and keep 'er cranking!" Chris yelled.

As the engine cranked, the starter motor settled to an odd, yet quieter noise as the engine cranked. With a loud pop and sputter, it caught hold and revved up as Ben held the clutch and pumped the gas.

By now, several locals had gathered on the sidewalk near the intersection. Some pointed, others laughed, while some even clapped. This was the best entertainment the town had in weeks. They'd always found the city-slicker invaders of their fair, cow town to be rather humorous. It was the damnedest Chinese fire drill they had ever seen.

The crewmen explained that this was the fourth time the Dodge "six-pack" had died from the same issue in the last two weeks. Ben put the truck in neutral and moved to the backseat while Chris swaggered back to the driver's seat and nodded to the crowd as he climbed behind the wheel.

"Boys," –Ben was learning that Chris always addressed crewmembers this way— "Boys," Chris said. "I think we beat our old record."

The process seemed to last at least twenty minutes as cars and trucks lined up behind them. The episode lasted only a minute or two, which was something for Chris to brag about!

After dropping Bill off at home, Chris turned the six-pack east and headed to the work center. Once again, they set off on the long drive up the steep, winding highway. Traveling through open meadows and cool mountain creeks, they finally arrived at the bottom. This ten-mile section of highway climbed 2,500 feet in elevation. The harrowing stretch contained numerous switchbacks, 1,000-foot drop-offs to the valley floor below, and no guard rail the entire way to the top. Ben's memory flashed back to the previous week when he'd first come up the mountain with John.

Chapter 5

Ben gripped his door handle as Chris maneuvered the old Dodge around the first set of hairpin curves. Swallowing his fear, he shifted in his seat and focused on the scenic vistas of the valley below. *Man, I cannot imagine driving this in the winter with three-foot snow drifts.* He was observing the beauty of the mountains when Chris laid on the horn and cursed. Ben's eyes flew to the logging truck barreling toward them, his hand gripping the door handle tighter when the loaded truck barely made it around the curve, forcing the Dodge halfway off the road.

"Damn," Chris exclaimed, "that guy is cutting all these curves too close for comfort."

Halfway up the mountain, the boys rounded a hairpin curve and screeched to a halt at the sight of one of their engineering rigs sitting at a 90-degree angle and blocking half the road. The ugly Willys Jeep, with its signature back end shaped like a box of Nabisco Crackers, was missing its front right wheel, and the front axle seemed to have come off. The front of the Jeep had slammed into a solid granite wall above the roadside drainage ditch. The front end of the passenger side was caved in a foot or two. The driver and passenger stood outside the wreckage, shaken by their accident.

"Hey, that's Jay and Walt!" Chris yelled. "Jay looks shook up!"

Ben remembered Jay from the Fire Guard School he'd attended with the rest of the summer crew members. They'd spent several days of fire training together.

Jay's eyeballs were as big as saucers and his body trembled as they approached.

"What happened?" Chris asked.

"A logging truck tore around that curve up there and was taking up both lanes! We had to go over the canyon edge or cut a hard right into the ditch and rocks. We chose the ditch, and when Walt turned a sharp 90, we pitched over on two tires and came back down on all four. When we landed, something up front snapped and sent us sideways. It felt like the whole front came loose, and we skidded into the ditch and hit that granite overhang on the other side."

"Need a ride back to the center?" Chris asked.

Walt shook his head. "Nah. I just radioed the Forest Supervisor's office downtown. He said they'd send someone to take photos and talk to us about what happened. The County Sheriff is on his way, anyway-

-said they had another driver on this stretch stop at a ranch house and call in a complaint about a speeding, out-of-control logging truck."

"We'll leave you to it, then," Chris said, motioning for his crew to follow him back to the truck. Once inside, he addressed them, his eyes serious. "Boys, remember what you just saw. This stretch of road has claimed more lives than any stretch in the entire state!"

Made a believer out of me, Ben thought, as they headed back up the narrow, winding highway to the work center.

As they pulled into Mineral Creek, the boys were surprised to see that the latest member of their crew had arrived. All eyes were on the man, who looked more like a beach bum than a rancher. At six feet tall, his bleach-blond hair hung long and loose, his tanned skin causing his observers to wonder if he'd come straight from the beach. A collective gasp echoed in the cab as the crew watched the man jump on top of a fence post and do a handstand. Like a gymnast, he walked the length of the fence without losing his balance before hopping down and bounding back to Ben and the boys like an excited puppy.

The damnedest thing I ever saw, Ben thought. *Damn cool, though.* The man reminded Ben of one of those guys in the beach blanket movies.

As soon as the crew piled out of the truck, the man started talking.

"Hey, I'm Kit from Southern California. You guys can call me Kahuna—all my friends do." A grin stretched across his face as he offered Ben a handshake.

"Good to meet you. Where did you get a nickname like that?" Ben asked.

"You ever read *Playboy*? There's a cartoon called 'Little Annie Fannie,' and one of the main characters is 'The Great Kahuna.' Some friends said I remind them of him since I love the beach and spend most of my time surfing and chasing girls!"

"Well, there you have it," Chris said. "We've almost got a full crew, with Kahuna, Ben, Wes, Bill, and, of course, me, the best-damned crew boss in the world. One more guy is expected to arrive later today or early tomorrow, from somewhere back East. Maryland, I think. Maybe Baltimore or Virginia, not sure. The plan is to have John bring him up here as soon as he arrives in Riverton, either on this afternoon's bus or tomorrow's early."

"I know none of you have your own wheels, but who owns that old beat-up Honda 50?" Chris asked.

On the corner of the driveway, Ben spotted a dilapidated, red, Honda 50 with white trim that looked like it had been tipped over one too many times.

"That's mine," Kahuna blurted. "I bought it from this guy back in town. John was nice enough to haul it up the mountain in the back of his old jalopy when he brought me up today. I had to spend an extra day at the supervisor's office to sign some papers, and I saw this for sale in the front yard of the house next door. I only paid $35 for it. The guy said, *'It may be ugly, but it runs great, and there's nobody left at home to ride it anymore, so it's yours now.'*"

Chris scoffed. "Looking at this beater, I don't think 'You meet the nicest people on a Honda' applies to your old junker. Not what Honda had in mind when they created their slogan."

"That's OK," Kahuna replied. "It runs pretty damn well. It goes forever on less than a gallon of gas—around 140 miles, according to the guy who sold it to me. You guys can borrow it if I'm not using it on the weekends, or even after work!"

Ben thought this might be a cool way to ride around on some of the flatter forest roads in the Blue Hills National Forest. He knew the

Deer Valley Ranger District where the work center was located had some nice forest roads.

Chapter 6

Sunday morning started like any typical summer day at the Mineral Creek Ranger Station. Everyone had settled in, falling into a flow of laundry, and preparing their work clothes for the following day. Most of the guys had brought lunch boxes and thermoses or purchased some along the way. Most lunch boxes were black, barn-shaped affairs made of sturdy metal—which proved beneficial since stuff was often thrown around in their six-pack.

Chris took his boys around the compound again, showing them how the gas hand pump worked to fill up the Dodge. While out, he showed them the various types and colors of flagging ribbon rolls they would be using to mark their thinning perimeters, and which paint colors they would use to mark the trees to either thin or leave standing. They also got a quick lesson in caring for and cleaning the Nelspot paint guns and the backpack units that held their marking paints.

All this was new to the crew, and there was lots to remember and learn. While out and about, John dropped off the last remaining member of their Timber Stand Improvement—or TSI crew, as they were called. Chris informed the crew of the new member, explaining that his name was Rob Kurtanz.

"That's 'Kurtanz,' with a 'Z,' boys. Pronounced like the word curtains," Chris explained.

The crew would soon discover that this would be repeated throughout the summer.

The boys followed Chris back to the old Ranger's house, which had affectionately been renamed "The Cookhouse." Almost all the crews joined them for meals there, and the name had seemed appropriate. Everyone chipped in for food and, of course, Randy's list of mandatory chores. Entering the front room of the cookhouse, they all stopped short and stared at the man lounging on the old, beat-up couch with the local newspaper in his hands.

Rob Kurtanz.

That's Kurtanz with a z of course, Ben thought.

Smooth-skinned, with a fair complexion and narrow eyebrows, Rob held the newspaper with pale, white hands—but his manicured nails were what captured the guys' attention. This guy had never experienced a single day of physical labor. Ben doubted he'd even been outside much. The boys exchanged looks, the message in their eyes clear: *what the heck do we have here?* In their world, no one except their mothers and sisters got manicures.

Seems to me this guy is more like them than one of the boys—perhaps even more sissified, Ben thought.

Rob was a thin young man, about five foot nine and 145 pounds. He wore khaki pants, a polo-style shirt, and fancy, all-leather sandals. Not the kind of outfit you would see in the forest.

The guys introduced themselves and found Rob to be a rather friendly chap, though he had probably the limpest handshake in the world. When it was Ben's turn to shake his hand, he noticed something strange—startling, even—as Rob returned to his newspaper.

"Damn-n-n-n! Did you see that?" Ben asked, joining the others in the kitchen.

Ben only swore or cussed out loud when excited or spooked, and he'd definitely been shaken up by what he'd witnessed. "Next time you walk near Rob, take a really good look at his eyes. I swear, he has the weirdest eyes in the world. One was fixed on reading the newspaper and the other followed me across the entire front room. He never even moved his head! You gotta see this for yourself," he stated shakily. "Damndest thing I ever saw."

41

Later, the boys learned that Rob grew up on the East Coast. He told them his home was about 50 miles north of Baltimore, but the exact location wasn't given. When questioned further, Rob seemed hesitant to offer information about his home and family, answering vaguely when pressed.

"Someone told me this dude came here from some kind of institution or hospital," Wes whispered.

And, of course, they all quickly jumped to the conclusion it had to be some kind of nut house. Whatever it was, Rob had been recently released and cleared from whatever problems bothered him, whether mental, physical, medical or whatever else could've been wrong with the guy. According to Randy, Rob's father had been elected to Congress. He served as a Senator, at either the state or federal level and was supposedly very influential back east. Rob's father had somehow gotten him assigned to the Blue Hills National Forest for the summer and, as a result, he'd landed at the Deer Creek Ranger District with the boys.

Randy strolled into the kitchen after Rob went to unpack and looked at "his girls." "You all better watch out for that one. He doesn't look quite right to me and is as much a greenhorn as I ever seen in my four summers here at Mineral Creek. I think he's softer than my pillow and probably about as out of shape, too. Mark my words, don't let him around anything sharp, hot, or steep without someone watching what he's doing, cause he's a walking accident waiting to happen.

"I swear, if you look into his eyes you might turn to stone. Even Medusa isn't as spooky as he is. You guys better get started on lunches for tomorrow while I go give the new 'sissy-dude' his kitchen and cleaning duties."

****

After the third week of work with a full crew at the Mineral Creek Ranger Station, Randy gathered his "girls" into the living room and reminded them to stay out of the drawer he'd marked off-limits in the dresser. Now it was time for an explanation.

"Look, girls," he said. "There are only a couple of us in this room old enough to legally drink beer. And, just so you know, I make my own. You saw that gray, heavy-duty, vinyl garbage can with the tightened lid in the kitchen. Don't mess with it, or you'll be messing with me. It's my latest batch of ale brewing. It should be enough to last me for the rest of the summer and see me through another long season. Gonna make it a lot easier to put up with you freaks.

"I'll be bottling it in the next week or so, and those quart bottles will be stored in what used to be your fourth drawer. Don't screw with any of it, or you'll be doing the worst of the camp chores for the rest of this summer. Got it!? I keep a careful count of every bottle, so consider that this my only warning.

"OK, girls," Randy bellowed. "Now that we've had you guys working for these past weeks, Monday will be our first monthly safety meeting here at the Work Center. The three district lookouts will be coming down, and the engineering crew will be joining us. The district ranger, Ned Bash, will be here to personally kick it off and meet everyone, so be ready. He takes safety too damn seriously, so make sure you're on your best behavior and this whole damn house is ship-shape—any questions?"

Randy yelled out Rob's new nickname. "Hey Kotex, it's your turn to cook breakfast, so get your butt up early and be sure and make an extra pot of coffee for the meeting Monday."

A few of the guys had started referring to Rob as the "Kotex Kid," some even choosing to call him "the moron." Neither name sat well with Rob. Any time his nicknames were used, the feminine features of his face slowly faded into a rather bizarre expression of subdued

rage he couldn't hide, scaring the mess out of those around him.

Chapter 7

Monthly safety meetings were a nice way to start the work week since the crews could sleep in later. The workdays were long. The time clock didn't begin until the crews were on the job site, no matter how far the drive was. If they had to drive an hour to their job sites, they had to get up at 5:00, cook breakfast, clean up, and the TSI crew had to ensure all their equipment was loaded and ready. They inspected their six-pack to ensure it was road-worthy, loaded up their lunches and gear, and then left the compound at about 6:45 for an 8:00 time stamp at the job site.

The days ended pretty much the same. They worked until 4:30 PM, loaded up, and arrived back at the work center after about an hour—just in time to start dinner. They received no overtime pay. When a rare opportunity for overtime occurred, it was only straight time. There was none of that time and a half stuff the logging and road building companies were paid.

They had a 10 or 11-hour day but only received pay for eight hours. Any chance to sleep in longer was great for the boys. They also like their weekly "tailgate" safety meetings because those occurred in the field and cut down their work time for that day. These meetings were held with the tailgate of the six-pack down. Chris would perch on the tailgate like a rooster surveying a henhouse and lead the discussion on the safety topic of the week and discuss any safety violations he'd observed. He loved perching high on the tailgate and letting his crew know his safety prowess.

On this particular Monday meeting, everyone gathered in the kitchen and living room to wait for Ranger Ned Bash. He arrived about a quarter to eight, drawing stares from all the boys as he walked in. A short man, Nash wasn't at all what they'd envisioned. Barely five feet five, he couldn't have weighed over 130 pounds.

"Got any coffee?" he asked. "That drive up the mountain is rough without coffee in the early morning. It's been on my mind the whole way up."

His coffee need satisfied, Ned kicked off the meeting and discussed some of the same things that had been covered during their tailgate sessions: proper use of hand tools, no horseplay during work, keep tools covered with their protective sheaths while walking. He talked about making sure the boys carried tools so they pointed down while walking on steep side slopes so they could throw the tool

47

downhill if they slipped. "An uphill throw might be your last," he explained.

The boys could see he took this safety stuff very seriously. He was quite interesting and a good speaker. He even exhibited a fatherly demeanor toward the crew. When someone asked a question, he found out their name and asked about their job for the summer, and what kind of experience they had in the woods.

As he concluded the safety meeting, he invited everyone to join him in the kitchen for a final cup of coffee before he returned to town. Ranger Bash poured himself a cup of coffee and promptly propped himself up on top of the gray vinyl garbage can, much to the horror of Randy and "his girls." Weighing 130lbs turned out to be a damned good thing, because he perched on top of the garbage can like he would a barber chair and talked to the boys about their summer at Mineral Creek. He asked several boys how things were going, and Randy began to sweat.

Little did Ranger Bash know—he'd straddled 20 gallons of "Randy ale."

"Guys," Ranger Bash said, his eyes roaming. "This place looks great. You've done a good job keeping it clean. Everything is put away where it should be, but something in this kitchen smells moldy. Or maybe musty… I think you need to scour out these garbage cans and check the sink drains for clogs. The smell in this kitchen is just way too much."

He hopped off the 20 gallons of ale that could have cost Randy his job—not to mention any subsequent future references had the ranger fallen through the lid and into the bubbling liquid.

That would have been some sight, seeing our district ranger fall into a garbage can and take a beer bath while talking safety, Ben thought.

As Ranger Bash walked out the front door, he yelled over his shoulder at Randy, "It looks like we have a pretty good chance for an early fire season. We have a lightning storm predicted for later this week. Make sure all the tailgate safety sessions cover lightning safety. Talk about what to do in a lightning storm, both out on the job and here at the work center."

On that note, the crew—along with their ever-swaggering crew leader—headed off to start another week of thinning projects in the forest.

On the way to the job site, Wes informed the crew that he'd completed his lookout training and could now offer his service as an alternate so the guys and gals in the district fire towers could enjoy a day off in town. He was eager to work the tower all day Saturday and Sunday while the crew got some much-needed fun and relaxation.

"This Saturday, I'll be up on my first relief assignment on the Slip Mtn. Lookout. Ben, if you get bored, come up and visit and see the view. I heard it's spectacular, even for an old hippie like me. Since there's a chance of lightning, I expect it will be interesting."

Chris, unimpressed, threw in his opinion. "I am amazed they would have some long-hair like you up in any lookout watching for fires, considering your draft-dodging background."

"I believe in that old saying 'make love, not war.' Going to 'Nam was not dealt in my cards. Even hippies like me have flat feet," Wes snapped.

Chapter 8

About 45 minutes from their next job site, Wes turned to Ben and asked, "You were in Vietnam not too long ago. What was it like? Did you kill any Viet Cong or their families?"

Ben tensed. This was the one topic he'd hoped would never come up. All he wanted to do was distance himself from his time in Vietnam.

"So, Ben," Wes pressed, "what happened when you were there? Riding my flat feet all the way to 4F turned out to be a good deal, right?"

"You know, Wes," Ben smiled, "4F also refers to someone mentally unfit. You are sure the bottom end of your body received the 4F, not the part between your ears?"

Ben's eyes grew serious. "Listen guys, it hasn't been that long since I got back home. I've hardly spoken to anyone about my tour in 'Nam—for good reason. Let me give you some background. I was there during the Tet Offensive. The media ignored the fact that we caused heavy casualties to the VC across the country. However, none of this was reported here in the States. The only thing the news cared to broadcast were stories like the massacre at My Lai. Every newspaper in the world covered the Court Martial of Lt. Calley, who was accused of mass murder. All this stuff keeps me awake at night. I wasn't on the front lines, but that didn't spare me. Bad crap can happen to anyone.

"You know, the world is a messed-up place right now. People see a soldier in uniform or a Vietnam returnee and automatically brand that soldier as a trigger-happy murderer. This is one of the few times you'll hear me talking about this, so let me tell you why I feel this way. My time in Vietnam was a normal tour length plus the extra time it took for basic training and graduating from the Army Intelligence school. Don't laugh, Wes," he cut his eyes to that man. "It's not an oxymoron. That school had some of the best damn education I've ever experienced. I was fortunate enough to get good grades in photogrammetry. That paid off when I was trained to become an imagery interpreter in Vietnam.

"I ended up as an aerial photo and imagery interpreter of all kinds of stuff like radar and infrared photos. I also helped prepare troop movement studies. That's about all I can say. We all had top-secret security clearances, and I can't talk about some stuff even though I'm out. However, we were told that we could discuss what happened if our family and friends read about it in the newspapers. Otherwise, I can't say much.

"Listen," Ben continued. "Like I said earlier, I was a noncombatant. That's another reason I don't talk much about my tour. Friends from back home were dying, and there I was having it easy for the first half of my tour. I worked twelve hours a day, six days a week, and then had a day off and to see the sights, drink beer, eat good food, and shop for my family back home whenever I visited Saigon.

"A few months ago, when my tour ended, I arrived at the bus station near a park in River City. Protests were going on—some of your buddies, Wes—the long hair, Hippie types. A bunch of wannabe students full of pot and booze if you ask me.

"The protesters were angry. Yelling and nasty with their anti-war signs waving by the openly stoned and drunk. So, I got off the bus dressed in uniform since it got me discounts on airfare and bus tickets. A couple of these long hairs must have spotted my uniform because they wandered over to me. They began to spit at me and called me a baby killer, fascist pig, and murderer. If you can think it, they yelled it. I got the heck out of there, met my brother, and headed home. I vowed I wouldn't talk about my service again, at least around people I didn't know well."

The conversation ended just as they arrived near the Little Meadow Road where they would be laying out some new thinning units.

Once again, the crew worked their butts off in the increasing summer heat. On the way back to the work center, the boys continued with their line of questioning.

"So, Ben," Chris yelled from behind the wheel. "Did you ever kill anybody?"

Ben cursed. "We weren't even allowed to have live ammo during guard duty. They kept that stuff locked up. We were an Intelligence Battalion numbering over 1,000. We were stuck in this tiny, old, French plantation compound not far outside of Saigon and probably less than two or three acres in size. Supposedly, we all had a small price on our heads, and we had a phony unit name at the front gate so no one could guess what we really were. No live ammo seemed kind of weird. The major in charge didn't want some trigger-happy intelligence dude firing off a live round and drawing attention to us.

"So no, I never killed anybody—at least not up close. I did have to fire my M-14 one time. Some things happened that I don't feel like talking about. But it's safe to say we're responsible for killing hundreds. After all, we plotted targets for B-52 bombing raids as well as napalm drops, Agent Orange, and other types of shelling and missions. In that instance, we might have killed hundreds in one bombing run. We never knew the actual results on the ground."

"Did you have any close calls?" Bill asked.

Ben thought for a moment before responding. "Damn straight. Being in a war zone affects everyone. Ground-pounder or not. There was one close call back when things were still sort of quiet. This was way before the game-changing Tet Offensive last year. couple of us were spending our day off in Cholon. We had a favorite restaurant there –you could get a huge bowl of clams steamed in garlic and white wine, with a large piece of fresh French bread and a glass of wine or beer all for $1.25," he grinned.

"We decided to have a quick beer at the bar area next door and a couple of the tea girls came over and asked us to buy them a Saigon tea and chat with them for a while. We decided to skip the expensive tea buying. The girls sat with us anyway, watching for their Mama-san, and chatted with us on the sly.

"Out of nowhere, there was this loud explosion. The blast appeared to come from across the street, where we'd just walked. Some of the front window glass shattered and debris rained down across the street. Before I could even think, this girl shoved me to the floor and huddled over me under the table until it was safe to come out. I couldn't believe she did that without any hesitation whatsoever. And guess what? My two buddies said the other girls did the same for them. All six of us ended up under the table."

"So, what happened?" Bill asked.

"It turned out to be a random thing, but it was damn scary. I later learned it was a bicycle bomb, and these things were set off all over the city. In this case, we were told the explosives—probably a small chunk of C4—had been hidden in a loaf of bread that was in a bicycle basket and parked down a few buildings.

"The scariest part of this is, we walked right by that bike not 5-10 minutes earlier. We all saw the bicycle and the bread but didn't think a thing about it since it was a common sight in Saigon.

"We did finally have our clams—and lots of wine—but we were plenty shaken, I can tell you that. I will never forget those three girls. Especially the one who pushed me down."

Chris started to say something, but Ben interrupted. "I think that's enough of this. Let's talk about something else, OK? Maybe we'll discuss it more over a beer someday, as long as you keep things to yourself. If anyone asks about my military service, you don't know a damn thing—OK?"

****

The next morning, after they'd finally arrived at the thinning unit, Kahuna yelled, "Hey Chris, all those pickups we saw on the way out were full of hunters. Is it deer season?"

"Well, boys," Chris answered, strutting around to the tailgate where they were getting their gear out. "We're in an area where they've allowed a special hunt to help control the overpopulation of mule deer. I think they only have 15 or 20 tags, but the area in and around Little Meadow has too many deer. This part of the forest can't sustain such a heavy population."

"Wow," Kahuna's brows rose. "You used 'sustained' and 'population' in the same sentence. I'm damned impressed by all those syllables. Just think what you could say if you went back to school," he teased with a smile.

Chris glowered as the boys all laughed. "Get to work, or I'll make sure Randy gives you girls his dirtiest chores. Buncha damn, city-slicker, smart butts," he grumbled under his breath.

After realizing they were in an active hunting area, the boys tied yellow and red ribbons around their pants legs and hard hats. They also tied them on their belts to make themselves visible to any dumb "city hunters" who might accidentally put them in their sights. The thinning unit ran parallel to the Little Meadow Road. They walked 10-20 yards from the road into the thick undergrowth to tie the boundary ribbons. The dense unit contained too many small trees three to six inches in diameter. In some areas, the trees made them impassable. Many were stunted and would never end up part of a healthy forest.

This morning, their goal was to mark the boundaries, survey the distance around the unit, and figure out the acreage contained within the unit. Then, they would map it out and give it a letter or number designation for the thinning contract. Once inside these thickets, they definitely needed those colorful ribbons tied up and down their pants legs and on their belts for hunters to see them, dumb city hunters or not. Chris marked the thinning unit by chopping a mark with his cruiser axe. The boys followed behind him, tying ribbons to mark the unit and completing the survey to determine the acreage.

Ben tied the yellow ribbon up high every 10-20 feet so the contractor could see the boundaries. Continuing around the corner of the unit heading back toward the road, he paused when he heard a gunshot. *Hmm,* he thought, *some hunters must have filled their tag. Usually, it means they were successful if there was only one shot.*

About a minute later, loud gunfire exploded through the air, sending a shocking jolt through the crew. *Bang! Bang! Bang!*

Ben's ears still rang when he heard *ping, ping, ker-ping!* His gaze flew to the ground, eyes wide-open as dust and pine needles went flying from a spot where the third or fourth bullet entered the ground just above his right foot. A mere two inches closer, and he'd be dealing with a serious gunshot wound.

Ben cursed. "Did you guys see that? Did you see that someone nearly shot my damned foot off?"

Ben ran, full tilt, toward the camouflaged truck parked on Little Meadow Road, screaming the entire 20 yards. Before he could reach them, the hunters beat a hasty retreat down the road, leaving Ben breathless in their dust.

Picking up a rock, Ben yelled after the truck. "You dumb pricks!" Throwing it as hard as he could, he hurled every four-letter word he could think of as the pickup sped away. Anger burned his neck as he marched to his supervisor. "Get on the radio and call this in, Chris. These guys need some jail time!"

"I didn't get a good look at the truck. Were they hunting, target shooting, or what?" Chris asked.

Exasperated, Ben threw up his hands. "You're not going to believe this. I could see the driver drinking beer, and get this, the guy in the back sat in an easy chair—a damned recliner—with his gun on his lap and a beer in his hand."

"What happened?"

Ben worked to slow his breaths. "I'm sure they heard us out there in the brush and started taking 'sound shots,' thinking one of us could be a deer. Damn it, I did not spend all those months in Vietnam only to come home and have some stupid city hunter, shoot me. Damn, those jerks!"

Turning to the crew, his brow relaxed as a slight grin appeared. "Thank goodness they were drinking. If they'd been sober, one of us might be hanging in their camp in a deer bag!"

Chris stared at Ben before his gaze rested on the crew. Relieved they were all in one piece, he let out a rushed breath as he thought about how close his "girls" had come to getting shot. "You know, boys, I think we've had enough fun for the day. Our last safety meeting turned out to be damned good. But this afternoon tops anything I could ever think to discuss. Let's go home. Forget that it's an hour early. We've earned it, for damn sure."

Chapter 9

Lightning across the Blue Hills National Forest happened all the time. Nonetheless, everyone respected the fact that forest fires could spark at any moment as a result. The mountainous Blue Hills National Forest was one of the top ten places in the world for recorded lightning strikes. On Tuesday evening, the boys discussed the upcoming possibility of a lightning storm and fires.

Overhearing their conversation, Randy stepped in. "Look, you guys are not a regular fire crew, but you've been trained to do the initial attack on small lightning fires, so you damn well better be ready. If required, you'll go out as a two or three-person lightning fire initial attack group. We need to get this place storm ready. Make sure all the Coleman lanterns are full, and the mantles are in good shape because we always lose our electricity when these storms hit. Kahuna, Ben, Wes—you three go through all the lanterns, check them out, and test them. Kotex, watch and learn, but don't touch, you hear me?"

Rob cast a hate-filled glare at Randy, his brewing anger evidenced further as he cursed him under his breath. Though Randy didn't seem to catch it, the boys saw the rage.

On the front porch, Ben went through the supply and ensured all the mantles were OK, the pumps worked fine, and each lantern was fueled up. He'd used these many times before when the power went off during the coastal storms back home. After he'd finished, Ben went back inside.

No one noticed Rob sneak onto the porch. Since no one was around to stop him, he ignored Randy's warnings and checked the lanterns anyway. In his infinite wisdom, he felt he knew exactly how to clean the lanterns, check the mantles, and fire up each Coleman without help from his detractors. *Crap*, he thought, *I'm not an east coast greenhorn! I've camped before! Well, in a cabin, anyway. Well...a summer home, rather,* he reminded himself.

Grabbing a lantern, he sat in a rocking chair, did the appropriate burning off the mantle, and checked the lantern's fuel level. He then pumped the lantern with the short push pump on the side.

He cursed as fuel shot onto his jeans and spilled onto the porch.

Doing a quick assessment, he saw that the tank wasn't sealed tight enough. Rob tightened everything up, re-pumped 20-30 more times, and determined things were OK. He grabbed a match and struck it, placing the flame inside the glass and carefully lighting the lantern mantle with the glass lifted. Instantly, flames whooshed up from the mantle outside the lantern. The fire swiftly spread, lashing out like a huge tongue from beneath the glass and catching fire to Rob's kerosene-soaked pants. Flames soon leaped across the careless spill on the concrete front porch, soaking up the fuel.

Having heard the cry, Ben ran out the front door just as Rob noticed flames on both his pant legs. Small flames were burning from the knees down. Rob screamed for help, and Ben yelled for the first aid kit. He quickly pulled off his sweatshirt and snuffed out the flames before they could spread or cause more serious burns.

Ben cursed as fear pulsated through his temples. "What were you doing?"

Randy raced out to see if an ambulance was needed. The crew was hot on his heels,

The Kotex kid sheepishly looked up. "I knew what I was doing. This damn lantern is screwed up. Randy, why the heck is it even in service? You're supposed to be the big king of the camp—what's with you, dumbo?"

All eyes went to his smoking pants and the scorched porch.

"Tell me exactly how many pumps you pumped into that lantern," Ben ordered.

"Oh, 20-30 the first time, then with the mantle readied, another 20 or 30 times," answered Rob, grimacing from the pain of his new battle wounds.

"You are so damn lucky. You put way too much pressure in that lantern. On top of that, you didn't bother to clean up the spilled kerosene on your clothes and on the porch. You could have blown up the whole area. You may not think much of our camp boss, but he knows these lanterns. No one has ever had a problem until you didn't listen and damn near pumped your butt into self-destruction. Are you that stupid?" Ben gaped at Rob. "From now on, you do what you're told, else you're heading back home—got it?

"Listen," Ben frowned, not satisfied he'd been understood. "You and the others need to understand I'm in this job for a long-term career, while *you're* here for some kind of western movie adventure. By now you should understand this is the real deal—not some move script. You scared the heck out of all of us. We all look out for each other, but you damn well better start looking out for yourself!!"

When Ben finished his lecture, everyone went back inside to prepare for another early morning and long workday. It was only 7 PM, but it had been a tiring day for all. The idiot hunters—along with the idiot easterner almost burning his legs off—had everyone exhausted.

****

With the work week winding down, Bill reminded the crew to be "lightning-careful" as he got ready to go home for the weekend. "I have seen plenty of close calls with lightning storms, even where I live down in the valley." Glancing out the window of the six-pack, he noticed a small, black plume of smoke off in the distance. "Damn, look at that smoke. No storms yet... I wonder where the smoke is coming from?"

"I got a sneaking feeling I know what all that smoke is about," Chris stated emphatically. He nodded his head as though he knew something they didn't. "Once in a while, the district honchoes will have one of our old, abandoned cabins burned down, or an old line-shack. I hear they're burning down all the old, abandoned sheds, barns, corrals, and cabins that are no longer safe for the public—usually when no one's watching.

66

"Not sure if this is 100% true, but I heard someone in Colorado, either a mom, dad or their kid, was snooping around an old mining cabin. All of a sudden, one—or all—of them fell down an old mine shaft. This kid, according to what I heard, died. At least, I think that's the story. I don't know. Anyway, since there's no way to make these places safe, and there are so many, district folks are just burning them down. The shafts are filled immediately, and all the buildings are bulldozed over. Same thing is happening here. This isn't the first one of these fires Bill and I have known about. I'm sure more will be burned. Who knows how many have already burned? I know it's all rumor, but I remember hearing from some of the old-timers talking down in the supervisor's office. They said they did the same damn thing to abandoned cabins way back in the 30's, so who knows? It sure as heck wasn't a lightning strike."

Chapter 10

"Hey, you guys, wanna hear something funny?" Chris asked. "You all met John, our district forester, right? Now, I'm gonna tell you this, but you guys have to remember that, even though we hardly see him, he's our boss and we work for him. After all, he heads up all the timber programs, including our thinning work. Anyway, from what I've heard, he gets way too carried away when it comes to enforcing contracts. He doesn't trust any of the contractors who do thinning on the units we work on. I'm not sure why, but he's definitely a strange guy. I oughta know, since I've been working with him for three years now.

"You guys know they're changing how we contract out the thinning stuff. We're going to go from marking every tree with blue paint that needs cut to writing a "Choppers Choice" contract, in which we tell the contractors what we need them to leave and at what spacing. They cut the rest on their own. John hates this idea and is fighting against it, so he sneaks out on weekends to watch ongoing trials of this new thinning work to see if they're screwing up.

"So, in the story I heard, John snuck out to spy on a contractor near here last weekend, while he was supposedly on a picnic with his family. They were near a contract site, and he left them along the road to pick up bottles, cans, and any other kind of prized junk he collects. While they were doing his scavenging, he crept through the woods and hid on a hill behind an old log where he could observe the thinners. They couldn't see him, or so he thought. He stayed there and quietly watched the thinning crews working for a while. They were pretty much cutting down everything exactly as we'd marked it—nothing seemed out of the ordinary. As he continued to spy from his perch, Old Windy Johnson, the contractor, spotted a flash of sunlight coming off John's horn-rimmed glasses.

"Old Windy decided to leave his crew and do some sneaking around on his own. Picture this: Old Windy creeps way up around the backside of the hill where John thinks he's undetected. Just when John was feeling real secure, Windy snuck up behind him.

"Now, John still hasn't seen him at this point, nor does he have any clue that Windy, who's getting on in years, is right behind him. Windy always uses a shovel handle as a walking stick. Because of the sound of the chainsaws, John never suspected Windy was just a few feet away from where he'd sprawled out behind the log and was spying.

"When Windy got close, he took the shovel handle in both hands, like it was a baseball bat, and swung hard. *Whack!!!* The handle ended up right across John's butt. John, thinking he'd been attacked by a crazed nutcase, yelled out every profane word in his vocabulary. As old Windy was dying laughing, John beat a hasty retreat as fast as he could back down to the road. Windy's crew watched him grab his butt the whole way. He quickly ended up back on the road where his wife and kids were still looking for his favorite trash. They were all puzzled at the sight of him running down the hill toward them. He cursed out loud, holding his butt and muttering more swear words as he approached. His face had turned as red as the town's fire engine.

"After the shovel whacking, Windy made sure he spread the story around town. That's how I heard about it," Chris grinned. "The guys in the office left a pink whoopee cushion on John's desk chair the next Monday morning. They also left a message that read, "Hope your butt gets well!" on a card that had been attached."

This was exactly what the boys needed to hear after the week they'd had. The laughter continued all the way back to Mineral Creek.

Funny stuff, Ben thought. *Sometimes true stories are way weirder than anyone could dream up.*

When the boys got back to the work center, they unloaded their equipment while keeping an eye on the sky as anvil-shaped clouds formed in the distance, southwest.

"Looks like a pretty good build-up starting to form. I suspect we're in for a thunderstorm either Saturday or Sunday," Chris warned. "We may not be a fire crew but remember what Randy said earlier: we can be sent out on initial attack on small lightning fires anytime— day or night. So, make sure all the tools are sharpened and ready."

Like every other Friday evening, they decided who would stay at the work center to take the weather readings. This week, Ben would stay, while the others were free to go.

Before anyone could leave for the day, a car pulled up to the cattle guard in the driveway and honked. The boys all stared at the two cute girls in the car. Decked out in tight, cut-off jeans and tank-tops, they both laughed as the driver honked her horn.

"Who the heck is that?" yelled Wes.

Kahuna broke out into a smile as he looked at the car. "That's my ride into town. I'll see you guys Sunday evening. Should be a damn fine time in town, boys! Sorry you can't join me. On second thought," he grinned, "I'm not. Ben, here's the key to the Honda. You can ride

71

it over the weekend—she's got a full tank in her. Just don't speed and wreck her," he laughed, knowing full well his "gutless wonder" could barely hit 40 MPH downhill.

Cool, Ben thought. *In between weather readings, I'll drive around the local county roads and head onto some of the easier forest roads.*

Chapter 11

"Ben," Wes called. "I'm providing backup on Slip Mountain this weekend. I'll be going up bright and early tomorrow morning and coming down Sunday night. Why don't you come up and see the lookout later tomorrow and have lunch? It's the closest lookout to the work center, and since you have Kahuna's 50, it should be an easy ride. I don't think it's more than six miles total from here. You just take the county road back toward town and take that first left; there's a sign with the mileage to the lookout."

This excited Ben. He'd been looking forward to exploring the hills on the old Honda. Suddenly, it felt like Saturday morning would take forever to arrive. Looking outside, Ben noticed those large thunderheads developing weren't so anvil-shaped anymore. They were now building up high into the atmosphere—a good indication of an approaching lightning storm. The LAL (lightning activity level) for tomorrow was predicted to be LAL3, meaning there was a good chance for lightning. *Might turn out to be an interesting day to visit Wes up on Slip Mountain,* Ben thought.

Due to the impending storm, Ben wasn't the only one to stay at the work site. Chris, Rob, and a couple of guys from the engineering

73

crew were also told to stick around in case of fires. The group passed the evening playing poker and telling dumb jokes. The cloud cover kept the temperature down and the humidity higher, making the evening cool.

"Feels strange," Ben observed. "Kind of smells like rain. Chris, you know this country—what do you think?"

Chris strutted around the room in his usual display of self-importance, like some rooster on a vitamin overdose. "Yeah, we'll be getting thunderstorms tomorrow. Perhaps settling in across the whole ranger district. Better plug your ears, Kotex, 'cause your mommy ain't here from Maryland to protect you," he said with a huge grin.

Chris never had liked Easterners. He wasn't overly fond of anybody unless they were from a farming or ranching country.

"You ignorant beet farmer! Quit calling me 'Kotex!' Use my damn name or you're gonna be sorry," Rob fired back.

Chris cursed. "I'm sorry *now*! Sorry you're such a damn greenhorn, Balti-*moron*. You damned near burned your legs off and set the porch on fire all because you didn't listen. You're so damn dumb about the outdoors. What did you do outdoors when you were younger, play with your sisters? Just shut up and do what you're told,

74

Kotex. You're starting to irritate me more than a little." Chris sauntered to the chair by the old couch and leaned against the wall.

Rob leaped to his feet, his smooth, feminine facial features conforming into a distorted, twisted mask of fury. His eyes squinted and the veins in his neck bulged as his face flushed red. "Chris, you prick, don't mess with me anymore! And never call me 'Kotex' or 'moron' again!" He leaped onto Chris, wrapping his hands in a chokehold around his neck. Shoving Chris against the wall, he tightened his grip.

"Let go of me, you maniac!" Chris yelled, his face turning purple. "Get him off me, you guys!"

Ben and Wes ran over and attempted to pull Rob off. They grabbed his wrists and tried to pry his fingers from Chris's neck, but they wouldn't budge.

"I can't free his hands," Ben yelled.

"I can," Joe, an engineer, exclaimed as he grabbed a small chair in both hands and swung it like a baseball bat, catching Rob right in the ribcage and causing him to loosen his grip. Seeing their chance, the rest of the engineering boys jumped in and restrained the enraged Rob.

Rob looked at Chris with a distorted sinister smile. "Whatsa matter, Chris, did you think this sissy easterner was going to hurt you? Trust me—if I'd wanted to, I would have. That's just a warning. That goes for the rest of you, too. Don't mess with me unless you're ready to pay the price."

Rob had everyone convinced he could take care of himself. But the way he'd handled Chris also sent a clear message to the boys that he was most assuredly some kind of mental case. They'd never seen anyone else settle arguments by choking the life out of someone.

Everyone settled back down as Chris mumbled a muted "sorry," his eyes watching Rob. "Your sissy-butt deserved it, though," he muttered, feeling the need to come out on top, even if it was only in his mind.

When they started another game of blackjack, Chris worked to change the atmosphere in the room. "Ben, what's the weirdest thing you remember during your time in Vietnam?"

Ben scowled but thought for a minute. With a slight grin on his face, he replied, "You know, one of the damndest things I remember is watching a fish walk out of the damn river right up toward where I was standing."

Ben moved on to the explanation without waiting for them to question him. "We had a club on the compound where we could drink beer, play cards, and watch live shows. The shows were mostly Filipino bands that imitated popular bands worldwide. Some good, some bad. Anyway, one night I remember watching the band. I'd had a few beers—maybe a few too many. When I grew tired of the band, I walked back to my barracks. Since the monsoon rains had started, the Saigon River had risen quite high and started to run into our walkways.

"I looked down and, underneath the lights, there was this damn fish walking straight toward me across the bank above the swollen river. It stood on what looked like two front legs with the back part resting on his tail. He just kind of wiggled back and forth on the leggy-looking things up front and pushed with the tail, I guess. Damn, it was a big one—over a foot long and probably weighed a pound. I found out from some guys who'd been there a while that it was a SE Asian Walking Catfish."

The boys listened intently.

"I find that to be bull," said an engineer. "I have never seen a fish with legs."

"Hey, you don't have to believe me," Ben grinned. "Go look in the Encyclopedia Britannica. It has a great story about those types of fish. I had to go back and look it up, myself, just to make sure it wasn't the beer clouding my memory."

Taking advantage of Ben's talkative mood, one of the guys asked, "What did the country actually look like? Saigon, for instance. All we see on TV is dead people, the jungle, and planes dropping bombs. All we hear on the news is how we should win the war right away as they talk about numbers of dead Viet Cong."

Ben thought before responding, hating to discuss the perils of war in light of his relatively easy time in Vietnam. "Look, the people there are amazing. They have these ugly, old yellow and blue taxi cabs that I swear were left over from the late 40's, but they keep them running with wire, tape, chewing gum and who knows what else. The country had been left with a pretty good infrastructure from the French. I saw maps of parks. There were sewer systems in place, water systems, roads, and bridges. People were friendly to me, and I never had someone threaten me while walking in the city. Of course, that was when we could go into the city on our day off.

"Saigon had city parks, a university, a wonderful zoo, botanical gardens, and a golf course. The city remained relatively safe until the Tet Offensive attacks. What I remember most is the stifling heat when I got off the plane at Ton Son Nhut airbase. When you first hit the ground, it hits you like a blast furnace blowing through a hot shower. Listen, each morning when I got up and polished my boots in the barracks, sweat ran down my butt like a river. I didn't believe I'd ever get used to the weather, but we all did. All in all, the area that had not been touched by the war consisted of a beautiful, old French city with lots to see and do."

"Now that you and so many others are home, do you think the war will be over by end of summer? We should have the Viet Cong and North Vietnamese kicked out of there by then, right?" Wes asked.

Ben thought for a minute. "No, it's pretty clear to me by all the war hippies protesting and getting all the news coverage around the world that people are sick and tired of seeing so many kids our age killed. I think it's pretty much over for us. And then you have the likes of Hanoi Jane, with some people accusing her of committing treason. We're too moral to win a war. Look, all we had to do was bomb the dikes along the rivers by the cities of Haiphong and Hanoi. But since that would have been an immoral act against the civilian population, we shied away from it. There are dikes along the Red River protecting numerous industrial sites and facilities. We could have bombed those and flooded their entire industrial complex during the monsoon season and that could have helped end the war immediately. But, of course, we would have killed thousands of civilians. Once again, we were too moral, politically speaking.

"Let me tell you how I learned how hard this war would be, even after being in an intelligence unit. I had access to all kinds of information—you guys wouldn't believe it—and I, too, still wondered why we hadn't won already. When I got to Vietnam, I'd never considered myself naïve, but from news reports, I thought for sure we should be kicking butts and going home quickly.

"I remember asking one of the lieutenants in our group, 'Shouldn't we have this over and done with before my tour is up? We have superior everything from what I can see.' That lieutenant answered, 'I thought the same thing, but I found out things are never as they appear. Here,' he handed me a book and said, 'Read this book. It changed how I thought about this war and how I looked at things from then on. The book was titled *Hell in a Very Small Place—The Siege of Dien Bien Phu.*"

"What was that?" Chris asked in his usual blustery manner. "A bunch of commies pinko-written crap so we would leave in defeat?"

"No, listen," Ben replied. "In the 50's, the French were cornered at this place up north and, even though they were superior in every aspect of war, weapons, technology, military training, equipment, and money, there was one thing they couldn't figure out. That thing was the resolve of a people with less. They were protecting their heritage, their history, their country. That turned out to be stronger than any war machine. Listen, they had hundreds—at times thousands—of their countrymen walk hundreds of kilometers south down those jungle trails. They'd picked up a howitzer round or other munitions or supplies, whatever each could carry, turn right around and carry the load on their backs, trekking the hundreds of kilometers back up North to help their General Giap and the Viet Minh who had the French surrounded.

"Each of them would make the grueling trip, drop off their load, and guess what they would do next, Chris?'

"Probably go have a beer or that gross sake mess and see the family?" Chris guessed.

"Not at all," Ben said. "After a short rest, they headed back hundreds of kilometers back north. They returned with fresh supplies and repeated the journey over and over to resupply the Viet Minh. This effort finally helped the Viet Minh defeat the superior French forces, forcing their surrender.

"What's really funny," Ben added, "is the bus driver who drove us every day from our compound SE of Saigon over to the Intelligence Center was a member of the Viet Minh forces who helped defeat the French. He told us the funniest stories imaginable, a new one on every bus ride, it seemed. He spoke great English, Vietnamese and, of course, he spoke fluent French. He thought the French were too self-assured and proper to win the war and that perhaps we Americans were too rich and too improper to lose. Boy, was he wrong.

"Listen, guys," Ben stated tiredly, "it's getting late, and I'm not much on war stories but you know it's just how I see things. We're too moral to do the things we need to do; we don't have the will to kill thousands of civilians where TV can cover the story, but we can sure kill them one on one for a body count. I remember reading casualty reports about kills from different units. The reports would state: suspected VC age 12, or suspected VC age 9, or suspected VC age 83. You get the picture. Newspapers reported like it was a scorekeeping exercise, and dead bodies were our wins. But what do I know? I'm just guessing. I think that's probably all I should say about my opinions. You never know who's listening out there to people like me who were in a unit like mine. I'm heading to bed," Ben said finally. "Listen, maybe some other time I'll tell you more about the things I experienced in 'Nam, but not tonight. See you guys in the morning."

Standing and stretching his back out, Ben shot a look at Rob. "Kotex, you damn well better cool it. We all have nicknames we didn't ask for but that's how we are in this camp, so get over it!"

Chapter 12

The morning's weather was exactly as predicted. Lightning was on the way. The clouds were steadily building, looking ominous and threatening. Ben made a quick lunch and stuck it in the saddle bag of the beat up, ugly, old Honda as he got ready to ride up to the lookout and see Wes. Ben told everyone at the station to radio him via Wes if they needed him.

As he rode down the driveway, carefully crossing over the cattleguard, the lack of shocks chattered every bone in his body and jarred every loose part of the old bike. He hoped the damn thing would hold together. Relief washed through him when he turned onto the paved county road where the bike quieted and offered a smoother ride. It was only a couple of miles until the turn-off for the lookout, but soon the old bike began to sound like a lawnmower engine with no muffler. Way too loud, rattly, and gutless. Despite this, Ben managed to get it up to 35 MPH on the flat, paved road. At last, he turned left onto the road to the lookout. He groaned as he made the turn and realized the pavement turned into gravel for the remainder of the three-mile-long, uphill run to the Slip Mountain Lookout. The lookout was one of the nicest lookouts in the West, offering fantastic views of two valley floors below. Around 6,500 feet in elevation, it provided far-reaching, 360-degree views of the forest surrounding it, making a great fire lookout.

The old bike did damn good, Ben thought as he started up the steepest section of his journey. As though protesting his praise, the motor started winding down and his speed began a rapid decline. 30 MPH...20...15...then down to 10. The bike grinded its way uphill another hundred yards before coming to a stop. Ben cursed, his eyes wandering up the steep hill. With a half mile still to go, he knew there was no way he'd be able to coax the bike to finish their journey.

Frowning, he realized the only way to make the last half mile would be to get off the bike and walk beside it. And so he did, giving it whatever throttle it needed to move up the hill without its rider. It took him another 30 minutes to get to Slip Mountain but, as Ben looked around and marveled at the view, he felt it had been worth it. The lookout rose some 80 feet above ground. He looked up at the tiny cabin perched on top. The only access was by several flights of metal stairs. At the bottom of the lookout was an outhouse, a small storage building, and a single tower with several sets of antennae pointing toward Riverton, 10 miles below.

Riverton could be seen way down below at the end of the long, beautiful, green valley. Almost 180 degrees West, Ben saw another high-country valley, which he assumed was the valley where the Mineral Creek work center was located. He yelled up at Wes, letting him know he'd arrived. The trip had taken about an hour, despite the last half mile of pushing the old 50. Wes yelled for him to bring up the water in the stainless-steel can sitting at the bottom of the stairs.

That's just friggin' wonderful, Ben thought, *now I gotta lug 50 pounds of water all the way up those four flights of stairs.* Resigning himself to the task, he grabbed the bucket and began the trek up. *This isn't so bad*, he thought, until he hit the last section. *Damn, I forgot we were at 6,500-foot elevation.* The journey wore on, but he finally reached the small cabin perched on four supports. A catwalk-style balcony about three feet wide, equipped with metal railings, surrounded the cabin and one entry door on the east side.

Inside, Wes thanked him for bringing up the water. "We were almost out, and I can't leave for a break unless someone is here to monitor the radio and telephone or one of the other lookouts can see this direction," he explained.

"Cool, man! You have a real telephone up here! We still have those old crank telephone machines. I can't believe what I'm seeing," Ben exclaimed.

Wes kept his eyes on the horizon as he answered. "This is one of the few lookouts in the West with electricity. If you look down there, you'll see a power line that goes to all the ranches and the work center. There's also a new telephone line following the power line through the forest. That goes right by here. See? Just a hundred yards that way. I heard crews will remove all the Number 9 wires as new lines and current telephones are installed at all the ranches and the work center. No more dry cell operated lightning rods."

"What's the deal with the insulators on the bottom of the legs on the furniture?" Ben asked.

"Those are our safety net. When lightning gets close enough to hear, you'd better hop up on a stool and keep your feet off the floor. Better keep from touching anything metal while you wait out the storm," Wes commented like a seasoned vet. "Otherwise, you could end up toast—or worse. I was told one lookout had to stay put for six hours, with no food, no water, and no peeing. Look at my cot. There are insulators on it, too, so I can ride out the storms in comfort if they hit while I'm here.

"Remember, the lightning can shock the mess out of you if you touch anything metal. I can't even use the fire finder until the storm has passed. But" Wes stated, "you can't spot any fires until the storm clouds clear anyway. Notice what's in the corner," he grinned.

"Wow, I can't believe you have a TV! Can you really get a picture up here?" Ben asked excitedly as he spied the tiny set.

"At this elevation, and being the only lookout with electricity, the TV can pick up a couple of channels via repeaters. Snowy, but still watchable," Wes answered.

As Wes and Ben dove into their lunches, they kept a watchful eye on the lightning storm as it rolled in from the Southwest at a very fast clip. By the end of their meal, huge, dark gray, cumulous clouds had formed straight overhead with rising, dark black tops. They walked around the lookout, and Ben saw the first lightning strike about three miles away, across the canyon.

"Damn, Ben, look at that storm moving our way. And damn fast," Wes said. "It'll probably hit us within a half hour, so we need to get everything off the catwalk that could blow away. The wind gets pretty strong up here during lightning storms, even small ones, as high as 50-70 MPH from what I've been told."

They quickly secured everything, then closed and latched the windows. Closing the door, they bolted themselves in and prepared for the oncoming storm. Fifteen minutes later, thunder boomed across the distant valley, the noise increasing like a jet engine as it neared the lookout.

Ben spotted the next flash, estimating it to be approximately a mile away. He counted seven seconds from when he'd first spotted it until it was heard. "It's heading right for us, Wes. Do we have to get on the stools?"

"Damn right! We sure don't want to wait any longer. A mile is close, and it could hit the lookout next time," West answered. "We do have lightning rods, and the lookout is grounded, however, we aren't necessarily safe from getting shocked at any time if we touch metal, like the stove, heater, or fire finder."

The sun was blocked by thick, black clouds as darkness invaded the light. Visibility shrunk down to a half mile. Lightning could now be seen streaking across the last patch of visible sky.

What a truly beautiful but scary sight, Ben thought to himself. *Damn, this is so cool.*

Bright flashes were now visible throughout the sky, thunder almost instantaneous and deafening at times. This meant the lightning was within a quarter mile. The two perched on their stools, glass insulators firmly attached to the legs and floor as they surveyed what they could see out the windows.

Ben became lost in thought. Memories of his time in Vietnam were visiting more often than usual. They weren't nightmares…just flashbacks to things he'd experienced. His mind took him back to the night of the Tet Offensive. The VC and North Vietnamese regulars were staging nationwide attacks on dozens of major US and South Vietnamese installations across the entire country.

The memory became more vivid. He was back at the Intelligence Center near the airbase in the safety of a building with no windows. The building was designed with a roof and wall system that could withstand direct hits from 220 MM rockets and most mortars. But, according to his commanding officers, none of that mattered.

"Some of you will be sent to the roof to guard this compound against attack. Sandbags are set up in an L-shape at each corner of the building. I'm sending several of you up there for guard duty, and you'll stay until ordered to stand down. Ben, you'll go up with Sgt. Williams and Spec Inswell on the SW corner. Get your weapon and ammo, go down to the corner of the building, and climb up through the hatch."

Once on the roof, Ben thought, *what now?*

Sgt. Williams looked at Inswell and Ben and said, "Odds are, we're going to be just fine. The air base is a couple hundred meters away. The Joint General Staff Compound is to your left another 200 meters, and the South Vietnamese HQ is next door to them. Those are the main targets of possibility. We're just here, a small, unassuming support building. At least, that's what we want the enemy to think. No one knows there are 700 of us inside doing intelligence work. You are not to fire unless I give you the order to shoot."

Ben's eyes opened wider as he snapped back to the present.

Glancing at him, Wes asked, "Are you alright? You look a little unsettled. We're perfectly safe here."

"I'm fine," Ben answered. "Sometimes I just get hit with all these memories from Vietnam. Some good, some bad."

Crack! Boom!! The noise echoed throughout the cabin as it lit up in a bright, white light.

Rubbing his eyes, Ben looked over at the fire finder, his jaw dropping. Dozens of tiny balls of white and yellow electricity rolled around the top. Then, out of nowhere, dozens of miniature fireballs rolled over the top of the metal cook stove. They stayed there for a short while as they bounced like jumping beans. Just as quickly as they had appeared, they vanished.

"Did you see that?" Ben yelled. "Have you ever seen anything in your life like that? That was so darn cool! I cannot believe we just watched balls of white electricity roll around the lookout. Is that what they call St. Elmo's fire?"

Wham!!! Another lightning strike hit close to the lookout, causing the support structure to shake. This was followed by another huge strike, which crashed by the lookout and struck a granite outcrop 200 feet below. Ben watched it hit, then witnessed one of the most amazing examples of nature he could imagine—a once-in-a-lifetime event. A yellow-orange, basketball-sized ball of lightning bounced off the side of the granite, bouncing to the ground and rolling a few yards downhill before it disappeared. Ben stared at the granite outcrop in disbelief, shaking his head. The storm continued, becoming more intense than he'd ever witnessed.

Lightning began to flash non-stop as thunder roared like an out-of-control freight train. Strong winds lashed against the four walls and windows.

"Stay up on that stool!" yelled Wes as another bolt of lightning hit close by.

I hope these windows are strong, because that's all that's stopping us from getting blown off this friggin', overgrown power pole, Ben thought as everything in the room trembled from the last thunderous boom.

A few minutes later, the lightning storm began to subside and the thunder slowly faded away. The storm appeared to be moving toward the Mineral Creek Work Center.

"I better get back to the work center," Ben stated. "Some of those ground strikes were getting close down there and I think all of us will probably be sent out."

"Except Kahuna, of course. He'll be having a fire of his own to deal with." Wes stated, giggling like a schoolgirl.

Chapter 13

Ben hopped on Kahuna's rusty, trusty Honda 50 and headed back downhill to the work center. Since this was a mostly downhill ride, he made the return trip twice as fast and much easier. As he bumped across the cattle guard and entered the compound, he noticed the engineering crew loading their pickups. Bill was back from town early, getting tools and water loaded, and Rob was busy filling the large orange canteens and canvas water bags.

"Hey, dipstick," Randy bellowed. "You'd better get into your work clothes and get your gear ready. We're being dispatched chasing smoke this afternoon and tonight. We've had dozens of ground strikes in the district. It's all hands-on deck, even if you are a bunch of sissy hands. There's going to be enough fire for everyone."

The phone rang from inside the quarters, and Randy ran to take the call. After about five minutes he came out, face grim. "OK, here's the deal." He handed assignments to everyone, including a list of locations prone to fires and lightning strikes.

"Ben," he pointed, "you and I are staying behind. Smoke was reported about a half mile from here on that hill just behind the work center. For now, the smoke has laid down, but the lookouts will crosscheck the location the next time it appears."

The men vacated the work center, each on an assignment or set to stand by on the district at different locations.

After the crews had gone, Randy came running out of the house, yelling for Ben. "I got a location for that fire! Get your butt ready to go and meet me by the gas pumps in five minutes."

Ben grabbed his gloves, laced up his boots, donned his beat-up hard hat, then headed to the gas house.

"Here, put these C-rations in your pack. Grab two canteens, a shovel, and a Pulaski," Randy bellowed before heading inside the gas shed and returning with an old-fashioned, 6', two-man, crosscut saw.

Ben stared at the antique for a minute, then shook his head, cursing. "What is that for? Don't we have any power saws?"

Randy, with his typical mean scowl in place, replied, "Listen, you idiot, the district only has five power saws available, and they're in use by the fireguards. This is it for you and me. The fire is approximately 1/3-1/2 a mile up the fence line above the work center, so let's get moving. We have at least five or six more hours of daylight—plenty of time."

They headed up the hill above the work center, walking along a fence line that was an allotment fence between two cattle grazing permits. It was a nice, open path through the ponderosa pine forest.

The afternoon sky displayed a buildup of clouds, promising late afternoon or evening thunderstorms. The storm Ben had survived during his earlier adventure was an unusually severe, early storm for this area.

Randy and Ben were quite the sight as they hiked toward the fire. Ben carried his canteen, C-rations, and two tools with relative ease, while Randy was laden down with the crosscut, oil, tools, water, and whatever else the six-foot, five-inch behemoth deemed necessary. The big jock of a basketball player strode effortlessly up the hill toward the smoke report.

And the report was right on the money.

Ben cursed as they hiked over the last rise. Directly in front of them was a 30" diameter ponderosa pine, about 100 feet tall. Their eyes wandered three-quarters of the way up to the burning section. Small flames lapped at the tree trunk, and smoke curled above the tree line.

"Crap. Look at that damn thing up there," Randy bellowed. "The problem is, we have to fall this damn thing, buck it up, then work on whatever is still burning after it hits the ground."

Glancing at Ben, who weighed all of 140 pounds, Randy pondered aloud. "Have you ever used a crosscut? Here's the deal. We're going to fall this tree right over there, away from the fence line. After it hits, we'll put in a scratch line around anything burning, then buck the damn thing up in two or three sections."

Randy looked at the tree and put his finger about 12" up. "Here's where we'll start the bottom of the undercut. We'll cut a pie out of the face here, then do a back cut behind it and fall it over where I pointed earlier, OK? I'll get the saw started, and you grab your handle. Back and forth we'll go for these two cuts of the undercut pie."

Ben watched in amazement as Randy began to see. He could not believe how easily he'd been able to get a smooth glide through the wood, as though the saw was working on its own. Back and forth through the face of the tree, the boys guided the saw, spitting out large sawdust chunks as they went.

"Get your butt in gear and grab on! Let's get this thing going faster," Randy yelled.

The saw sang through the first horizontal part of the undercut. They finished it up rather quickly, with Ben mostly just hanging on to the damn saw as Randy kept the whole thing moving back and forth under his own power most of the time.

As they repositioned the saw to start the top part of the undercut, their eyes went to the darkening sky. Thunder rumbled in the distance. Randy took out a file and started knocking down some rough edges on the saw's teeth. He bent over the saw blade and filed away, his hard hat barely hanging on and his cruiser's vest hanging down on his neck.

As Randy was hunkered over this filing operation, a noise caught Ben's attention. Listening harder, he heard it again.

Thunk. Thunk. Thunk.

Ben's eyes widened when he spotted the embers and tiny burning branches hitting the back of Randy's cruiser vest as he continued to file.

When a larger ember hit Randy on the hardhat, he angrily yelled, "You stupid idiot! Quit playing while I'm getting this damn thing sharp—no more kidding around when I'm not looking!"

After his outburst, the largest ember fell from the burned area high above, hitting Randy right on top of his hard hat as he looked at

Ben and cursed. "That tree is starting to burn hotter up there and the wind is blowing those friggin' embers right down on us. We'd better get a move on and get it on the ground. Crap. I thought you were screwing with me," he stated sheepishly.

The boys finished the undercut, and Randy grabbed the Pulaski. With the axe end of the tool, he chopped out the tiny bit of wood holding the pie-shaped cut.

"All right," Randy said, "let's get the back cut going and get this damn thing on the ground."

He placed the blade horizontally at the back of the tree, with the undercut facing the targeted drop area, and started the saw horizontally toward the front. Once again, Ben was barely holding on and not doing anything other than keeping the saw going back and forth. He served more as a guide than a sawyer as Randy muscled it through.

As the saw blade approached the undercut, there was a loud cracking noise, and the tree began to slowly tilt toward the landing zone. After another, louder crack, Ben heard the loud swooshing noise as the 100-foot ponderosa pine crashed to the ground. At first, its descent was slow, but then it finally crashed down for an accurately planned landing.

"Quick, grab that shovel and start a scratch line up where the burned-out area is," Randy yelled.

The thunder was now too loud for normal conversation. Instead of answering, Ben ran the length of the tree and started a scratch line around the burning area while looking for embers on the ground scattered near the fallen tree. He shoveled dirt on the most dangerous embers and then continued digging down through the layer of pine needles. Quickly, he built a narrow fire line around the burning area, up around the treetop, and back down where Randy was working a few yards out around the fallen tree. Figuring he'd scratched out about 150' of line, he smiled to himself with more than a little pride.

Randy chopped some of the smaller limbs off the tree and used the narrow hoe blade of the Pulaski to scrape away burned material, keeping everything inside the fire line that Ben scratched right behind him.

"Hey," Randy yelled, "you did a good job getting that line in as quick as you did. Not bad for a skinny runt!"

After about three hours of scratching at the burned areas, bucking the downed tree into three sections, and checking around the fire line inside and out looking for any burning materials, Randy stated emphatically, "I think this puppy is pretty much out. Let's grab a bite to eat now. There's not going to be any dinner down below, and we'll need to keep an eye out for another hour for any smoke, then head back down to the Center. I'll call in from there and tell them the fire is out."

Randy and Ben walked back along the length of the fallen tree to the fence line, leaned their tools up against the barbed wire, hung the two canteens over a post, and sat down to eat some C's.

A thunder cell had built up overhead, bringing with it gusty winds. They both quickly jumped up and walked around the fallen tree, taking one more look around the fire line, checking for smoke or flames before settling back down to eat. Flashes were getting closer as they finished their c-rations, and both were getting anxious about being so close to the top of the hill, leaning up against fenceposts during their meal.

"You know," Randy yelled, "I think we'd better move away from this barbed wire and go over there near that small thicket of trees, away from these tall ones. They're like lightning rods, and we're the grounding."

No sooner had they started to move away from the fence line than Ben felt his hair stand on end. His skin felt prickly and out of nowhere, a white, bright, intense flash of blinding light lit up the darkened forest. The thunder sounded like a hundred screaming locomotives. An explosion of sound and light, all happening at once.

Chapter 14

The flash sent Ben's mind back to Vietnam, where he looked over at Specialist Inswell, who was lying beside him. The two were hidden behind sandbags near the corner of the building they'd been assigned to guard. The sandbags were piled three or four high and there were around eight in each direction at a right angle along the corner of the roof.

"You know, this is damn serious. This is the first time we've been given live ammo in seven months," Ben whispered.

They both had older M-14s rather than the newer M-16s, which was fine with them since they'd used them in basic training. Bright flashes could be seen several hundred meters out, along the perimeter of the airbase, followed by explosions. Red tracer rounds went off everywhere as the explosions got louder and their flashes lit up the night sky.

Ben and Inswell kept a tight vigil, watching for any VC who might try and scale the 10-foot, electric fence surrounding their compound. The tracers were coming more frequently, and the cracking of automatic gunfire was now only 100 meters away in the compound next door. A firefight was in progress on the other side of the building, causing Ben's and Inswell's hearts to thump wildly in their chests. Their breathing grew loud enough to be heard between the explosions, and they wondered if the VC would head toward their fenced-in compound.

They were sure a lot of the explosions were from incoming rockets that had most likely launched from somewhere near their barracks compound. The terrifying sounds of war continued for a couple more hours before things finally settled to an occasional explosion.

"I think we're going to be OK here," Ben whispered shakily. "Not so much gunfire now, and those heavier explosions have almost stopped." Ben had no more than finished his sentence when complete terror pierced his soul. Movement along the barbed wire fence had captured his attention. He broke into a cold sweat as he watched three VC approaching the wire. One was beginning to climb.

Ben cursed, his eyes huge. Grabbing Sergeant Williams' attention, he pointed. "Look down below."

The sergeant spotted the three VC and cursed. Two were carrying satchels, while one had an RPG. "What now?" Williams whispered, thinking. After a moment, he had a plan. "OK, here's the deal. Put a round in the chamber—both of you. Ben, on my command, you take the top guy. Inswell, you take the one in the middle. I'll take the guy at the bottom. Unlock and load now!"

They chambered a round, and Sergeant Williams held his hand flat before he raised it and whispered, "NOW!"

The three aimed at their assigned targets, and Ben opened a rapid-fire sequence with a tracer showing on the fifth round. His target immediately slumped toward the wire and fell to the ground. As Ben looked up and down the wire fence, the VC he shot disappeared from view, somehow managing to crawl away, leaving his rifle and pack behind. Inswell fired at his target, hitting him several times, with the final round piercing the VC's satchel and setting off a large explosion. The third VC was thrown to the ground by the blast, and Sergeant Williams finished him off.

Two sets of eyes shot to Sergeant Williams as he radioed the major, letting him know what had happened and that it was all clear. The three sat in silence, shaking as though it was 32 degrees outside.

"What did we just do?" Inswell's eyes were huge as he looked at the others.

His comrades could only stare back at him, each shell-shocked by what they'd done.

The crackle of the sergeant's radio startled them as their commander ordered them to go below and three others replaced them.

After the fact, Ben learned that the airbase had suffered heavy damage to planes, supplies, and several hangars, but most of the casualties were VC with scores killed along the perimeter fencing. Very few had breached the perimeter. Those who did had only made it a few steps before being gunned down. The Tet Offensive was a wake-up call to everyone across the country though, in the long run, American and ARVN forces were the victors as tens of thousands of VC were killed.

Ben's tour of duty would never be the same. The war had now come to him and his unit. There were no more leisure Sundays from this point on.

A loud clap of thunder jolted Ben back to the present, and he looked at Randy. "You all right?" he yelled hoarsely. For some reason, he now had a sore throat.

"I'm OK but, man! That was close. And the smell—can you smell it? Ozone from the heat of the flash, I guess," Randy exclaimed, his voice unsteady. "I remember reading about lightning-created ozone in chemistry class."

They shakily got to their feet and checked their clothing and boots.

"I'm OK," Ben offered. "Nothing singed or burnt. But man, that whole thing made my skin crawl. I felt it a split second before it hit."

The thunder cell dissipated as quickly as it had formed, with the remnants moving off to the northeast.

When they walked to the fence line, Ben exclaimed, "Randy, look at our tools!"

The wooden handles of the Pulaski and shovel still leaned against the barbed wire. Long, black burn marks ran down the handles toward the metal part of the two tools.

Randy cursed. "That could have been us had we stayed close to the fence. It looks like the lightning hit the barbed wire and traveled along the whole thing. And look at the canvas straps on the canteens— shoot, look at the damn canteens!"

They peered at what used to be bright orange canvas covers. The orange on them was now tinged with black marks and soot near the aluminum edges.

Ben looked at Randy, who looked paler than ever. "Well, the good news is we can show these singe/burn marks to anyone we talk to. Without this proof, I don't think anyone would believe what just happened, no matter how we told 'em—I can hardly believe it myself, and we just experienced it! Let's get out of here before another thunder cell forms."

Checking the fire one last time, they headed back to the work center, each looking forward to the comforts of the old ranger's house. On the trip back, both thought about how close they'd come to being singed toast, like those two wooden tool handles. The storms had rolled over the valley area, covering the neighboring ranches and the work center in lightning strikes.

Randy anticipated a long evening. With all the new ground strikes on the district, new fires were sure to continue popping up.

Back at the work center, Ben plunked himself down on the living room's well-worn couch and took off his work boots and socks. Spitting a curse word into the air, he yelled, "Look at this."

When Randy rushed in to see what was wrong, Ben pointed to his feet.

"Look at those burns on the top of my feet and toes," he exclaimed. They weren't bad burns—more like a light sunburn. Nevertheless, they were remnants of their close bout with the lightning bolt.

"Damn," Randy said, staring down at the redness on both feet. "It's a good thing we moved when we did. We could've had some of the more important parts of our body singed." He grinned and laughed, causing Ben to join in, lightening their nervous moods.

The shock and amazement remained on their faces long after they'd settled down.

As Ben rested, he worried about the recurring memories of his time overseas. Though not all bad, the timing was bothersome.

His thoughts were interrupted as a few of the engineering crew wandered in, as well as his crew members, Bill and Rob. They'd worked on several small lightning fires, with most not much bigger than a 50' circle, and others no bigger than a garbage can lid. It was a typical summer fire season.

After hearing Ben and Randy's incredible story, Bill spoke. "In keeping with today's strange lightning events, you wouldn't believe what happened here. We got back here fairly early, around 4:30 or so, and even though the district was still getting lightning, a lot of it was right around here. We were ordered to stand by here at the center in case we had another fire close by. Well," he continued, "there we were, sitting around waiting for the phone to ring. Now and then it rang, but it was most likely rings that were set off by lightning around the area. I told our dumb greenhorn not to answer the phone, especially since there was lightning in the area. We needed to be damned sure it was our rings, loud and clear, not an electrical charge from the storms. Otherwise, we could end up as toast. Needless to say, Rob, in his infinite wisdom, did not listen. The phone rang one long, rather loud ring. It was obvious that it wasn't our ring, but no, he had to run up and answer it.

"Like a dummy, Rob ran and picked up the phone in the same instant that a loud crack of lightning flashed throughout the house. Get this: it knocked him across the kitchen over by the cookstove, near the garbage can. I yelled at him to see if he was all right—stupid question, he's never going to be all right. I ran into the kitchen as he was getting his dazed, dumb butt off the floor, and he kind of sheepishly stammered, 'Randy was right. Don't go near the phone in a lightning storm. My ears are still ringing really loud. You all sound like you're talking from inside a tin can.'

"I'll bet it was the same ground strike you guys barely dodged on the hill. That fence comes right down here to the compound next to the house," Bill offered.

Randy had been standing in the hallway, listening to Bill's story. He burst into laughter, his voice loud and jovial. "Did you think I was friggin' kidding when I told you girls about that phone, metal housing, dry cell batteries, and the metal number 9 lines? You need to listen closer and remember what I tell you." Randy went back into his bedroom, still giggling as he thought. *Will this summer ever end? I need a beer!*

Chapter 15

"I think we should go to town this weekend," Ben told the crew. "Maybe we could go to the drive-in. I think we could all use a diversion."

They had collapsed in the living room after another long week of work. Though the last week had been much calmer than the stormy week before, the boys had worked themselves to exhaustion.

"We don't have a rig big enough for us all," Wes stated.

Bill wandered into the room and eyed the crew. "I'm batching this weekend. The wife and kids have gone over to her mom's house so the kids can see their grandparents. We can take my extended cab pickup. It'll hold six."

Randy wrapped an arm around Bill's shoulders. "I know I've been a jerk to the girls, but you know what? They've done really well these past couple of weeks. Take a couple of quarts of my homebrew with you. They've earned it. I'll trust it to you, but don't let them think I'm getting soft. And make sure they stay out of trouble."

Bill smiled. "Thanks. We'll enjoy some at the drive-in. I'll make sure no one gets carried away."

Bill had no clue that his words would come back to haunt him.

When Saturday evening rolled around, Wes, Bill, Rob, and Ben traded their work boots and clothes for street clothes. Kahuna had left earlier, carried off by two local girls who'd picked him up in their parents' Eldorado convertible. Chris was heading back to Beeton for his sister's birthday party.

"Hey," Bill said with a grin. "Look what I have." He pulled out a cold quart of beer from his portable cooler. "We can have a small glass for the road!"

Rob raised a brow at his comrades. "I don't do rot-gut crap," he stated emphatically, as though he knew good homebrew from bad. "You guys try it first. If you don't barf it up, I might have a glass—a small one, for sure."

Taking a quick drink, Bill cursed. "This is really good. Randy's got something like a cross between Country Club and Heidelberg here—I like it!"

Rob watched him, warring with his thoughts. He didn't want the guys to find out he'd only had alcohol once in his life when he was given a tiny sip of the family's Mogen David on Christmas Eve. Relenting, he pointed at the container. "Hey, pour me a small glass.

You guys don't look like you've been poisoned." He grabbed the glass of foamy homebrew and gulped it down in two swigs. "Geez, that's not bad. Not bad at all." A light buzz was already kicking in.

There was about an hour and a half before the ticket booth opened at the drive-in. With a 45-minute drive ahead of them, Bill decided to kick them into gear. "Let's load up and get down the mountain."

Off they went, with their small cooler in tow. On the way, they discussed the last weekend's activities, each counting themselves damn lucky to have their first taste of real firefighting behind them.

Rob, feeling the effects of the glass of beer he'd chugged, looked at Ben with a lopsided grin. "Hey, how did you really get your toes sunburned? You and Randy take a nap with your boots and socks off?"

"Not funny," Ben frowned. "Not funny at all. At least I didn't get my tail knocked off trying to be an indoor lightning rod."

"What do you expect from a moron?" Bill piped up.

Fury ignited in his bones as Rob light-headedly reached in front of him and grabbed Bill around the neck, choking him.

"You prick!" Bill cried out, his hands gripping the steering wheel tight as he fought to keep them on the road. "Get your hands off me before we crash down that canyon, you stupid clod!"

"Take it back, you hick cowboy loser, or I'll make you sorry," Rob growled. He loosened his grip slightly and Bill gasped.

Ben turned toward Rob and slammed him with a kidney punch. Everyone jumped at Rob's loud, guttural cry as he released Bill, who slumped forward in his seat.

Rob cursed, gasping for breath. "Why'd you do that? I was only kidding!"

Wes turned in the front seat and shook his fist at Rob. "Listen, you idiot, we do not kid around on this road. You know how many people have died down in that canyon? Keep your damn hands to yourself. Choking is not kidding. If you ever do that again, you'll be answering to me. And you'll get a lot more than a punch to the gut, do you understand me? Never do that again!' he repeated, slowly, his eyes boring into Rob's.

Rob slowly pressed himself back into his seat, his right side still smarting from Ben's fist. "You guys need to quit calling me moron and start treating me better." He stammered his words, like a little kid. "I think the beer must've made me do it. I'm feeling dizzy."

"More than dizzy," Bill stated. His shoulders shook with laughter now that things had calmed.

Rob tapped Bill on the shoulder. "Sorry, OK? Sorry."

Chapter 16

With the drama of the drive behind them, the boys arrived at the drive-in movie ticket booth. They hid the small cooler to avoid getting caught with alcohol and the beef jerky they'd snuck in. The drive-in had a strict policy prohibiting alcohol or outside food. Bill collected the ticket money from the boys and paid the young lady inside the ticket shack.

They were told to go toward the back, since the pickup had a high cab. When she read their disappointment, she grinned and told them, "Turn your truck around and back into your spot. It's easier to see from the bed than those front and back seats."

Good idea, Bill thought. He had several wool blankets under the back seat they could use for cushioning.

They found a place in the middle near the last few rows and slowly backed the truck up near a speaker stand. Once parked, they stretched the speaker into the bed where they could all hear the music playing before the movie started.

"Hey, Ben, why don't you go up with me to the concession stand and we'll get four small cokes?" Bill asked.

"I don't like Coke," Rob stated.

"That's OK, we'll use the cups for our beer," Bill grinned. "No one will suspect we have beer in a red or green soda cup."

When Ben agreed, he and Bill walked the 20 yards to the concession stand. On the way there, it seemed like everyone they'd ever met was at the drive-in. They saw the big boss, old, hook-nose John, and his wife Jeane. Ranger Bash was ahead of them at the concession stand.

Bill nodded at Ben. "Isn't that Red, the married engineer who lives next door in the green cabin? That must be his foxy wife, Rina."

Shrugging, Ben focused on the concession stand attendant and gave her their order. Stepping up beside him, Bill helped him grab the cups of pop and tubs of popcorn. Carrying them back to their rig, they settled in and waited for the movie to start.

"Bullitt," starring Steve McQueen, was going to be a great movie. Ben could hardly believe this small-town drive-in was already showing such a top-rated, popular movie. Steve McQueen was one of his favorite actors.

The first half of the movie was the greatest. During the 15-minute intermission, the boys stretched and sat up straighter as the lights around the drive-in slowly lit up.

Ben pointed over his left shoulder, toward a solid black Eldorado. "Hey, isn't that Kahuna over there?"

Bill and Wes both turned to look.

"Sure is. And look at the two good-looking girls with him," Wes pointed out. "And in the back seat, no less. I just cannot believe it. He has some kind of knack for conning those locals into whatever the heck he wants. Amazing!"

"Let's enjoy that other glass of beer now," Bill volunteered. "We've earned an extra glass this week. Hold your coke glasses low below the pickup fender and I'll sneak a pour for all of you, then we can take the bottle and hide it in these popcorn tubs. One of us can dump it in that garbage can by the concession stand after the movie starts up again." Bill did his best to pour equally into the four cups while keeping it all on the sly.

"You OK, moron—er, Rob? Sorry!" Bill grimaced and hoped his mistake didn't set him off.

"You know," Rob answered calmly, "I could actually get to like this stuff."

What a picture that would be, having this dude drinking beer all the time. No, thanks, Ben thought.

The movie was about to start again, so Ben quickly offered to take the evidence to the garbage can and get rid of it before someone got wise and turned them in. He took off, slowly walking toward the garbage cans with the empty beer bottles hidden in two paper tubs from the popcorn. As he approached the dimly lit concession area, he noticed the local version of Barney Fife.

Crap, he thought.

Sergeant Dusty, as the locals had deemed him, was standing next to the closest concession window, trying to order a soft drink. Ben sauntered up and dropped the beer bottles into the can.

Thump! *Clang!* The glass bottles rang out as they hit the side of the can. And good old Sergeant Dusty, always looking for a non-existent crime, peered over the top of the can and spotted the empty homebrew bottles.

Ben turned and slowly walked around the corner toward the men's restroom at the back of the concession stand, all the while glancing back to see if the good sergeant was following.

And wouldn't you know it, he was.

Ben's mind raced as he wondered if it was illegal to drink beer at the drive-in, or if it was just a local rule. He did not want to be on the wrong side of the locals, no matter what. He wanted to remain in this forest for quite some time. He was starting his career, after all. It wouldn't do him any good to be confronted with the smell of beer on his breath. The sergeant would connect the dots to the empty homebrew containers instantly.

Despite the clouds obscuring the moon, it was still light enough for Ben to see a narrow cow path leading up the slight rise behind the concession stand. He quickly turned away from the restroom and stepped onto the path, following it for about ten yards over a slight rise, then down toward what looked to be another narrow pathway.

The moon was now completely covered by a cloud, and Ben hightailed it over to the next pathway. It turned out that this trail was not a trail at all, but rather a four-foot wide, five-foot deep irrigation ditch that ran for several miles parallel to the highway behind the drive-in. Ben was glad he spotted it before the light faded as he hopped over the ditch, clearing the water to the other side. Glancing behind him, he spotted none other than Barney Fife's twin, Sergeant Dusty, slowly coming over the rise. The good sergeant approached the ditch, and Ben veered off to the left, quickly putting some distance between the two.

Sergeant Dusty, being the clueless dude that he is, sped down the path, oblivious to any hindrances to his journey.

Ben heard a loud splash, followed by loud cursing as Sergeant Dusty fell into the ditch.

The sergeant was greeted by chest-deep, cold water, clear up to his badge. His boots were stuck in the clay mud on the bottom of the ditch, his gun and ammo were soaked, and his flashlight was nowhere to be found.

Ben stopped and hid behind a small juniper, watching Sergeant Dusty grab at the grass or brush clumps and pull his way up the steep banks of the ditch. But all he managed was to slip back each time and get muddier and muddier.

Finally, after several more outbursts of four-letter words, he gave up and sloshed through the water, walking along the ditch for a few feet until he found a small juniper tree near the edge. He slowly pulled himself up on his belly, landing on the bank on the wrong side of the ditch. He spat a curse word into the air. "Now I gotta jump back across the damn thing," he muttered to himself.

Ben quickly slipped away as the good sergeant looked for an easier route back to the concession stand area. Jogging quietly along the ditch toward the drive-in front gate, he slipped past the closed ticket shack and back to the truck. The whole thing could not have taken more than six or seven minutes, but to Ben, it felt like an hour.

"Where have you been?" Bill whispered loudly.

"You would not believe what just happened," Ben offered and burst out laughing. He explained the story to the boys, telling of the clanging beer bottles, the slow pathway chase to the ditch, and of "Barney Fife" in the water up to his eyeballs.

The boys expressed their disbelief in the story, but the laughter took a while to die down.

When they'd calmed down, Rob piped up. "Hey, I'm still woozy from that beer, and I need to go whiz, I'll be right back."

Chapter 17

The drive-in, filled with half the town's cars and trucks, started to unwind when the movie finished. Slowly everyone made their way down the rows toward the exit.

"Damn," Wes exclaimed, looking around. "Where's our idiot partner in crime?"

It wasn't until then the boys realized Rob had been gone a full 15 minutes to "go whiz," and he'd still been feeling the effects of the homebrew.

Bill's brows furrowed with concern. "I'm willing to bet that tenderfoot-greenhorn hasn't ever had much alcohol. I'm beginning to think it may have him a little out of kilter."

"Really," Wes gaped at him. "How could that numbskull get any further out-of-kilter than he already is? Even without beer, he isn't close to normal."

The crew waited a few more minutes, watching as the drive-in continued to empty as cars made their way out the front gate.

Finally, Bill grew exasperated. "I'll go to the restroom and see if the idiot fell in. If he's not there, I have no clue where he could be."

"We'll take a look around here," Ben volunteered. "I see Kahuna and his chicks are still here. Maybe he wandered over there."

Ben sauntered over to Kahuna, who still sat in the backseat between the two girls. "Hey, Kahuna," he called. "Did our idiot crewmember come see you guys? He left the truck about 30 minutes ago and we haven't seen him since. He said the alcohol made him woozy, but dang, he only had one glass of beer, and that was over an hour ago!"

"Haven't seen him," Kahuna grinned. "I've enjoyed the time with these two lovely young things. I sure as heck don't want any of his drama."

"OK," Ben nodded. "We'll wait as long as we can but we have to leave after the last car because they shut this place down and lock her up."

Ben returned to the truck, noticing Bill had already come back from looking for Rob.

"We need to leave right after that last car over there, because they'll lock the place up right after," Bill reminded them. "We can take a look around the entrance to the drive-in and see if he wandered up or down the road toward the mill."

Following the last car out, the boys drove slowly down the gravel road that led to the highway, peering into the trees. They looked closely, hoping to find Rob hiding, passed out, or wandering around. Disappointed when there was no sign of him along the drive-in access road or highway, they drove slowly away from town hoping to find him in all his stupid glory. When they still could not find him, they turned the car around and headed back toward the direction of the sawmill near town, passing the drive-in entrance once again.

About a third of a mile from the drive-in stood the county's largest sawmill with its huge millpond shining in the moonlight. The millpond was left over from an old rock and gravel site and was over 100 feet deep in places. It was full of logs ready to be drawn up into the mill by the log conveyor. The large parking area at the mill was empty—the workers long gone for the day.

Bill looked over at the millpond, thinking. "Look how that fog is hanging over the water. See that light pole and that outhouse-looking shack? There's always a night watchman on duty. Let's go see if he's seen our missing in action idiot."

The boys drove close to the guard shack, and Steve Johnson, the 75-year-old watchman, slowly limped out to see what these "punks"—as he called all young people—wanted.

"What are you punks doing here? You ain't supposed to be on mill property. Nobody is allowed around here; what do you want?"

Bill explained about their missing friend and told of his suspicions that he may have wandered away from the drive-in. He further explained that the beer might have made him weird, more so than he already was.

Lightning flashed in the distance, and clouds formed overhead.

The watchman responded, irritably, "Haven't seen anyone. Just me and my trusty transistor, listening to music. Now get your punk butts out of here before I call Sergeant Dusty."

As the boys turned and headed back to the truck, they heard faint muttering and humming.

"What the heck is that noise?" the watchman blurted, whipping his head around. "Sounds like it's coming from the pond. It's hard to see with that fog hanging over the water."

The four wandered to the pond's edge and stopped short, staring in shock. Toward the center of the pond, was their resident idiot,

127

himself. Rob was straddling a large log in the middle of the water, oblivious to the world and just as happy as he could be as he muttered and hummed to himself.

Glancing through the fog, Ben noticed a walkway near Rob's watery perch. It consisted of two logs cabled together with a couple of boards nailed along them. The walkway covered four or five pairs of logs with boards. Along this walkway, other logs floated nearby. Ben figured the walkway was used to sort the floating logs for cutting.

"We can walk up here and get within 20 feet of the idiot and pull his log over with that pike pole," Ben called to Wes. "I think it's one of those 24 footers—should be long enough to reach."

Though Rob was less than 20 feet from the walkway, the fog, and thunder clouds covering the moon, made it hard to see him.

"Come here and help me," Ben yelled to Wes.

Turning to Rob, he called, "Hey, idiot, I'm going to reach out with this pike pole and pull your log over here so you can get out on the walkway, OK?"

Rob's answer was barely audible. "Leave me alone. You guys hate me; you don't want me around, so just go and let me be."

Watchman Johnson's face burned. "Get that little prick off my millpond right now or I will call the cops!" he yelled. "I have no time for this. That punk needs to get off my pond—now!"

"All right, all right, give me a minute," Ben responded. "Wes, come over here while I reach out with this pole."

Ben grabbed the aluminum pike pole hoping to snare the end of the log Rob was straddling. There was a small hook on the end for snagging and sorting logs. He tried to hook the end of the log to no avail. The long pole had quite a bit of sag to it, making it nearly impossible to snag his goal across the distance.

The storm was getting closer, with rapid flashes of lightning making Ben's need to snag the log even more urgent. The floodlight over the pond was starting to flicker, threatening Ben's only source of light. Determination driving him, Ben reached out one last time and caught something, pulling it hard.

Just as the hook latched on, the lights flickered out. Ben felt the pole snag the log as a muffled, sloshing sound caught his and Wes's attention. They both squinted through the haze and darkness as the lights resumed their flickering.

"Where is he?" Ben's words were clipped with frustration. The light remained on for longer this time, and Ben blurted, "He's not on the log and I can't see him in the water!"

Wes cursed. "What did you do, Ben?"

"What do you mean, what did I do?' I just snagged the front of the log. The hook was in the bark, then something made it turn loose. It almost felt like that dumb prick might have pulled the hook out of the bark. Even with the lights back on, I can't see anything, can you?" Ben exclaimed, peering over the water.

"What's going on? What happened out there?" the watchman demanded, even though "out there" was only 50 feet from the guard shack. "Did you grab that log and pull him in?"

Ben, starting to feel sick to his stomach, yelled back, "You better call the cops; that idiot's not on the log and I can't see him anywhere."

Bill returned from searching for Rob around the millpond's edge. He listened as Ben and Wes recounted their attempts to hook the log, nodding his agreement when Ben explained his suspicions that Rob had pulled the hook out to avoid being pulled in.

"Old man Johnson just called the cops to come down and help us search for him," Ben said. "I can't figure out what just happened. I had the damn log!"

Bill looked at them and frowned. "Now listen you two, I know we don't like Rob's worthless butt, but you didn't give him a push with that pole, did you?"

Ben gaped at Wes before turning to Bill. "Jeez, no! He might be a dumb peckerhead, but I would never do anything like that. You gotta remember, I want to complete my probation period on this job and continue here with a full-time career. I would never do anything to jeopardize that. Man, I could be so screwed now," Ben worried.

A few minutes later, Sergeant Dusty drove up to the guard shack and came over to the boys. "What are you all doing at the mill site this time of night?"

Johnson looked at the Sergeant. "Well, seems like these punks lost one of their buddies out there, playing on my mill pond. I was told he was out on a log babbling and humming. These boys reached out with that pike pole over there and tried to hook the log he was riding and pull him over there." He pointed to the log walk. "Somehow, they lost him. He either slipped off the log, slid off the log, or was shoved

131

off the log. I have no clue. I heard it all, but it was really hard to see over there from where I was with all the foggy haze hanging over the water and the power going off and on. At times, it was pitch black out here with that stupid like flicking all the time."

"Which one of you was the pole operator?" the sergeant asked with a smirk on his face. Without waiting for an answer, he narrowed his eyes at Ben. "Do I know you? You look familiar. Have I had you in jail before?"

"No," Ben stated emphatically. His eyes went to the sergeant's clean and freshly pressed uniform. He had no pistol, no ammo pack, and no flashlight. Just cuffs and a night stick hanging from his belt. He was also sporting brown loafers that were not part of his uniform. He hid the smile that threatened to expose his secret and explained in great detail exactly what had happened.

When he'd finished, Sergeant Dusty rushed to his squad car and radioed his headquarters, which was located on the other end of town. He asked for a search party, the bloodhound they had trained as a tracker, and a diver for the morning. Riverton police had two volunteers that were certified as qualified divers who could search the pond after sunrise. Briefly, the sergeant explained over the radio what had happened.

Of course, the boys never mentioned the homebrew, or the fact that Rob might be a nutcase, or at the very least, slightly unstable.

Chapter 18

It was almost three in the morning, and Ben, Wes, and Bill sat slumped in the pickup with the doors wide open wondering what could possibly have happened to Rob. There was no thrashing sound coming from the water. No sounds that might be attributed to someone in distress or, worse case, drowning. While the three were deep in thought, and starting to get more than a little scared, the tracker bloodhound and its handler showed up at the scene.

The handler was a tall, thin kid. He was an auxiliary-type volunteer, Ben thought. Couldn't be more than 19 years old. He came over and introduced himself, a smile spread across his pimpled face. "Hey, guys, I'm Jack Smith, and this is Beau, my hound. As soon as it's light enough, I'm going to take him around the end of the millpond and see if we can pick up a scent. Do you have anything that belonged to this dude? Beau will need to sniff it to search him out."

"I don't think so." Bill glanced around the truck. "Wait, I think he left his baseball cap in the backseat. Let me look around." He went back to the truck, finding Rob's hat where it had been kicked toward the corner of the pickup bed. "Here, this is his hat. He left it in the back of the rig when he went to the bathroom at the drive-in. At least, that's where he said he was going."

"That will work just great," Jack responded, holding the hat under Beau's nose.

As the sun rose, Jack and his hound took off. They circled the truck and then headed for the edge of the millpond. The pond was around five acres in size and would take the hound less than 60 minutes to cover its perimeter.

The two disappeared around the far side of the millpond, with good old Beau sniffing, snorting, and eagerly searching along the water's edge. After about 10 minutes, Beau's howling barks could be heard from the other side of the pond. He'd picked up on a scent and dragged Jack about 25 yards away from the pond, toward the foothills surrounding the mill. Just as quickly as the hound had picked up on the scent, he lost interest. Beau circled the area, sniffing every square inch and found nothing.

****

Forty-five minutes later, Jack and the hound returned to the group.

"Look, Beau never misses. About two-thirds of the way around, he caught the scent of something he thought was related to the smells from the hat. We headed toward that hill over there, and he lost the scent. It just plain ended. He couldn't find a trace anywhere to start up again."

"Does that mean Rob crawled out of the pond and took off somewhere?" Ben asked.

"Not necessarily," Jack answered. "Beau and I have only been doing this on 'practice training' cases. This is the first time we've tried to find a real person. It could mean anything. I think we're going to have to call in a more experienced tracking dog from the sheriff department. They have a pair of dogs that have been successful in searches for missing hikers, kids, and other cases around the county. I'll have the station call the Sheriff's Department when I get back down there, then I'm heading home. Us volunteers still have to work real jobs, you know."

Sergeant Dusty told the boys to head to the police station where someone would take their statements. He wanted to hear everything that had gone down that day. He was determined to solve the mystery of Rob's whereabouts. Had he run away? Killed himself? Or had something horrible happened to him?

****

The boys walked into the police station wearing the weight of Rob's disappearance on their shoulders.

A young duty officer glanced at them as he poured himself a cup of coffee near the back of the room. "You three come over here and sit around this table. Do not talk to each other or look over each other's statements. I want each of you to separately write down what happened. Include anything from that day you think is important. Make it as detailed as possible."

After about an hour, they'd completed their statements as directed.

"Can we go back to work enter now?" Bill asked.

Sergeant Dusty walked in, his eyes looking Bill over. "Yeah, you can take off. I got your boss, Ranger Bash, out of bed earlier and explained the situation as best we know. I told him I needed you three back here later this morning. You'll come back here at 10:00 AM. We'll have the sheriff's hounds try and figure things out in the meantime. If we find nothing, I'm going to have to call this punk's parents. Do you know who they are?"

Ben told him what he knew. According to Rob, his dad was some kind of congressman or judge—some high-falooting political type. He lived somewhere within 100 miles of Baltimore, Maryland, though the exact location was unknown to Ben.

"You can call the personnel people at the district office," Bill offered. "They have all that in his personnel file from when he signed up. We all had to put our home addresses, next of kin, or nearest relative information on the forms."

Chapter 19

The truck cab was silent as Bill drove up the winding mountain road back to the workstation. At last, Bill broke the silence. "Listen, Ben, I'm only gonna ask this once more. Did you shove that S.O.B. into the pond on purpose? Don't feel guilty for admitting the truth—-we've all wished he'd disappear at one time or another over the past few weeks—I just need to know if you did it."

Ben didn't answer right away. He was busy working to reign in his frazzled thoughts. The beer at the drive-in, narrowly escaping Sergeant Dusty's clutches—he was sure the man had figured out it was he who'd led him ditch swimming. And then there was that idiot, Rob. Ben was sure he was screwing them over once again but how? Why? Where *was* he? Ben wondered.

"Ben?" Wes prodded, curious to hear his answer.

Snapping from his thoughts, Ben gaped at his comrades and cursed. "No! As much as I dislike that sissy little worm, I would not harm him. Besides, other than that last bit of crap when we were heading to the drive-in, he was finally acting halfway decent. I have no clue what happened out there, so don't ask me again!"

Bill's thoughts shifted to his wife and four kids. He was beginning to worry about his future. He wanted to believe Ben but wondered if Rob's latest antics had been enough to cause Ben to shove him right off that log with the pike pole. Shaking his head, Bill welcomed the wave of reason as it washed through his mind. *Ben loves the local area,* he thought. *He says he wants a career here, and I believe him. Perhaps tomorrow will bring more answers regarding what happened out on that pond.*

****

Morning came without much sleep, but Ben felt rested when his alarm went off at 8:00. Remembering they didn't have work today, he smiled. And then he remembered why.

After scarfing down a late breakfast, the three headed back down the mountain to the police station. There, they met Sergeant Dusty, who had them follow his squad car to the millpond site.

The mill ran under the watchful eye of the only other full-time cop in the small town. He observed the logs' entrance to the mill, ensuring nothing was attached to any of the logs, such as the missing person's clothing.

Nearby, a millpond worker sorted logs with the pike pole Ben had used the night before, keeping an eye out for anything suspicious. The plan was to shut the operation down for their 10:00 AM break and have the two divers in the water, searching for Rob's body. No one knew for sure if Rob drowned or if he was anywhere near the millpond, or he just took off somewhere drunk as a skunk. He could actually be anywhere.

"The sheriff's two volunteer divers and their hound team will be here within the hour. Is there anything else you guys can think of that might give us a clue as to what went down—or why?" Sergeant Dusty asked the boys.

When they shook their heads, Dusty continued. "I got ahold of this punk's father. He's a New York state senator. Quite wealthy and influential. He's extremely upset. He took a Redeye flight last night and is driving straight here from the airport. Said he should be here before noon."

****

The two seasoned bloodhounds and their expert handler had the same results as Beau—there was no scent to follow around the mill site. The scent traveled away from the pond and back toward the water

141

before disappearing. The divers, too, had no luck finding anything in the pond. Although the water was murky, they'd been able to see most of the bottom of the pond with their underwater lights and had searched around the sunken logs and any other obstacles where a body might be lodged. By the end of the search, Rob's disappearance remained a mystery.

Sergeant Dusty stared at the three boys as though they were now suspects. "All right, you three. I want you to go down to the station and wait. The missing person's father will be there in about an hour. Don't talk to each other about this investigation or anything written in your statements. I want the facts fresh from your own peabrains when the father talks with us. Understood?"

Ben looked at Wes and Bill, his eyes displaying his worry. "OK, we'll do as you ask, but look, we've got no clue what happened to Rob."

****

The boys hopped into Bill's pickup truck, heading across the small town, past their favorite "Fire Drill" highway intersection and back to the Riverton Police Station. Once there, they sat in silence, fighting nausea as they awaited the arrival of the rich, Eastern politician.

Ben was feeling especially anxious. *Could I have accidentally shoved that little S.O.B. into the water with that pole and not realized it? After all, I'd had a couple of beers, myself, and he is a screaming prick...*

His self-doubt was soon interrupted by a loud voice from the police station entrance.

"Who's in charge here?"

Chapter 20

The boys' eyes went to the tall stranger who filled the doorway. A handsome, older gentleman named Adam Katz was dressed in a dark, red suit and red tie and sported expensive, custom-made leather shoes.

Wow, Ben thought, staring at the man's manicured hands, *this guy has to be Rob's dad.* The soft, white, callous-free skin and styled hair was a dead giveaway. It was obvious he'd never worked outside of an office setting a day in his life.

Sergeant Dusty walked over and introduced himself to Rob's father, Adam Katz, before leading him into his office and explaining what he knew about Rob's disappearance.

The boys watched nervously as the man's face turned red. He gestured and pointed, loudly exclaiming his dismay at the lack of information regarding his son. Katz demanded to know what had been done and why Rob had yet to be found in this Podunk community.

"Where could anyone possibly hide in this damned dump?!" the father yelled. "If you can't find him, bring in the state police or FBI; anyone besides you small-town idiots! You obviously have no experience whatsoever. I demand to talk to those three boys who were with him."

"You three get your butts in here and talk to this man," Sergeant Dusty yelled. "He needs to know what happened and you three were there, so it's on you."

Once the boys were in front of him, Rob's dad let loose. "Alright, you three, what happened? Where is Aaron?"

Exchanging confused looks, the three answered in unison, "Who's Aaron?"

Adam Katz, losing his patience, grew more red-faced by the minute. Tiny beads of sweat dripped from his white, perfectly combed hair. "What do you mean, 'who's Aaron?!' He's my son—the one you've been living with. The one *you* did something to!"

"You mean Rob?" Ben asked cautiously. "We don't know any Aaron. The guy who's missing is Rob. He's from somewhere around Baltimore, or back East somewhere, a typical greenhorn, and is on the crazy side."

Adam Katz slumped into a chair in front of the desk and cursed. "I thought he was going to get better out here," he murmured. "His name is Aaron Katz; we live in upstate New York. He was having some emotional issues after his mother died two years ago. He's been under psychiatric care most of the time since then. If he takes his

145

meds, he's just fine. If he doesn't..." He glanced at them, sadness reflecting in his eyes. "Well, I'm sure you've seen his changes in behavior and rapid mood-swings."

The boys took turns explaining what they'd witnessed over the summer. They left nothing out, especially all the stupid things Rob had done. Finally, they talked about their trip to the drive-in on Saturday, and of the couple of glasses of beer they all had. They ended their tail with the subsequent disappearance of Rob—Aaron—that evening.

"Look," Ben cautiously explained, "I don't have a clue what happened. Like I said, I put the pike pole on the log to pull him in. The lights went out, and we heard a slight muffled sloshing sound. It didn't sound like someone was out there drowning. There was no cry for help—just a slight water splash. I wouldn't do anything to hurt anyone," he restated. "I want to work here permanently, and I wouldn't jeopardize that."

Katz's eyes were wet as he responded. "I think I believe you. Aaron has had so many emotional issues these past two years. He's done some things that—well," he hesitated, embarrassed, "—someone 'normal' wouldn't do. If he'd been drinking—which, by the

146

way, he's never done—then took his Valium close to the same time, there's no telling what the effects would be. He was warned by his doctor in New York to never mix anything with his medicine. He was taking a rather large dose, and alcohol doesn't mix well."

Remembering something he hoped would comfort the father, Bill offered, "If it makes you feel any better, after that choking incident, Rob, er, Aaron, apologized, so there was some semblance of normalcy as we headed into town."

****

Ater their discussion with Aaron's father, the three boys were finally released back to Mineral Creek. They were physically and mentally exhausted from what had transpired. As though Rob's disappearance wasn't enough, they now had his big lie to comprehend. Near the end of their conversation, Aaron's father had seemed half-way gracious, even thanking the boys for their honesty. But Ben could tell he still suspected they weren't being straight with him.

Ben's thoughts were interrupted by Kahuna's chariot. The big, black Eldorado drove up to the gate, and the beautiful young ladies from Saturday kissed Kahuna on the cheek before he bounded out of the car, smiling from ear to ear.

"Another wonderful time was had by all," Kahuna blurted. Amused by his own words, he was not worried that he could have missed work on Monday if he stayed with them longer, which he'd seriously considered.

"How do you do it?" Wes asked.

"Not sure," Kahuna answered. "Could be my good looks, my great hair, or my muscles and suntan."

Ben rolled his eyes. *What an ego. Whatever it is, it works for him.*

"Didn't any of those olive-skinned, black-haired beauties in 'Nam share some of themselves with you?" Kahuna asked Ben.

"Really? Ben gaped at him. "That's none of your damn business. I'm gonna head to bed. It's been a heck of a weekend, and I'm glad we're working tomorrow. You guys can explain what Kahuna missed while he was playing tongue-swap with his two new friends."

As Ben drifted off to sleep, Bill and Wes filled Kahuna in.

Chapter 21

Sleep didn't come easily for Ben. He tossed and turned, thinking about the weekend's events. When his mind had tired of tormenting him with Rob's disappearance, it shifted to thoughts of Vietnam, fixating on a woman he'd befriended while there.

Her name was Mia, and she was beautiful. She was a little thing—only standing around five-foot-one and weighing no more than 110 pounds. She had beautiful, long, black hair—the kind seen in pictures of Asian women. Her skin was lighter than most of the women there. Her mother was half-Vietnamese/half-French, while her father might have been Chinese. That made for an interesting combination. Her eyes were almost as round as Ben's and a light hazel color.

She always wore the traditional *ao dai* dress, consisting of long, silk pants under a long, silk, tight-fitting dress. He thought about how beautiful those colors were on all the women, with blues, pinks, and other pastels mixed in with white. That dress hung on her every curve like it was molded to her body.

He'd first met Mia in the restaurant bar near where he and the boys had almost been bicycle-bombed. Even though her parents were well off, she lived alone, attended the University of Saigon part-time, and earned her own money by working weekends.

She wasn't the typical "tea girl" looking for some GI or fat cat contractor to pay for play. Ben had made friends with several bar girls and learned some came to the city from the countryside to make money however they could, whether in the bar, the bed, or as some officer's hootchmate.

When Ben finally drifted off to sleep, his dreams were as vivid as the day's events. He was suddenly back in Cholon—with Mia.

It was Sunday—his day off. He returned to the restaurant bar where Mia was working. The old mama-san in charge of the girls gave Ben her usual dirty look. He smiled and nodded as he withdrew some piaster bills and handed Mia around 200 for her tea.

That should keep the old girl shut up for at least an hour.

"I am so glad you come today. I not do good on some of my English. Hard time in class," Mia said awkwardly.

"Why don't I try to help with your English? I can come by where you live and help. Maybe next Sunday, if I'm off duty. Unless, of course, you're working."

Mia responded with a warm smile. "Maybe more than study…
You like me?"

Ben, in his usual shyness, responded, "Of course I do, I just…"

"Shhh," Mia whispered. "I good girl, but you nice to me. Unlike
GIs who just want boom-boom then disappear—gone forever after
bed."

****

Ben continued to toss and turn as his dreams of Mia continued.
That next Sunday, he'd followed the directions Mia had given him to
her house.

"Take left at alley," she said. "When you reach canal, turn right
and count number of doors. I am number four doors down that alley,
away from the canal."

He found the alley without much trouble and walked around a
hundred meters down. The walk seemed like forever but, at last, he
reached the canal and turned right. He counted four doors, knocking
lightly on the fourth one.

When Mia answered the door, Ben's eyes were transfixed on her.
Dressed in shorts and a pink t-shirt, she was barefooted and gorgeous
as the full moon lit up her smiling face.

"Come in quickly, before anyone see you," she whispered. "Not everyone here like Americans. Sometimes, if they see Vietnam girl with GI, they report to VC."

Her small shack consisted of a couple of small rooms. There was a tiny entry room with a large crockery jar of water on the floor and a bedroom with barely enough room for a bed. Behind her, was a tiny kitchen area next to a bathroom. The bed was a short, homemade platform with a mattress on top. The bathroom—if one could call it that—was the size of a closet, consisting of a stool and some buckets

Mia grabbed Ben by the hand and gently led him into the bedroom. He looked at her as heat rushed up the back of his neck, coloring his cheeks. He hoped she hadn't noticed...

Mia smiled, teasing her lips with her tongue. "Hey, nice GI Ben, you not have woman before?" Her voice was mischievous and caught him off guard.

"Yes, I have," he answered. "...once..." His voice trailed off and he ducked his head.

With a laugh, she pulled him onto the bed. Giving him a quick peck on his flushed cheek, she whispered, "Take off your clothes. I be right back."

Forgetting all about helping her with her English, Ben nervously shed his clothing and laid the pile neatly by the door before plopping beneath the old sheet that was spread over the bed. The only other thing on the bed was a worn pillow. It was a rather crude room, but he knew Mia's presence would change that.

He was right. From the moment she reentered to the moment they fell asleep in each other's arms; Ben knew nothing but bliss.

The morning quickly arrived, and the cramped house became like a steam bath as the day heated up.

Mia woke up first. "Come," she said, shaking Ben. "You must go. I must work later and you need to go now before anyone sees you. Remember what I say: GI's not welcome here. Cholon can be dangerous, and we all have been watched by the VC everywhere in my neighborhood. I have seen them."

Ben leaned over and kissed Mia goodbye, not knowing that would be their last encounter. "I'll come to the bar next week and see you again, OK?"

"You my one and only number one. Yes, you my only one, but you must buy more than one tea or Mama San will fire me."

And with that Ben left, never to see Mia again.

****

The next morning, Ben rolled over in his bunk and rubbed his eyes. Groggily, he realized he was soaked in sweat.

From where he sat on the edge of his bed, Wes watched him as he pulled his boots on. "Are you all right? You were talking in your sleep all night long. Moaning and groaning and carrying on like you were with someone."

"I think I *was* with someone last night, at least for a while," Ben smiled.

"Who's Mia?"

"What did I say?"

"You were carrying on a ripe old conversation with someone by that name," Wes grinned.

Ben gave him the short, non-sexy version of the story of Mia. He that she was a friend who he'd helped learn English, while she taught him about Vietnamese culture and history—and sex, but he skipped those details.

"So, what happened to her? Did you finish your tour and leave her there?" Wes asked, his curiosity piqued.

Ben looked at Wes, moisture filling his eyes as he told him the rest of the story. Toward the end of his tour, the Paris Peace Talks were beginning. He'd helped with the United Nations damage assessments as they assessed the damage caused by the rocket attacks by the VC and North Vietnamese. There were rocket and satchel bomb attacks carried out all over Saigon and the surrounding areas, especially in the Cholon area.

Ben had learned the rockets were being launched across the Saigon River from the jungle near their compound. At night, the rockets could be heard overhead. They made *whisper* sounds—*whew, whew, whew*—as they went over Ben's barracks and slammed into the city.

"One day, while I was looking at the latest aerial photography of where the rockets were landing, it became evident to me that most were landing in the Cholon area," Ben said. "The VC and NVA hated the Chinese and targeted that section a lot. I looked at those latest photos and was shocked. I could make out a familiar part of Cholon. It was the area around the alley where I walked down to get to Mia's place."

He sighed. "I could see where it ran into the canal. But when I went to look where her house should be, there was nothing left but rubble. Her house was gone. Nothing left but large pieces of tin, wood, and rubble. It stretched along that pathway to a dozen or so other huts, all completely wiped off the face of the earth. There was nothing.

"Her neighborhood of tiny shacks had been wiped out. They must have been hit with more than one rocket. After things had calmed down and we were allowed to return to the city, I went back to the restaurant bar where she worked. I was told she disappeared, and I'm afraid that was the end of that story." Ben's voice was shaky, and he wiped his eyes. "Enough of this. I gotta get ready to go to work, and so do you."

Chapter 22

As Ben and Wes finished breakfast, Randy popped his head in and asked, "No word yet on Rob? I mean Aaron... It's been almost two weeks and not a damn explanation of anything."

"I haven't heard anything," Wes stated. "I just don't get it. How can anyone disappear off the face of the earth like that? Especially in this county, where everyone knows what everyone else is doing. And Aaron—or whatever his name is—is such a greenhorn, I don't get how he can survive anywhere. He must be holed up in someone's empty house or some abandoned shack. He sure couldn't survive out in the woods."

Just then, the wall phone clanged. Two long rings, a short ring, then another long. Randy grabbed the phone and spoke quietly into the receiver for a good five minutes.

He hung up the phone and then turned to the boys. "Guess what, girls? You know most of the West has been having large fires. Well, right now they're running out of crews and equipment. John just told me the forest is sending a mop-up crew to a fire in Washington. They want the crew to go up there to free up some of the more experienced crews stuck on mop-up and replace them with project crews like us.

We'll put a crew together, 15-20 of us from the district, and head up there tomorrow."

Ben gaped at Wes. "Wow, that's amazing. But, Randy, are we qualified to do that?"

Randy scoffed at him. "We've all been to Guard School. We've put out several lightning fires and know how to do mop-up. Every one of you has been on those small fires, so this should be easy. The hard work is done. The fire is essentially contained, so all we will do is patrol, keep an eye out for fire near the line, and put out all smokes a chain or two inside the fire line—simple, right?

"So far, the plan is for us to load all our tools, five or six cases of C-rations, canteens, and bedrolls, and then we'll drive over to Beeton and catch a plane to Central Washington. They have some six packs waiting for us to use that are parked at the airstrip."

Thoughts of their missing crewmember faded to the background, at least for the moment, as they readied their packs for tomorrow's big adventure.

****

The district crew loaded three six-pack Dodge pickups and were out on the road early, heading to the airport. Bill, Wes, Ben, Kahuna, and Chris were all excited about a new experience. This time they'd be teamed up with engineering crew members and other guys in the district, making up a 16-person mop-up crew. They would also need to be ready to respond to any new, small, lightning fires if needed.

They arrived at Beeton airport and stared out over the one, long runway. It was a white DC4 with a black stripe down the middle and *Western Fire* written in bold letters across the upper middle of the fuselage.

"Wow, would you look at that," Kahuna blurted.

Approaching the plane, a loadmaster showed them where to place their tools and gear, then escorted them to the front. There were several rows of seats, with stacks of water and other supplies behind the last row. The boys were pleasantly surprised to see the plane also equipped with two stewardesses.

The plane quickly filled as another crew boarded, having been at the airport for the last two days. They all loaded in, the engines fired up, and they taxied out.

"Damnit!"

The boys's heads spun to one of the stewardesses.

159

"What's the problem?" Kahuna asked. If he was really nice to her, perhaps she'd give him her phone number.

"I forgot my darn belt, and my jeans are about to fall off," she worried.

Kahuna quickly reached into his carry-on pack and pulled out a piece of nylon rope. "Here, take this and tie your pants on. We wouldn't want any embarrassing accidents at 15,000 feet., would we?"

Everyone laughed as she threaded the rope through her belt loops and tied it into a bow. "Thanks," she said with a smile. "I'll see that you boys are comfortable on this flight."

The plane rumbled slowly down the runway, fully loaded. It moved awkwardly, like a weirdly gaited camel with wings bouncing as they rolled down the pitted asphalt runway. It seemed to take forever as it slowly left the earth behind, climbing at a snail's pace into the morning sky. The excited firefighters strained to see out the windows as they rose above the fields and forests, leaving Beeton behind. They continued the slow ascent, circling and headed Northwest.

The stewardesses brought the boys water and snacks to take the edge off a very bumpy flight. The morning was heating up, and thermals were pitching the airplane around quite a bit. Thankfully, it didn't take more than a couple of hours for the captain to announce they would land in about 30 minutes.

Ben looked out the window, but all he saw were deep, hilly canyons. There was no sign of civilization, and definitely no airport. They flew a while longer, and then the plane descended, bouncing around like a bucking bronco. First, it went sideways and then bounced up and down. Suddenly, they began a quick bank to the right.

Ben looked out and stared straight down the wing as the plane banked. In the bottom of one of the hilly canyons was a single, long, line—the runway. He could see it snake along the canyon bottom, surrounded by steep sidewalls. At the upper end of the runway were a bunch of trucks and some people standing around piles of equipment, pumps, hoses, and other supplies.

Ben looked at the boys, a worried look on his face. "I have no friggin' clue how we're going to land in that canyon."

As he spoke, the landing gear was lowered abruptly with a loud thump. The DC4 quickly descended to a precariously low altitude, dropping off the deck a few hundred feet above the steep canyon walls along the runway in the opposite direction, heading downstream toward an area where the terrain flattened out. Then, out of nowhere, the pilot quickly banked the plane an absolute 180 degrees and dropped the last few hundred feet, swinging around in a tight flight path. He plopped the DC4 down for a perfect landing on the beginning of the narrow runway and maneuvered the plane for a safe landing.

Wes looked at Kahuna, eyes wide. "Man, I thought I was going to crap my pants!" Everyone laughed out loud in a somewhat fear-dampening response. "I cannot believe we just 180'ed that landing in the opposite direction and plopped this sucker down between those steep canyons, down onto the bottom."

Chapter 23

The boys were still shaken when the plane landed. On wobbly legs, they disembarked and went to the luggage compartment to get their gear. They stacked the luggage alongside the pickups waiting for them. The keys were found on the back-rear tire just as John had said. The local district fire control officer, who'd introduced himself as Fred, was there to let them know where they were going. After providing maps for each vehicle, he grabbed Randy and briefed him on what fire they would be working on, informing him that there were three major fires in this forest, alone.

To Ben's surprise, a film crew was set up down the runway. "What's with the Hollywood film?" he asked the officer.

"It's for some new show they're doing," he replied.

Several members from other fire crews wandered over and watched the filming of firefighters as they sharpened their power saws and hand tools.

The camera operator was engrossed in his filming, oblivious to the crowd gathering around him. A long-haired hippie, the guy was dressed in a colorful shirt, wild boots, and brightly colored tie-dyed jeans. He swatted his hair away from the lens as a man approached him and started a conversation.

Ben watched the exchange from where he stood with his crew, noting the cameraman's body language—he was angry about something. Before he could think any more about it, a loud eruption of screaming and cussing ensued. The crowd leaped back when the fire crewmember suddenly cranked his chainsaw and started chasing the cameraman down the runway, revving his chainsaw as he ran.

Ben and the guys burst into laughter as they watched, amazed by how fast the cameraman could run.

Wes cursed. "What's that all about?"

Fred, the district officer, raced toward the two, yelling at the crewmember as he ran. Once he'd gotten his attention and ordered him to shut the chainsaw off, he proceeded to chew him out for a solid ten minutes.

Fred stormed back to his pickup, where Bill cautiously approached him.

"What the heck just happened? Do those two know each other?" he asked.

Fred cast a glare over his shoulder at the two. "That idiot cameraman insulted that crewmember. Said he looked like some kind of Paul Bunyan wannabe with a large dose of hick thrown in. Asked him if he spoke English or just one-syllable logger talk, then dared to ask when his last shower was. The crewman wasn't about to take more of that and told him he better run for his life or lose everything below the knees. He scared the wadding out of that guy." Despite his agitation, he laughed.

Having had their fill of entertainment, the Blue Mountain Forest crews hopped into their six-packs and headed up the mountain toward the Knife Fork Fire. It was named after Knife Fork Creek, where the fire had originated. They faced about a 45-minute drive, followed by a hike into the part of the fire line where they would mop up, patrol, and monitor.

They arrived around 11:30 and gathered their equipment before hiking through a large area that had been previously burned. They hiked through a thick stand of Lodgepole Pine, which was completely blackened. For miles, all that could be seen were burned-out trees, void of most of their needles. The hillside looked like a bunch of black telephone poles scattered about with light brown tops. Any brush or grass that had been there had been devoured by the fire. In many places, every bit of vegetation and forest litter had been burned down to bare mineral soil.

It took them about an hour to walk through the portions of forest that quietly smoldered, having been devoured a couple of days before. When they arrived near the fire's edge, they stopped for a quick lunch of C-rations. The day was warming up quickly.

Wes' gaze wandered the terrain as he ate, his eyes fixing on active fire downhill. "Is this a safe place to be right now?" he asked Randy.

The fire had burned the area they'd walked through, then shifted with the wind and burned up the ridge to their right, leaving a large, unburned island below them. Wes guessed the area to be around 100 acres of green overstory trees and heavy brush. Further down the mountainside, smoke rose higher than when they'd arrived. They had one two-channel radio and monitored whatever fire reports they could hear.

Randy thought about the question as he assessed the situation, weighing it against his experience. "We should be safe, especially since we have that large safety area we just walked through but just keep watch for any wind shifts. That heavy smoke below us could carry some flying embers; so, watch for any flareups near the line. Look, guys, the mop-up work here looks pretty easy. Just make sure you flip any burning debris into the black, not downhill."

With that, the boys went to work. It was a long, slow, hot afternoon as they fought the small flareups and smoke within two chains of the fire line. They widened the fire line where needed, ensuring one person acted as a lookout above them the entire time.

At 3:30, they stopped for a break. They'd completed quite a bit of the mop-up they were assigned to complete during their shift and were growing tired. Wes and Bill returned from patrolling a quarter mile up the fire line from where the crew had been working.

"Nothing out of the ordinary," Bill stated. "We noticed the smoke was a lot darker below us, though. You can't really see it from here because it's not a huge, tall plume above the trees yet."

"OK, we're now entering the most dangerous part of the day. Burning conditions are serious. It's dry, getting hotter by the hour, and I can feel the wind picking up, so let's be careful what we do. No dumb moves. Keep an eye out for quick changes," Randy warned.

An engineering crewmember called out to Randy, radio in hand. "There's a lot more radio traffic than earlier. Sounds like several parts of the fire are getting very active."

The crew perused the fire line, scanning the unburned island below them. The radio crackled with a dire report—a crew could be cut off or burned due to the active fire.

Randy's heart pounded in his chest as he stared downhill. He cursed around the lump in his throat. "I think they're talking about us. Look way down there at the plume of smoke—toward the bottom of that unburned area. It's risen visibly, just within the last few minutes."

The boys observed the strengthening flames in the distance as the wind grew stronger.

Randy cursed into the air, panic seizing his muscles. "Wes, you and Bill go down each section of the line you were on earlier and tell everyone to hightail it back here. NOW!"

Although the crew was spread out, they weren't far away. Bill and Wes herded them back to the rest of the crew.

They watched in horror as trees were torched below them. The wind, now hitting around 10-20 MPH, pushed the fire straight up the hill toward them, expanding in all directions. The roar of the fire grew louder as it crowned across the unburned island below them.

"Follow me back the way we came!" Randy shouted. "We should be safe in the black. Call them on the radio and let them know we're heading into the safety zone in the black. Tell them we'll hike back to our rigs."

The crew breathed a collective sigh of relief once inside the safety of the previously burned ground. They began their hike back, terror nipping at their heels as the 100-plus acres behind them were engulfed in flames that reached as high as a hundred feet above the treetops. The sound was deafening—resembling a half dozen, screaming freight trains screaming. They picked up the pace as they hiked several hundred feet inside the burned-out forest but soon discovered a new problem.

The wind had picked up and was now blowing a steady 25-35 MPH, with 50 MPH gusts.

Wes cursed over the sound of the increasing winds. "This isn't a good place to be right now. The fire area might have been safer."

"Why is that?" Ben asked.

Before Wes could answer the question, a loud whooshing caught their attention as one of the burnt-out snags crashed to the ground.

Randy gathered the crew around him, working to keep his fear from showing. "I'm not gonna gloss this over. This could be the most dangerous one-mile hike we ever have to face. There's little to no soil anchoring these burned-out trees to the ground. To top it off, the wind is getting worse. At any time and from anywhere, one of these trees could fall. Watch your step and watch your heads. We'll take that deer trail back to the rigs—it's only about a mile."

They followed him back toward the rigs. The trail was rocky in places, and full of tree roots at times. The trail narrowed in places as it wound through the blackened forest skeleton. Up ahead, the radio operator stopped to answer a call. His words were cut off by a loud *whoosh*! *Crash!* All eyes shot to the 50-foot tall lodgepole as it blew over and struck the radioman squarely on the right shoulder, knocking the radio 10 feet away.

Randy, Wes, and Ben shot forward and began digging beneath the branches, searching for the man.

Wes cursed; his voice tight with panic. "He's bleeding really bad. There's a big gash on the right side of his head."

"Grab that faller! His crew was right behind us—get him up here quick! We have to get this weight off of him, but be careful," Randy yelled.

The faller raced toward them, immediately working his chainsaw as he cut the limbs away. As the second cut was completed, the crew quickly pulled a short log off the trapped man as Randy checked for a pulse.

"Bring that first aid kit over here," Randy shouted above the wind. "Pull out the large compresses and tape and we'll dress the wound as best we can. I think I feel a pulse. Bill, you head back to where we parked. The district has a first aid tent set up down there. See if they can radio for an ambulance or helicopter for evac. We need to get this guy to a hospital ASAP. He's lost an awful lot of blood in a very short time. Unless this wind gets more dangerous and we have to move to avoid getting hit by another tree, we'd better not move him."

A short time later, the wind subsided. Everyone huddled around their fallen crewmember just as Bill arrived with two guys from the First Aid tent. They had a stretcher and another radio.

Bill looked at Randy as they approached. "How is he? Is he going to be, OK?"

Randy's voice tremored as he answered. "Not sure, he's lost a lot of blood. Let's get him out of here. He has a very faint pulse."

Bill turned to the medics. "OK to go?"

The lead first aid responder answered, "We've ordered a helicopter. It should land at the parking area in about 15-20 minutes. If four of us grab a corner of the litter, we can get out of here before the wind picks up again. Let's get going."

As the four litter bearers carefully wound their way through the blackened forest, helicopter blades sliced the air as they reached the parking area. The injured man was quickly loaded onto the ship's attached side-stretcher and the ex-Vietnam helicopter pilot wasted no time heading toward the nearby hospital.

It was almost six in the evening. The crew stared at each other, shocked at the amount of blood on their pants and shirts. Most of the guys slumped to the ground, while all fought back tears.

It was a day they wished they could forget but knew they never would.

Fred drove up and screeched to a halt. Leaping from his vehicle, he approached the crew. "You guys did an outstanding job out there, under extreme and dangerous circumstances that most of us will never see in our careers. I just got word he appears somewhat stable. They're about ten minutes from the hospital, and the emergency room is standing by with a trauma team waiting to take him in. I won't lie. His chances aren't good. But without your quick attention, he would be dead right now. You guys really did a great job out there today. I'm cutting orders for you and the other crew to go home late tomorrow morning. We still need you here, but going through this kind of trauma is not easy. The fireline isn't the place for you right now. I have rooms reserved in town for you tonight. In situations like this, you need to decompress and just get home to your families and friends. Take care of each other, OK?"

Everyone nodded, though each was numbed by thoughts of their dying comrade.

They would be heading for home—but one of their crewmen might not make it out alive.

The next morning found some crewmen out for an early run, while others milled aimlessly about, weighed down by yesterday's cloud. Breakfast was on the district's dime at two of the finest restaurants in town, but thoughts of their fallen crewman overshadowed any joy. The men picked and poked at their food, unable to rouse an appetite.

"Look," Randy began, "what we did yesterday was pretty amazing when you think about it. I don't know the guy. Found out his name is Jim. We don't see much of him because he lives on a ranch two miles from the work center. Since he's local, and from a well-known family, we may be getting a lot of questions. I suggest everyone refers any questions about his condition to the family or hospital. Any questions about what happened, should come to me unless you're OK answering."

"Any word on his condition?" one of the guys asked.

Randy smiled. "Glad you asked because I was told earlier this morning that Jim is alert and can sit up on the edge of his bed. He had over a dozen stitches to his scalp and a couple broken ribs when he fell on the root wad. But that radio that was slung over his shoulder took most of the impact. The radio caused the small tree to slightly glance away just enough to avoid what could have been critical head injuries. It sounds like he will be able to go home in 3-5 days."

Chapter 24

Later that morning, the DC 4 brought the crews back to Beeton, where they loaded their parked rigs and headed to Mineral Creek.

"You know, it's been over a month since Rob, I mean Aaron, disappeared. We haven't had any updates since," Ben mused. "There's been no word from his father, or Sergeant Dusty. What do you suppose is going on? I wonder if they still think I shoved him off that log."

When no one answered, Ben cursed. "I didn't. You guys know that, right?"

Randy glanced at him. "You need to relax. If they thought you were involved, y'ou guys would have been quickly brought back to the station and tossed in a cell, trust me."

Taking Randy's advice, Ben watched the country roll by. Observing the tin-roofed hay barns and ranch outbuildings, his mind wandered back to Vietnam. The big Tet Offensive had made international news. He'd extended his tour an extra two months to avoid being discharged with less than 90 days of military service after his tour ended. There was one day in particular that stood out in his memory. Another VC offensive—a day that brought the war closer than he would have liked.

Ben remembered leaving the Intelligence Center to catch his usual bus, nicknamed the "green monster," back to the barracks. Phil, his new bunkmate, had rushed up and breathlessly informed him of trouble.

"Something's wrong," Phil gasped. "There aren't any buses coming. Just deuce and a half. I didn't hear why, but it sounds like there could be big trouble all around Saigon and the surrounding countryside."

He'd no more than finished his sentence when the trucks rolled into the area parking area. They were the typical deuce and halves, except the wooden seats that go along both sides of the bed had been removed. The driver was armed to the teeth, and the soldier riding shotgun had an automatic weapon and enough ammo for half a war.

"Everyone counts off as you get in. I only want 14 people in each deuce and a half. I want seven of you to get as close to each side wall as you can and keep your heads down until I tell you it's ok."

Phil cursed, nervously. "What the heck is happening?"

They found out soon enough. As they pulled onto the traffic circle to Highway 1, all hell broke loose. The streets were empty. No mama sans carried baskets, there were no cycles, pedicabs, motorbikes, or bicycles. Only one or two locals were out on the street. Quiet streets like this only happened when the VC were in the area.

When they turned off the highway and onto the back road toward their compound, the driver yelled, "Remember: keep your heads down. Do not try to get up or look around!" He put the deuce and a half in high gear, pushing it to go as fast the engine's governor would allow.

From where he was hunkered down, Ben saw huge chunks of tin blown all over the area. The tin had once made buildings. Storefronts and homes were now completely leveled. Some nicer, French-era, two-story homes had smoke pouring out of the windows. Bullet holes and RPG damage had torn the homes to shreds.

As they approached their compound, Ben looked at Phil and cursed. "Did you see that? The "two-story" is gone and so is the sawmill across the street."

The front gates opened, and the four trucks rolled quickly inside. Ben looked across the country road at the leveled sawmill and "two-story." "Two-story" was the nickname for the infamous bar and whorehouse where one could go right out the front gate and have a beer and spend some time with the ladies—a visit which usually resulted in the need for lots of penicillin. The bar had been flattened and rendered unrecognizable.

Inside the compound was a rather large tank from the Big Red 1. It was parked just a few feet from the Saigon River, next to the entrance to the barracks. Its main gun was pointed across the river toward the jungle beyond the river's edge. Sporadic gunfire sounded from not too far away. As Ben started to say something to Phil, a Cobra gunship arrived directly overhead, firing several short bursts with casings flying everywhere. No one knew what the ship was firing at, but Ben was grateful it had been there.

From the safety of their compound, they looked toward the large sawmill that had been destroyed, their eyes searching for the source of a distant firefight. Small arms fire continued, mixed with an occasional burst from an M-16. A couple of A1 Skyraiders appeared overhead, approaching the area behind the sawmill. These old training planes were still used by the South Vietnamese Air Force. They could hold a single thousand-pound-bomb or two five-hundred bombs and were amazingly accurate. The first Skyraider flew away from the back of the compound at around 3,000 feet in elevation, circled behind the old sawmill, and then dove straight down at about 1,000 feet off the deck. The pilot released his two five-hundred-pound bombs just before he took a hard-right bank. The concussion was so close that Ben felt it hit the pit of his stomach and the explosions that followed rattled his head and shook the compound. The second plane repeated the same drop, exploding an area behind the mill site, and then there was silence. No more gunfire, no more explosions. There was nothing. A couple of hours later, the tank rumbled out the front gate, and things inside the compound returned to normal.

For the next few months after the attacks, "normal" had a new meaning. The bus trips had to have armed escorts in the front and rear anytime they left the compound, and everyone was expected to be more on guard. Gradually, things normalized. The club at the back of the compound re-opened, and the 15-cent beer flowed, once again, like the river next door.

Ben was jolted back to reality when Randy's gruff voice broke through his thoughts.

"Ben, you with us or somewhere else? What the heck are you daydreaming about now?"

Heat crept up Ben's neck as. "I was just thinking about things I'd rather not think about. Why don't you turn on the radio? We're only 30 minutes out; we should pick up our local station."

Randy flicked the radio on, and he and the boys belted the lyrics to the latest hit. Wes had just hit a high note when the music was interrupted by a broadcaster. Live news was rare. It only I during emergencies, or when the usual recordings didn't cut it. It wasn't hard to pick up on the fact that this broadcaster was no professional.

Startled, the boys listened as he spoke.

"We interrupt this broadcast for a news bulletin straight from the Riverton Police Department. The sheriff's office has just announced that a body has been discovered in the millpond, west of town."

"Turn that up!" Ben yelled, his heart in his throat. "What did he say about a body?"

When everyone was quiet, Bill asked the question no one else wanted to voice. "Do you think they found Rob, er, I mean, Aaron?" He cursed. "I wonder what happened?"

The boys waved a hand to silence him as the broadcaster continued.

"According to unconfirmed reports, this could be the body of the missing Forest Service greenhorn that local law enforcement officers have been searching for in the last month or so. We have no further information, other than to report that law enforcement is on the scene now. We will try to get an interview at the mill site soon. We will now return to our regular programming. Stay tuned for further updates."

Shock settled around the boys' shoulders like a heavy cloak.

"We were just talking about this a few minutes ago," Wes said numbly. "And now this report? Do you think it's really him?"

Ben hung his head. "Not sure, but we're going to find out, whether we want to or not. I can't believe our return home is ending like this, after all we've gone through these past several days. At least we might finally have some answers—if that really is Aaron they found."

"Who else would it be?" Wes demanded. "Only one person has gone missing in this little burg in the last hundred years, so who else would it be? That old geezer in the guard shack?"

"Since we're near the district office, let's turn in our timeslips," Randy suggested. "We'll get paid more this time since we put in a few extra hours on that fire."

When they pulled into the district office's parking lot, the boys' nerves were on edge, and exhaustion weighed on their features. As they walked into the office, the district clerk took one look at their faces and asked, "You boys, OK? What brings you in today?"

Randy offered a tired smile. "We thought we'd go ahead and drop off our time slips since we were on our way through town. Figured it might be easier on you to have them early."

Before Helen could reply, Ranger Bash rushed in, his features grim. "Ben, you, Wes, and Bill are wanted in Sergeant Dusty's office. He and the sheriff would like a few words with you. Randy, you can go along with them if you want. They finished at the mill site about an hour ago."

Wes cursed as nerves wound his muscles taut. "What now? Haven't we been through enough already? Now this? We need to get back to the work center and get some sleep!"

Without a word, the boys loaded up and headed over to the police station. When they arrived, Randy looked at their grim faces and his chest tightened. "Do you want me to stay here or come in with you guys?"

"You may as well hear first-hand what he wants to say before the radio blabs it all over the place," Wes grumbled.

When they walked up, Sergeant Dusty was near the front door with the sheriff. Offering a polite smile, he ushered them in. "Come on in. I've got news about your friend, Aaron."

Once the crew was seated in the sheriff's office, Sergeant Dusty began to explain. "When the mill workers lifted a large pine log, they saw something underneath as it was pulled out of the water. They shut down the conveyor and went to see what it was." He paused and ducked his head, focusing on his clasped hands. Swallowing hard, he forced himself to tell them. "Aaron's body was underneath the log. The cold water had left him in good condition and enabled the coroner to make a quick preliminary determination of the cause of death."

"What happened?" Ben asked, shock rippling through him. "How could he possibly have ended up underneath a log in the pond? No one saw him? The divers? The watchman? The *workers*?" He was on his feet now. Pacing as he tried to make sense of it all.

"I don't know about that," the sergeant replied. "But here's what we do know. The log had some barbed wire attached to it. Probably from someone's range fence. The faller must have missed it when he bucked up the log. The wire, along with a couple of small branch knots, got tangled up with Aaron's clothing. It looks like he slid off the log and tried to come back up but got snagged by the wire and branches." Reading the guilt clouding their features, he shook his head. "There's no way you guys would have heard or seen anything with the storm that night. Add the flickering lights…it was a disaster waiting to happen."

"Wait a minute." Bill furrowed his brow. "What about the hounds? They tracked his scent on the other side, remember? The handlers said they tracked him away from the pond's edge and back to it."

"Everyone was looking for him for a good half hour before the dog was on a scent back to the pond," Sergeant Dusty replied. "We think he probably wandered around for a while before climbing on a log. He must've drifted, or paddled, toward the guard shack. It wasn't that far, even on the water. The hard truth is that the coroner ruled his death as an accidental drowning. Most likely resulting from his use of

184

prescription drugs, mixed with alcohol. His father agreed with this assumption just a few minutes ago. He was pretty shaken up, but I got the feeling that he wasn't surprised. The only thing the coroner noticed on the body was some trauma on the right side of his head, but he thinks that was from bumping into the log as he tried to free himself. Odd shape though, almost round. Alright boys, unless you have questions, you're free to go back to Mineral Creek. I doubt I'll need anything else from you."

The return trip up the mountain was somber. Wes, unusually quiet, asked, "Do you guys really think it's over? It just seems the coroner was too quick with his findings."

"Yeah," Randy responded. "But remember, the coroner here isn't a medical examiner. He can decide enough is enough and just go with his gut feeling if he wants to. There's only one doctor in town now, and I doubt he has time to disagree. I think he probably already signed off on the cause of death. I gotta tell you, though… It's really weird they found *round-shaped* head trauma."

Bill cursed loudly, startling the quiet in the cab. Wide-eyed, he asked the question on everyone's mind. "Ben, did you cold-cock

Aaron with the end of that pike pole? I remember you shoved the danged thing out there pretty doggone hard…

With a half smile that spoke of evil, Ben looked at Bill. "You know what? I…"

Many Years Later…

Chapter 25

Ben sat on the front porch of his parents' Sisu Bay, Oregon home. He was always *glad* to visit the great place where he was raised and never tired of the opportunity to marvel at another beautiful sunset. He missed the ocean. He missed Sisu Bay but was glad his career had taken him to new beginnings.

Wow, it's 1980, and I'm nine months into a new job in a new forest, with a new promotion. I'm glad I decided—we—*decided to stay in forest management,* Ben thought as he absorbed the yellow-orange rays of the fading sunlight.

The screen door slammed, and Ben's head snapped up as his wife of nine years rushed outside. Her features belied her fear as she spoke, her voice rushed and shaky. "They're o-o-outside, again. J-just sitting there in a big, ugly, black Suburban. It's the same one I saw drive by slowly this morning. What do you suppose they're up to?"

Ben frowned. "Are you sure they're the same guys, Gianne? Couldn't it be another version of that car you saw this morning? They're unusual but not rare."

Gianne, growing more upset, paused for a minute, then answered firmly, "I am positive it's the same one. How many black Chevy Suburbans do you think come this way twice in one day? You know we are too far off the beaten track to have much traffic, let alone see two of the same big, old, black tanks coming by here twice..."

Ben's dad had overheard the conversation and joined the couple on the porch. "I'll go ask them if there's something in particular they're looking for," he angrily announced. "That should prompt them to fess up to whatever's going on. For all we know, they could be selling something. Or looking for beach houses for sale. Or who knows what else!"

"Tom!" Gianne called after him, but the older man only rushed through the house to the back door and hurried down the sidewalk, toward the street.

As he stormed toward the black Suburban, Tom's face turned ashen when his eyes fixed on, what looked to be, a gun barrel pointing at him. He did a double take, relieved to discover it was a camera. Angrily, he crossed the two-lane street. When he was midway there, the vehicle sped away from the house and disappeared around the corner. Promptly, Tom gave the Suburban the "Italian salute" and rushed back into the house.

"I have no clue what the heck those two were after," Tom grumbled as he returned to the front porch. "They had a camera and were watching us. I'd like to know what's going on. Maybe later, I'll give my golf partner, Andy, a quick call down at the police station and see if something's going on. That Suburban looks a lot like the undercover rigs the FBI or state police use, the kind you see on all those TV detective shows. What do you guys think?"

The black Suburban mystery remained unsolved as the weekend ended and Ben and Gianne headed home. Though it was only a three-hour drive, it felt like ten with their two kids in tow. The twins, Joe and Joy, were now seven and were finally starting to enjoy trips to see Grandma and Grandpa, though they still had trouble staying on an even keel for the long, boring car ride.

Once home, Ben carried the twins off to bed and then he and Gianne spread out on the sofa, each breathing relieved sighs at being home again. Moving to Goldville from the tiny town of Riverton had been a wonderful change for the family. Goldville, once a thriving mining town, had a population exceeding 60,000 in its heyday.

189

Today's population count sat at 35,000, a far cry from the 2,500 Riverton population. Adding to the town's attractiveness, a new ski development was underway on Pine Mountain. Ben's new forest, Monument Pines National Forest, was a breath of fresh air, as was his new job title—Community Relations Officer. He loved the job. Working with kids, the local media and government had presented a set of challenges he'd embraced whole-heartedly. He was glad he'd gone to night school and finished his government relations degree. Aside from his work, he assisted the locals on fire assignments, something he'd loved to do as an infrared interpreter.

The rumors of his past had faded away years ago. Almost twelve years had gone by since his crewmate drowned in Riverton's millpond. The assumption of Ben's guilt had been an ever-present cloud for over a month after Aaron's body was discovered. It wasn't until the medical examiner released his findings that the rumors were put to bed. The suspicious mark on Aaron's forehead had tiny pine splinters and traces of pitch. It had been ruled that Aaron likely came up under the log and rammed his head against a pine knot or limb remnant, causing the wound. The pike pole Ben had used to get Aaron back to shore had nothing to do with anything.

"I wonder what the deal was with those guys parked outside your mom and dad's house," Gianne wondered. "I'll be quite honest, I'm still nervous something isn't right. I can't help but feel they were there for your parents…or even us…"

Ben started to say something but stopped short. Now was not the time to discuss this. Kissing his wife, he gave her a reassuring smile. "Don't worry." Standing, he went and checked on the twins, unpacked, and readied his briefcase for work.

It was close to 10:30 PM. Ben and Gianne were tired from their drive. An early bedtime was in order. Once the laundry was done and lunches had been made, the couple headed for their room, pausing when the phone rang.

Aggravated, Gianne cursed. "Who could be calling us so late? It's 10:30 at night!" She picked up the phone with a frown. "Hello, who is this please? Oh, Harry, hi. What's going on? Is everything okay?"

"I'm fine. The question is, is everything alright with you guys?" Harry was Ben's oldest childhood friend and had lived in Sisu Bay his entire life.

"Yes, of course," Gianne answered, startled. "Why do you ask?"

"Could you put Ben on? I have something I need to tell him."

Gianne handed the phone to Ben, worry dimming her eyes.

"Ben, here."

"I'm not sure what's going on—I'm not even sure if it's a big deal or not—but there've been a couple of men going around town asking a lot of questions about you guys. You know, background stuff, like whether or not you've ever been in trouble, asking where you live, who you married, whether you worked in Sisu Bay when you were young. Those kinds of questions. Weird stuff, don't you think?" Harry asked.

Ben thought before answering. "Harry, were two of the guys driving a brand new, black Chevy Suburban?"

"How did you know? That's exactly what's been seen around town!" Harry responded, surprise registering in his voice.

"You know, Harry, it's been almost fifteen years since anything remotely close to this happened to me it. Remember? I was being checked out for my top-secret security clearance after I got drafted before I was sent to Army Intelligence School. I had to have clearance for all the stuff we did in Vietnam. I think tomorrow, after our Monday morning staff meeting, I'll see if my forest supervisor can inquire through our administrative folks and see what this is all about."

When Ben hung up, Gianne cast him a confused look. "Do you think maybe you're being checked out again? Why would they do that?"

"I have no clue. But, like I told Harry, I'll start some inquiring in the morning," Ben assured her.

Monday morning found Ben weighed down with apprehension over the weekend's events. He was glad the staff meeting was a quick one. FS John Wolden had agreed to see him at 11:00, which gave him another hour to let his overactive imagination play mind games with him. He had all kinds of scenarios about people spying, stealing, and kidnapping, all involving the now-infamous black Suburban. *God*, he thought, *I need to get some work done and get a grip. I've got to get back to reality.*

Ben looked out his closet-sized office door as Larry Capps, the fire management officer, rushed in and barked, "You have a fire assignment. Be ready to go by 4:00 PM. You are to go to the airport in Brighton. Your infrared imagery will be dropped, then you're off to the Pine River Fire Camp about forty miles west of Riverton. You can do the IR interpretation in the camp with the incident commander and operations chief. The IC's name is Johnson. You will only be doing one shift, as your buddy, Tim Jackly, will be their regularly assigned IR interpreter, but he's tied up until the day after tomorrow. You'll be going with Alan Jinks; he'll be driving you to the airport and then to the fire camp. He will then stay as a time-recorder, and you can keep the pickup for your use while there."

Ben stopped for a moment, taking this all in. "Okay, I just have to let the FS know I can't meet with him in an hour. Then I'll go home and get ready to go."

Ben rushed to FS Wolden's office where his secretary, Sue, guarded his door like an army ranger.

"Can I see him right away?" Ben asked.

"He's tied up right now. You have an 11 o'clock with him, right?" she asked.

"I do," Ben answered, "but I got my dispatch order to a fire over on the Blue Hills NF and I need to go home and get ready to go."

194

"Hang on a minute. I'll sneak in and see what he's doing and tell him your plight," Sue responded.

A minute later, the FS called him in a gruff voice. "Ben, come in here quickly. I have exactly one minute."

Ben explained the problem and why he had to go, then added, "There's some really weird stuff going on back home in Sisu Bay. There've been some strange dudes hanging around my folks' home and around town asking questions about me and Gianne. They're addressing the questions to everyone—including my old high school teachers, employers, and friends. Do you know anything about that? The last time this happened to me was after I was drafted and being investigated for my security clearance before military intelligence school."

"Actually, I do," Wolden responded. "I know exactly what's going on and as soon as you get back from your fire assignment, I'll fill you in on what I know. At that time, you'll be meeting a few government officials who might surprise you. There's nothing sinister going on, and your inclination about updating your top-secret security clearance is right on. I've also been on the querying end of many questions about you, as have your former supervisors."

****

It was getting late when Ben and Alan hopped in their pickup and headed toward Brighton airport.

"Brighton sure is a nice airport for such a small town," Alan stated. "It's a paved runway with a pilot-activated light system in place for night landings. It's quite a long runway and can easily accommodate almost all twin-engine turboprops."

"How do you know all that?" Ben asked.

"My Uncle Jim is a pilot. He flies a King Air and has a lot of passengers coming into little old Brighton to do some trophy fishing and hunting, gold prospecting, you name it. It's actually a pretty cool airstrip. They even have a double-wide trailer for pilots and passengers. Pretty cool, I think."

After hanging around the so-called terminal for a couple of hours, Ben and Alan dove into the lunch-style dinners their wives had packed for them and watched the moon rise, as it would soon be time for the Infrared Aircraft to finish the IR run.

"What time is it?" Alan asked.

"Almost midnight. They were going to fly the fire about a quarter 'til, so I think they'll be here about 1:00 AM," Ben answered.

196

"Now, look, I'm going to tell you how this works so you won't be surprised. The IR plane won't land with the imagery from the fire. It takes way too long, and the flight plan is too much of a hassle."

"So what do they do?" Alan asked.

"Okay, here's what will happen. The plane will notify us on the radio air-to-ground frequency. They use our call sign as IR1 and contact us when they're thirty minutes out. When they're five minutes out, the pilot will activate the runway lights and then immediately turn them off again. We'll park over there, parallel to the runway about fifty yards. We'll turn on the pickup headlights, so they'll be able to see us when they're on approach."

"So, what happens after all this light crap?" Alan asked with a puzzled look on his face.

"Okay, Alan, the way this works is they have the imagery all wound up like a tight roll of paper towels coiled inside a heavy-duty plastic cylinder, with plugs on both ends. Inside, is a light and a noise buzzer, both activated either right before or upon impact with the ground. The cylinder never breaks, at least not during any of my fifteen assignments. The IR technician in the plane will shoot this cylinder from the approaching aircraft through a pneumatic forced-air

197

tube in the fuselage, shooting it to end up as close as safely possible near our headlights."

"Holy crap." Alan's brows rose. "That's so cool. I had no idea. This is going to be a fun night!"

It was about 12:30 AM when Ben and Alan, with the pickup in place and almost dozing off, heard a call over their radio.

IR ship to IR1, we are now thirty minutes out, on time, on schedule and should be close in twenty-five minutes. Acknowledge!

"10-4," Ben responded. "We'll see you in twenty-five... IR1."

With that, they knew things were on the right track to get the imagery to fire camp before the morning shift was sent out to the fire lines. There would be plenty of time for the imagery to be interpreted and the information passed on to the IC and ops chief.

It was a short twenty-five minutes before the lights on the runway suddenly came on and they could hear the plane's engines. As soon as the runway lights were activated, the pilot turned them back off and Ben turned on the pickup's headlights and clicked them on low beam. They anxiously for the drop.

"See you clearly," said a voice over the radio. "We're coming in for the drop. We'll drop to your east, about twenty yards." The twin-engine Queen Air came lower and lower, toward the pickup.

Panic seized Alan and he gripped the dashboard and cursed, eyes fixed on the plane barreling toward them. "Are they gonna crash on top of us? They're coming so low. I can't believe this!"

The plane dropped down to a couple of hundred feet off the deck.

Ben laughed a hearty laugh. "You are so funny. I've done this same drop a dozen times. Relax. It's going just as planned."

Suddenly, a loud *whooomph* broke through the air and a cylinder was fired out of the belly of the plane, hitting the ground about 50 feet away in the thick grass.

Ben and Alan were leaping out the door when the pilot radioed, "You guys go find that first cylinder and we'll circle around and take a long bank back toward you. We have another cylinder full of imagery. The first one was for your fire, the second is some lightning storm detection runs we were asked to make, covering a mile or two away to the north from our assigned fire."

Quickly, Ben and Alan ran to the grassy area in search of the cylinder.

"Shh, stop right here," Ben said. "Listen quietly. I think I hear the buzzer. Can you hear it? Over there, to your left."

Sure enough, as they headed that way, they could see a red glow in the cheatgrass and heard the buzzer getting louder as they approached. They quickly grabbed the cylinder and ran to the pickup as the IR ship returned toward the truck. Per their training, they opened their doors and hid behind them for safety.

Alan trembled as the plane approached. *Whooomph!* The cannon tube shot the second cylinder and instantly a loud crash sounded, and small shards of glass landed like hail over them both.

Ben cursed, unable to hide his fear. "Did you see that sucker? Look at that door! That tube went right through the driver's window above my head. They've never shot one that close to me before." He grabbed the radio mic, his nerves trembling. "Hey, guys, that was way too close. You shot that tube right through the driver's side window, above my head."

"10-4," radioed the pilot. "We'll make sure that doesn't happen again. Our apologies."

Ben and Alan exchanged looks at the slight giggle in the pilot's voice. Prodded by nerves, they both burst out laughing.

"I'm glad I was along for the ride on this one," Alan stated. "What a story it will make."

"Maybe not," Ben answered. "Probably better if no one knows about this. A lot of violations to explain. But I guess we're going to have to tell someone. The safety people are going to be angry, to say the least!"

Chapter 26

Ben and Alan had no trouble retrieving the last tube. It was on the ground right next to the passenger side back bumper, unnecessarily buzzing and lighting the way. They grabbed the second cylinder, hopped into the truck with the two tubes in hand, and then turned down the airport driveway to head to camp. When they neared the highway, a white van pulled up in front of them, blocking their way out.

"What's the deal?" Ben yelled out, cursing. "Why are they stopping us? We have some infrared that has to be in the fire camp in the next two hours!"

Two rather large individuals in blue polo shirts and jeans climbed out of the van and slowly walked over to their pickup.

"What do you two think you're doing?" the taller one demanded. "That scenario we just witnessed violates so many FAA procedural and safety rules, I have no clue where to even start. We've received a half dozen complaints about touch and go aircraft activities happening at all hours of the night at this airstrip. We've had calls from everyone from local ranchers to nearby homeowners. So, what in the Sam Hill is the deal here?"

Panic crept up Ben's neck as he forced his response. "Okay, here's the deal. We're here to pick up some infrared imagery and take it to our fire camp. We don't fly the planes or make the rules; we're assigned to the Pine River Fire and need to get going so the morning shift has the latest fire mapping. I suggest you contact our national aviation managers and tell them your concerns. We have never had any FAA issues in the past. Why now?"

"Rules have changed for these small, isolated airfields, and I would tell that to anyone you see. As far as we are concerned, your operation at this facility is shut down, as of this minute. I will ensure a Notice to Airmen is posted for every pilot in the area to see, including your people! There will be no more illegal approaches and cannon drops. The people who live around here will be a lot happier with this crap shut down."

"What happened to your window?" the second guy asked.

"It was an unfortunate tree-limb accident. No big deal. We really need to get out of here and get to the fire camp. Can we go?"

"Alright, we've got your names and everything we need for now. You're free to go about your business," the agent agreed.

"Hey! We need your names also!" Ben called out.

The man laughed and cursed. "Get out of here before we call the sheriff and have you two thrown in jail."

Unwilling to invite more trouble, Ben and Alan obeyed and drove for the highway, toward the Pine River fire camp.

When they were a good way away from the men, Alan looked at Ben and cursed. "That was absolutely bizarre. Do you think we're in trouble? Or just the aviation bigwigs?"

"Not us," Ben assured. "But I'm glad they let us get out of there. We'll be in camp in ten minutes, and I've got a lot of work to do. It's almost 3:30, and I only have about two and a half hours to get this imagery interpreted and mapped, and get the IC and operations people briefed."

After they arrived at the fire camp, Alan said his goodbyes, and Ben unloaded his equipment. He used a Coleman camping lantern with a fluorescent tube as his portable light table. He fastened a piece of frosted mylar drafting film inside the light window and *voila*, he had a light source, which was the right size for the width of the film. Ben found the large briefing tent and set up his work area. An hour and a half later, he'd mapped all the hot spots around the fire's edge. He estimated the fire size to be eleven hundred acres, with a lot of burning material near existing fire lines on the north and northwest sides of the fire. That was a three-hundred-acre increase from yesterday. One area near the river on the north edge, bothered him quite a bit, and he slid the film back over the light to that spot. There was a target detection mark on the edge of the film that indicated an active hot spot located at a right angle somewhere in that area on the image.

I think that spot could be at least ten acres, Ben thought. *It looks like it might be near the existing line. Crap. It's on the wrong side of the fire line!!*

He took another look, thinking it might be a rock outcrop or something else with a heat signature but, no, it was a pretty good-sized spot fire that appeared to be over the fire line and ready to head up the other side of the canyon. He quickly gathered the map and the IR film and headed over to the chow area to see if IC Johnson was grabbing an early coffee. It was 5:00 AM, but everyone got an early start at the fire camp.

Ben spotted someone sitting at a table alone and asked, "Are you the IC? I have the IR interpreted and mapped and there's something he needs to see ASAP."

"You must be Ben," the man answered. "Yes, I'm Jim Johnson, IC. Show me what you've got. We brief the shift change in less than an hour."

Ben breathlessly began to explain. "Here are the areas where the heaviest fuels are burning." He continued with his explanation of the complete fire perimeter. Finally, he ended, stating, "Now take a look at this. The worst thing I found is this right here." He pointed to an area he thought to be at least ten acres in size and was clearly outside existing fire lines. "See this area here on the map I've marked? It's across the fire line and over here, it shows quite clearly on the infrared film. If it's burning hot enough during the night to show up this intensely, you will definitely need to prioritize this, in my opinion."

Johnson cursed, his eyes huge. "I'll get this to the OP's chief right now. Good work. There's a crew in that area. I'll make sure they're warned to watch their backsides and find a safe way around and stop that spot where it is. Thanks for the good work. Anything you have mapped out on the detection run; you can leave with my deputy. Let him know if anything bad is happening around us, like new starts."

Ben left the detection mapping with the Deputy IC. There were a couple of small starts in that north quadrant, but they were surrounded by openings and rocks. He grabbed his stuff, headed to his pickup, and unpacked his air mattress and sleeping bag, in search of a few hours' sleep. He was beat. He was only doing one shift on this fire, as a friend and fellow interpreter from that forest would report to camp at about 4:00 in the afternoon.

****

Ben slept until around 1:00 PM, until the noise of the helicopters, coupled with the afternoon heat, made sleeping impossible. He briefed Tim on what he'd found and went over the two or three new fires he'd found on the detection flight, then discussed the briefing he'd given IC Johnson before he left for home.

Ben got home around 6:00 PM. His heart warmed when Joe and Joy came bounding out of the house, all giggles, to give him a big hug.

"How was your fire, Daddy? Did you put it out?" they both asked, wide-eyed.

"No," Ben said, "but there are lots of firefighters out there who will put it out. Where's your mom?"

"She's on the phone," Joe responded with childish enthusiasm. "I think she's talking to your boss."

Gianne popped into the room and gave Ben a big kiss. "That was John Wolden. He's still at the office and wants to see you first thing in the morning. So, whatever you had planned, you need to clear it."

"Wow! Still at the office at this hour," Ben exclaimed. "I wonder what the heck is going on? He mentioned my security clearance being updated, and the two guys in the black Suburban, so I think I'm about to find out. I'll make some calls and cancel a meeting and an interview I had scheduled for tomorrow morning."

The family settled in after a late dinner, watched a little TV, and then went to bed early, anticipating an early day.

Morning came quickly, and Ben headed to the office. He dropped off some papers to the timber and range staff he'd been working on before the fire, then headed to FS Wolden's office.

"Go on in," Sue told him upon arrival. "He's expecting you. He has some guests with him also."

"Thanks, Sue. Any idea what the heck is going on?"

Sue shook her head, impatiently waving him in, eager for him to quit wasting her time. Ben walked in and found FS Wolden at his desk. Two, rather professional-looking, young men sat at one end of John's small conference table.

"Ben, take a seat over there. I'll let these fine gentlemen explain what's going on. Agent Jeffries, would you go ahead and lead it off? Tell Ben what we discussed a few minutes ago."

"I'm Special Agent Sam Jeffries from the San Francisco office of the FBI, and this is Senior DEA Agent Peter Lutz from their Oakland office. I'm sorry for the mystery surrounding our background checks. We had to have those completed in order to update your security credentials, so you can keep your top-secret clearance," Jeffries explained. "Peter and I have been instructed to talk with you about working with us on some upcoming special assignments. Nothing dangerous; you would be part of a special task force helping us locate serious criminal activity in the national forests, parks, Indian Countrylands, and wherever else we are requested. The activities are mainly drug crimes, serious violations of the Antiquities Act, as well as marijuana plantations occurring on any federally managed public lands, or even on state lands."

Ben thought before speaking. "Wait a minute. What could I possibly offer in the way of help? I'm not law enforcement trained, and I have no police background. I don't understand."

DEA Agent Lutz answered, "We understand that. However, you do have a unique set of skills that we all think would help our newly formed task force. First of all, you don't have a big mouth, meaning you proved years ago in Vietnam that you are trustworthy with classified intel. That's half the battle for a member. That is why you now have a reinstated top-secret security clearance. But," he added, "we've been told you are an outstanding IR and photo interpreter, with a good cartographic background. And, from what I know of your intelligence training, you understand interrogation techniques, how to spot good sources of human intelligence, and your position here can easily merge with our needs as far as ordering you up and keeping your assignments on the QT."

"Well, what do you think?" Jeffries asked. "Before you answer or decide, remember one thing; no one outside of this room, including your wife, friends, or any other family members, can ever know about this conversation or anything about our task force. You will never be placed in any danger, but a slip of the tongue could cost one or more of our agents their lives. Here is what you can tell your wife about the need for a clearance update. Tell her you may be asked to do an assignment in Washington DC, perhaps involving White House briefings, and that is why the updated clearance is needed. So, Ben, what do you think?"

Ben looked over at his forest supervisor. "John, what do you think?"

"I can't answer that; this is entirely up to you. You will get a monetary bonus at the end of the task force assignment if you accept, but I have no idea what that means. It's your decision and yours alone. I will warn you, though… they have to know within the next hour so they can start setting things up. The approval process for this starts in Washington DC at the heads of our departments, so a quick decision is paramount. I will have some knowledge of what you are doing and where you are located, and I will be relaying to Gianne your assignment if she asks."

Ben's eyes roamed the room as a grin spread across his face, displaying his thoughts. "I have always been a bit of an adrenaline junkie and this sounds very exciting. I am in, and I think this could be a once-in-a-lifetime assignment for someone like me so, yes, I'm okay with it."

They shook hands and Ben received instructions about how he would be ordered up. the same as if he was dispatched to a real fire, flood, or earthquake assignment, or wherever he normally would be ordered to go.

****

Ben settled into the rest of July with ease—his love of his job helping to pass the time. He'd been on one other IR fire assignment and had helped teach fifty-six middle school-aged children during his environmental education classes. To top it all off, the local newspaper featured a story about the kids and the classes he provided.

Toward the end of July, Ben was called into Supervisor Wolden's office.

"The task force has been in place for several weeks now. They need you for an assignment in the central California foothills. They have confirmed reports of an extremely large marijuana plantation somewhere on national forest land. The operation is thought to be connected to a Mexican Mafia Cartel. You will go tomorrow morning. A small jet will pick you up and take you to the airport at Fresno, and from there, an agent will take you to your work location. How's that for excitement? They're sending you out on a Lear-type jet!"

"Wow!" Excitement pulsed through Ben's veins as he quickly jotted down the details.

This is for real. This is really going to happen.

**Chapter 27**

Ben arrived at the charter flight side of the runway and looked for the private jet he was to travel on.

"Hey, Ben," Dean Schmidt, a Forest Service contract pilot whom Ben had flown with at least a dozen times, sauntered up to where he stood. "Where you headed? Are you with me on this trip?"

"No, I'm heading to California on a different fire this time," Ben answered. "Wish I was with you, though. I always feel safe on your flights and enjoy the chats."

"Thanks," Dean answered. "You're always good company too. See you later." Dean walked over to his twin-engine Cessna, glancing back at Ben as he headed toward the chartered jet.

Ben looked at the private jet and marveled at how much it reminded him of the Infrared King Air turboprop. It wasn't much bigger but he discovered the difference as he climbed inside, leather seats, lots of legroom, coffee, Danishes, and orange juice were available, and he was eager to partake of the luxuries on the flight.

The pilot came and greeted Ben. "This will be a two-hour flight. Once we're over ten thousand feet, enjoy a little breakfast."

Ben grabbed a quick orange juice before take-off, poked a straw into the carton, and studied the information given to him by the task force. He read through everything, looked at some site maps, and finally read at the bottom where they would go from Fresno. The plan was to drive north to Jimtown and set up in a newly constructed business park location. Agents had set up a shell business—a mining exploration company. At least, that was what would be displayed on the large front window. That was where the task force would meet and work as the HQ for the operation. Before Ben realized it, they were at forty-thousand feet and cruising. After he'd enjoyed a coffee and Danish, and what seemed like only a few minutes, the captain announced their descent into Fresno.

****

After landing, Ben grabbed his gear and headed into the charter terminal where he immediately spotted FBI Special Agent Sam Jeffries.

"Hey, Ben," Sam said, "here we are, your first task force assignment, and it is a doozy. I'll explain on the drive up to Jimtown."

Once they'd settled into the drive, Sam jumped in. "Thirty miles east of Jimtown, on National Forest lands, a dove hunter

215

wandered into a large marijuana plantation. He said he could verify numerous sections of the plantation covering, what he thought were, several acres and stated there could be dozens of these plots. He was too scared to hang around for long. He also said he saw PVC pipes contouring around the hillside and large camouflage screens covering many growing sites. He reported this to the local sheriff and then went home. He told Sheriff Jennings that he feared for his life by reporting this and asked him not to let anyone know who he was or what he had seen—said he'd read about what drug runners do to snitches. The sheriff thought his use of the word 'snitch' was odd, especially if he was only some wandering-by dove hunter as he claimed.

"When the sheriff and his men went out to his home on the edge of town the next morning, they realized it was unlikely he was a dove hunter. They found him dead, with a gunshot wound to the back of the head. He had a small, packed duffle bag, and it looked like he was getting ready to get out of town as fast as he could. The interesting thing about that guy is that he had a record a mile long, including drugs, smuggling, and arson. The sheriff told me he thinks this guy might have been a local recruit and was in on the operation from the beginning. The evidence points to him being a disgruntled double-crosser or embezzler who bailed on the operation. Amazing that he decided to report the whole thing to the sheriff, then got everything packed, ready to skip town, and ended up wasted."

Ben cursed. "That is not what I had in mind for excitement. That's too much."

"Not to worry; this appears to be nothing more than an accomplice getting the short end of the stick and trying to get even. His cartel buddies were having none of that. We have a general idea where this operation is located, and when we get to Jimtown, I'll show you on a map what we know so far," Sam assured.

They arrived at the fake mining office, unloaded, and joined in a discussion on their suspected plantation site. Ben saw DEA Agent Lutz and said hello. Around twenty people crowded into the office for the afternoon briefing. The representatives came from a half-dozen law enforcement agencies, including the local sheriff, Steve Jennings, and the State Police.

Lutz went to the front of the room where a map had been set up on a display board. "Listen up. We know the location of this plantation network is in the area locally known as Venus. It is a left-over, ragtag encampment from the hippie days of 1960. In this area, there are druggies, draft evaders, and who knows what else kind of low lives escaping into these woods. Scores of campsites and vagrant-type residence setups consisting of tents, tarps, shacks, and old trailers are scattered over approximately a hundred acres. It's a 'no-man's land,' right in the middle of the forest. Local law enforcement leaves it alone unless a serious crime is committed there."

He paused a moment, giving them a moment to digest the information. "People have gone into that area and disappeared. We have reason to believe that this area is part of a drug cartel operation. There is a real possibility of extensive booby traps and automatic weapons. There's no telling what other attacks we're in for when we breach this criminal's playground—your guess is as good as mine. We've ordered an infrared flight over this area around midnight, so we have an idea about their latest activity. Ben, raise your hand. Ben is our IR interpreter. He will look at the infrared imagery and tell us what he can spot from the air. The plane will be high enough that it won't scare them off. Everyone, get some shut eye. The ground force part of this task force is already in place nearby. FBI Special Agent Jeffries has already left to lead the operations. They are prepared to go in at first light. So, get some rest. You're gonna need it," Lutz concluded.

Ben knew the photos and imagery he would finally get to see would be from the latest version of false color infrared, which will show green live trees, brush, and shrubs as one color and nonliving material as another. That way, he knew he could figure out the location of the camouflage netting if they flew over the right place. Ben had the IR imagery in his hands by midnight. After taking it from the messenger, he sat at a light table and started looking at the film, along with local topo maps, then searched through a pile of aerial photos. He unrolled the film, sliding it up and down the light table, looking at one section of country after another.

"All right," he called out. "I think I found where they're hiding everything."

Ben yelled for DEA Agent Lutz, and as Lutz rushed to the light table, Ben excitedly pointed to an area on the photo. "Look, see this black and white photo? A young, thick ponderosa pine stand is blending into some Douglas fir. See those grassy openings all through the thick stands of young trees? Now, look over here at the IR film where those thick stands of trees are. See those openings from the photos? See what has me so excited?"

Lutz cursed. "That orange color is non-living material!"

"Exactly," Ben replied, "non-chlorophyll material shows orange on this false color infrared. But we saw that tall grass vegetation in the areas between the thick, young stuff on the photos. That tells me the camouflage nettings are the orange-colored stuff blocking out the tall grasses growing below. You can almost make out the edges of the camo netting. I marked all this on these large-scale maps, along with some of the more important trails and roads nearby. You can also see deer trails, minor jeep roads, and unmapped trails heading in and out of Venus. This is what Agent Jeffries and his strike team need to help them bust this operation open wide."

****

The sun painted a beautiful red-orange sunrise across the eastern sky as Agent Jeffries and his ten-member strike team traveled to the grow site. Traveling down one of the deer trails Ben had seen on the imagery, they approached the site cautiously, hoping no one spotted them before the raid. M16s and Kevlar bulletproof vests were the equipment of the day. As they got closer to the center of the

220

plantation, the lead agent leading the group suddenly disappeared. Jeffries and his crew snapped to attention when his screams pierced the air. Rushing forward, the team came to a halt as at the edge of a deep pit that had been carved out in the forest soil by the cartel. Its express purpose was to maim or kill any unwelcome intruders. Peering into the pit, Jeffries was slammed with the horror of the agent's fate.

Several punji sticks had penetrated one leg, his lower body, and part of his right arm. He bled profusely, pulling all his strength to hold back his screams for fear of giving away their location.

"We have to get him out of there. NOW!" Jeffries whispered in earnest. "Get your first aid kits so we can make him as comfortable as possible. We've got to get that bleeding stopped as soon as he is up and out of there. When we pull him out, whoever has the drugs in their first aid kit, go ahead and administer. I'll go back down this deer trail and call for a backup medical extraction."

Two of the agents managed to get into the hole without encountering the sticks. One agent pressed a hand to his injured comrade's mouth as they slowly extracted him from the pit. Raising him up to ground level, they quickly stopped the bleeding and administered an appropriate-sized dose of morphine.

"Jones, you stay here with him," Jeffries quietly instructed when he walked back up to the men. "I've got a medical extraction team hiking in as we speak. I had them on stand-by just in case of a medical emergency and they should be here in around 30 minutes. How's he doing?"

"Actually," Jones responded with relief, "it looks a lot worse than it is. He lost a lot of blood, but the stakes were nowhere near any vital organs or arteries, so we've pretty much got the wounds cleaned out and the bleeding stopped. He got lucky."

Thinking about the path, Jeffries frowned. "Let's go around to that other trail about twenty yards out. It parallels the site and should avoid the possibility of any more booby traps along the way. Who knows what other surprises this bunch may have set..."

With the patient well in hand, the task force continued around the hillside on their new trail and approached the area marked as the main location of the plantations.

"Look down below, where we were walking. Do you see that?" The agent behind Jeffries asked.

Below their route, the team spotted a PVC pipe painted brown. It was snaking its way along the hillside, away from their target site.

"Good spot," Jeffries whispered. "That's their water system for the plantation. I have a feeling that this is one sophisticated operation—not some local yokels. This is definitely cartel work. There's too much money invested here for small timers."

Looking over at Agent Johnson, Jeffries commanded, "Johnson, you're our expert sharpshooter on this team. I want you to go toward the west edge of those thick stands and set up in that small opening. If any type of shooting starts, you have my approval to return fire at your discretion."

Johnson took off up the hill and quietly set up in a small clearing. Here, he had an unobstructed view into the thickets and throughout the scattered plantation areas. He could now see the camouflage netting between the thickets of small trees. Several individuals with shovels were working between those thick stands. Johnson watched them as they wandered into the more open areas. He quickly set up his sniper rifle, zeroed in his scope, and waited for the team to approach from the south and east. Jeffries and the unit had now circled back around within twenty yards where and spotted the netting and men scurrying around with freshly harvested plants in tow.

Crack.

A gunshot split the air. Automatic weapon fire answered the call as the team spread out. Before the M 16 rifle opened again, Johnson fired off a single round. Silence was his only answer.

Three men took off running, away from the plantation site. They turned and fired at the team as they ran. Johnson disabled the lead runner with a shot to the upper leg and yelled as loud as he could, "ALTO! ALTO!"

The men dropped their weapons, and Johnson, who spoke fluent Spanish, ordered them to drop to the ground with their hands behind their heads. Two members of the task force quickly approached the third runner as he lay on the ground. As soon as they were within a few feet, he turned and raised a pistol, ready to fire.

Whopp.

A bullet pierced the back of the shooter's head as Johnson shot him with accuracy only a trained sniper could pull off. The pistol-packing cartel member was dead in an instant.

"Holy crap!" Sam shouted. "That was a fine shot! Who else is in there?"

Johnson quickly yelled back, "There are four or five worker bees in there; they're sitting on the ground, waiting for us."

Entering the plantation, the team was amazed at what they saw. Each worker sat calmly and silently, waiting with their hands in the air. As Jeffries spotted the five, he ordered one of his men to take the two remaining cartel runners away and get the wounded one bandaged up.

A Mexican national slowly got to his feet. With his hands in the air—and speaking near-perfect English—he stated, "Amigos, do not shoot us. We are not part of this. We are not part of the Oso Negro cartel. We do not want to be here."

Jeffries responded, "Oso Negro—Black Bear. Is that the name for this cartel? Are there more members around?"

The worker shook his head, his voice trembling. "There are no more here and, yes, that is how they are known back home. They have kidnapped us from our homes in Northern Mexico and forced us to come here and work this place. You must arrest us and put us in your American jail."

"Why?" Jeffries asked with a puzzled look on his face.

The worker quickly answered. "Members of Oso Negro have our wives and children under surveillance. If they think we have escaped, or helped you, or given you information, their orders are to slaughter our families. They will have no problem carrying out those orders, so we must be jailed. Then the word will spread back to Mexico that we have been captured and jailed."

Jeffries radioed his contact at the sheriff's office, advising him of the situation and how to get into the site. He mentioned the wounded, the dead, and the captive, then sat down to take it all it all in.

Chapter 28

Sheriff Jennings and several deputies arrived within the hour. They took the two cartel members into custody and ordered a medivac helicopter to carry out the wounded member. The team was briefed on the wounded agent, now in the local hospital and in great shape, considering.

"Look," Jeffries addressed the team, "let's make sure this place is secure overnight. The sheriff has offered to leave some deputies here overnight and guard the site. We'll go back to our office and ensure everything is set in place for tomorrow. We'll haul out the plants for incineration at the mill and destroy or remove all the infrastructure and equipment in the morning. We did a preliminary estimate and believe there are close to twenty-five hundred plants spread out over forty to fifty acres. This will be one of the largest hauls of the year. I was doing some figuring off the top of my head, and I think the estimated street value is well into the millions. A fine bust and a huge economic blow to the cartel."

The task force members returned to Jimtown and began a hotwash, a critique of the day's activities, including a required analysis of the use of firearms.

Ben was bored. During the on-site activities with the cartel and workers, he had to remain in the fake office all day. He had a tactical radio and could monitor any transmissions, but the day was still long. Nevertheless, he wasn't complaining—he knew it had to be this way to ensure no one connected him to the drug operation.

"Hey, Sam," Ben called to the other man, "can I go with you guys tomorrow and see the site before it's destroyed? I'd like to take a couple of these newer aerial photos and infrared and compare them to what I can see on the ground. It might help me spot something like this a little quicker down the road. You never know what will show up on a fire assignment. It's often things that have nothing to do with the fire."

Sam thought for a minute before turning to his comrade. "Pete, what do you think? It sounds like a good idea. Might Ben in future operations as well. You never know when something like this will happen again."

"Works for me," Pete responded. "It's safe, and the deputies and agents all realize our identities are not to be spread."

In the morning, Ben, Sam, Pete, and a couple members of the team headed to the plantation site. Ben was excited to see what he'd picked out on the IR imagery, firsthand. As they approached the site, Ben asked, "Is that a waterline over there?"

"It is," replied Pete. "Why do you ask?"

"Look on the imagery. If you look closely, you can barely make out a faint line; it disappears into the thickets and then reappears in these open areas. Do you see?"

Sure enough, a faint line could be seen every now and then. Ben knew that piece of information had been important in helping to spot the plantation. He hadn't thought much about it when originally looking. He'd seen it, but now he knew how important it was. The brown paint on the normally white PVC pipe made the heat signature somewhat muted but the pipeline was not completely hidden.

They looked around the areas where the harvested plants were being crudely processed and readied for markets across the country.

I am amazed at the camouflage netting; it seems to stretch across the thicket canopy from one tree stand to another, Ben thought. Aloud, he said, "I had no idea how extensive this was. Man, this is an amazing operation. Water piped in for a drip system, all that netting hiding the workers—it's way more than I'd imagined. All those plants interspersed and growing amongst the pine and fir thickets…this was well thought out, for sure. No doubt they've damned up a natural spring around the hillside as their water source. Pete," he yelled, "I'm going to go up that way and get a different perspective."

Ben quickly walked a short distance up the hill. As he took a few steps, something caught his eye. He glanced at the ground and nausea slammed his stomach. There was a pool of partially dried blood and…parts of someone he didn't want to think about. He turned around, white as a ghost, and rejoined the group as fast as he could.

Pete took one look at Ben and knew what he'd come across. "Ben," he said calmly, "we didn't intend for you to see that. That's not part of your assignment with this task force but now you have firsthand knowledge of what this team is all about. And sometimes…" he sighed, "it is not pretty."

Ben shifted his gaze, working to regain his composure. "Yeah, Pete. I realize how serious these operations can be; it was just a quick, cold shower moment. I've seen the dead and wounded before but that was during my time in Vietnam. I guess I shouldn't have let it surprise me that much. I'm still glad I was able to come here and see this cartel operation and compare the ground to the images I could see from air."

"All right, folks," Sam yelled, "we need to get back to Jimtown. Everything is in place for local law enforcement teams to come in. You all did a fine job. I just heard that our comrade in arms will be out of the hospital when we leave tomorrow. Good news, all the way around."

In Jimtown, the office had been stripped and emptied. There was no trace of them ever being there, except for their personal gear which was stacked in the corner and ready to load. The team prepared to leave, and Ben was eager to get out of there and forget some of what he had seen.

****

Ben arrived home around 5:30 PM. He'd been on assignment for five days and had found it fulfilling and exciting. *Maybe too exciting*, he thought.

Joy and Joe greeted him at the door and grabbed him as they pummeled him with questions, asking if he'd put the fire out by himself.

Gianne came from the kitchen and gave Ben a big kiss, pulled away, and asked, "Are you okay? You look a little pale. Did you have to eat camp food, or were you able to go into town to eat?"

Ben nodded. "I'm fine. We put in a lot of hours in the last five days, and it was a lot of work."

"Really?" Gianne responded. "I thought you were on an assignment doing a bunch of fire detection work, not one fire in particular?"

"Well, it started that way, but we had a big start from one of our detection flights. I had a lot of work to do, until their local IR interpreter took over. Had to put in two overnighters."

After some storytelling to the twins and a quick pillow fight, Ben felt ready for bed. He didn't want to alarm Gianne as to how bad and taxing the assignment had really been, so he watched the 11:00 o'clock news with her, then coaxed her to bed.

Gianne turned over and looked at Ben. "I'll leave you alone until tomorrow night," she giggled. "But you'd better watch out tomorrow; I'm going to jump your no-fire-assignment bones! Okay?"

Laughingly, Ben agreed. "That's a promise; goodnight."

At 2:00 AM, Gianne woke to find Ben tossing and turning. He was sweating profusely and began mumbling under his breath.

"Ben, are you okay? You've been rolling around in this bed for the last hour. What's the matter?"

232

"Nothing," he mumbled. "I'm alright. Go back to sleep. I think I'm feeling some of the bad burritos we had for lunch."

Gianne rolled over but her instincts compelled her to reach out and touch him. She recoiled from the sweat drenching his body. *Something's not right*, she thought. When the black Suburban rushed to her mind, fear seized her soul.

But, why?

Chapter 29

On Thursday morning, the first-person Ben wanted to talk to was the forest supervisor. He was glad to be back from his last assignment and was ready for the normalcy of his real job. But, to be at peace with the changes in his life, he first had to find out a few more things about these "special assignments."

Sue, still guarding the front gate at the supervisor's office, ushered him in right before lunch and warned him the supervisor only had a few minutes.

Once inside the office, Ben wasted no time. "John, I've got something to ask you, and I want a straight answer. Exactly what is your role in all this cloak and dagger mess I'm suddenly involved in?" Shifting, he cursed. "I guess my real question is this: If this is all so danged hush-hush then why are you in the know? What's your connection to these assignments and other agencies?"

John steepled his fingers at his desk and gave Ben a long stare. "Sit down."

Ben obeyed without question, unsure if he was about to receive answers or a reprimand.

"When I was in the military, I wasn't what you call the 'typical ground-pounder' in Korea. I was a covert agent assigned to military intelligence. I had extensive training in undercover operations. I've worked closely with the FBI, DEA, and military intelligence at the highest levels, both during and after the Korean War. During the war, I helped work with the leadership of local villages to overthrow their local outlaws. After my military time was over, I remained in the active reserves and, over the past ten to fifteen years, have been assigned to the Pentagon at times. My bachelor's degree is in Natural Resource Management, but my master's is in Public Policy. I've also been working on a Doctorate in Internal Affairs. And now you know."

Ben narrowed his eyes as he took this in. When John continued speaking, he gave him his full attention.

"If this were a spy movie, you might say I'd be your handler. In reality, I'm here to offer you encouragement and guidance, and to give you someone to vent to. I will be briefed before, during, and after all your operational work. Remember," he pointed a finger at Ben, giving him a stern look, "no one can ever know any of this! Right now, you have some down time from assignments. Go do your regular job. Write that briefing paper I need by tomorrow for my meeting with the governor and have fun in your conservation class this afternoon. Look, I've been informed about what happened at the drug site. I'm aware of what was seen and not seen. If you need to download, that's what I'm here for."

Standing, Ben stared at John, then nodded as he walked out the door. "And now I know. I'm glad I have someone to discuss all this with. My main problem now is to figure out how to keep Gianne from guessing. She's pretty perceptive when it comes to my fire overtime and travel stuff. She won't be satisfied if it doesn't explain things to her satisfaction. Whenever I withhold information from her it makes her more curious about what I'm up to."

After leaving John, he went to his cubbyhole office and readied for his conservation education class of 7th graders. The students were fulfilling their teacher's assignments for extra credit summer work.

Today's discussion and lesson plan covered local tree species and Ben anticipated that it should be a lot of fun. The weather outside was changing quickly, and the local forecast called for a chance of thunderstorms. So, for safety's sake, the kids would be stuck indoors.

As he walked into the classroom and was met with the students' loud chatter, he knew it would be challenging to keep their attention. Thinking fast, Ben glanced outside as a thunderclap sounded in the distance. "Change in lesson plan," he loudly called over the students' voices. "Here's what I want you to do: as soon as you see the next flash of lightning, quickly count the number of seconds from when you saw the flash until you hear the thunder. After that, I want you to tell me how far away the lightning is from our building. Your math and science teachers will be proud of you next fall when you write this in your report."

There was a bright flash and, five seconds later, a loud, rumbling drumbeat of thunder that shook the building until the windows rattled.

"Five seconds, Ranger Ben, five seconds! Is that close? How am I supposed to know how far the storm is?" a boy asked.

"Good job, and good question, Tim. Right now, the storm is about one mile from us, and that is very close. The rule of thumb is that, for every five seconds, the lightning is one mile away. When you see a flash of lightning, count one thousand one, one thousand two, and keep going until you hear the thunder. Who can tell me why this is important?"

A girl in the back of the room stood and answered, "If we counted five seconds, that means it's only a mile away. When we count the next time, and count ten seconds, that means the lightning storm is now two miles away. We know the storm is going away from us. Right, Ranger Ben?"

"Good job, Lisa," Ben praised. "That is exactly right. Doing this helps us know if we are out of danger. It's vital to know if a storm is moving away from us, or if it is getting closer. If it's getting closer, this requires extra diligence in being careful to stay safe. Now, your assignment and report that you'll need to give to your teachers in September is a discussion on what each of you has learned. And for you to prove this is real, you must go to the science section of the library, do some research on information about the speed of sound, and use it to prove how five seconds is a good estimate of a mile. Okay, you're all done for the day. Much better than looking at pictures of trees, wasn't it? You're dismissed. The storm is moving away from us, but be careful on the way home anyway."

That day, lightning storms were prevalent throughout the range of the Sierra Nevada Mountains of California, spreading to the north, along both sides of the Oregon Cascades. The storms were intensifying at several locations, and Ben knew he could be called out for a fire assignment at any time. He didn't mind. The extra money would pay for an extended family vacation to Sisu Bay and the Oregon coast.

When it was almost time to go home, Ben looked up at the sky. *Man*, he thought, *that is one nasty looking sky. Way worse than during class—thunderheads everywhere and lightning all around...*

Chapter 30

Ben's evening was blissfully packed and satisfying. By the time he'd finished dinner, the kids' bedtime routine, and loving Gianne, his heart was full.

"How were the school kids today?" Gianne whispered as she snuggled against his chest. "Were they as fun as always?"

"Yes. Want to know something? The kids are what make this more than a job. This was a worthwhile career move." He smiled and breathed in the scent of her hair. "Listen to that thunder. From the looks of things, I'm thinking there's a high probability I'll get a fire assignment within the next day or two. These storms seem to be rolling in one after the other. It's so dry out there, and it looks like lightning is covering the west sky."

"You be careful out there," Gianne cautioned.

"Always." Ben pressed a kiss to her temple.

They rolled over and tried to get some sleep as the thunder grew closer.

Ben was in a deep sleep when a shrill ringing pierced the air around three in the morning. Heart pounding, he realized the phone was ringing—and the caller seemed to be relentless. Stumbling out of bed and into the kitchen, he answered the call.

"Hello?" Ben's voice was raspy. "Who the heck is calling at this hour?"

"Ben, this is dispatch. We have a fire order for you to report to. You'll never guess where—the airport next to Fresno where you're scheduled to meet the IR flight crew tomorrow night at midnight, with imagery of the Foothills Fire."

Ben snapped to attention, his thoughts racing. Was this an actual fire, or a task-force assignment?

His thoughts were interrupted by the dispatcher. "You'll have plenty of time in the morning to stop by for your fire orders and assignment info. You can also grab your IR gear before heading out for your flight. You'll be flying with your old buddy, Dean Schmidt. He's the contract pilot for your flight. Meet him there at 3:30 PM."

Crap, Ben thought, *this must have been one heck of a lightning fire bust for them to call me now instead of in the morning. There's almost twelve hours before I need to leave…* But he knew how chaotic it could be when forests and parks picked up as many as fifty fires all at once.

241

Gianne rolled over as he climbed back into bed. "When are you going, and what fire will you be on?" she asked sleepily.

"It's called the Foothills Fire, and it's somewhere outside of Fresno, California. That's really all I know for now, hon. But I'm sure it will be on the news tomorrow, along with dozens of other new fires."

The next morning, Ben slept in. Once up for the day, he kissed Joe and Joy and reminded them of their chores and to help Mommy while he was gone. Once he'd ensured his family was tended to, he headed to the office with his red fire bag in tow. It was loaded, as usual, with enough clothes and necessities for two weeks if needed. His red bag was a coveted possession since these were mostly given only to those who were on the fire line or working in a fire camp situation with fire credentials.

Leaving everything he needed in his office, Ben snuck around the corner to Sue's desk. "Hey, Sue. Listen, I know how busy John is but is there any way I can get in to see him? It will only take two minutes, promise."

Sue looked up at Ben with that devilish smile she was known for and answered, "Hang on. I'll call in and see. Since his door is closed, that usually means no."

She rang John and talked for a couple of seconds before motioning Ben to go in. "You must be one of his favorites; he never lets anyone in on short notice like this," she said with a wide grin.

Ben went into the office, sat down, and dove right in. "John, I need to ask you if this assignment I'm going on is another task force gig or an actual fire assignment. It seemed too coincidental that I am going back to the Fresno Airport."

"No," John responded, "it's a legit assignment, and I don't have any type of intel to clarify it as something more. Looks like IR time for that fire, as well as any others that come up down there, so good luck and enjoy."

When he left John's office, Ben grabbed his gear and loaded the pickup that would take him to the airport. One of the summer kids was assigned to drop him off. They parked near the charter flight terminal, a rather small, unassuming, old wood building, and Ben unloaded his gear.

"Thanks for the lift," he said to the teen before wandering into the terminal shack and dropping his stuff near one of the half-dozen old, worn-out chairs in the open lobby. There was a coffee room and small office in the back for the pilots, so Ben walked back there to ensure he knew who his pilot was, since they changed at the last moment sometimes. He recognized the tail numbers of the twin engine, Cessna. The plane had been carded and approved for federal flights for employees, and he'd been on it several times.

"Hey, you worthless punk," yelled a voice from across the room. "Am I taking you along for another one of your taxpayer-funded joy rides today?"

Ben glanced up and smiled when he saw Dean Schmidt.

"Are you actually going to do fire work this time 'round or screw around for a week or two?" Dean teased.

Ben grinned. "Great. They stuck me with a pilot who's on a temporary release from his retirement village."

They shared a laugh and shook hands as Ben joined him at the table.

"What's the deal with you and Fresno?" Dean asked, pouring himself a cup of coffee. "Nobody in their right mind wants to go there *once*, let alone twice."

Ben laughed. "Well, actually, it's the closest airport to where I'm heading. After we unload, I drive up along the foothills a short way and then up into the lower edge of the Sierras. It's only about forty-five minutes to get to the fire camp, so I can easily pick up the IR at the Fresno Charter Terminal. That way, the ship can get in, get out, and be on its way to the next target from an airport that can handle the King Air."

After a quick cup of coffee, Dean was ready to go. "Alrighty, let's get this show on the road. It's only you and me on the flight down. On the way back, I've got three returning home with me who've timed out from other assignments."

With that, Dean loaded Ben's gear into the plane, being careful to position it so that the the weight of the baggage balanced with their own weight. "You can sit up front, but like I've warned you before, don't touch any of the controls or I'll drop you off early," Dean warned with a laugh. He went over the safety features of the plane and showed Ben where the emergency window, door latches, and fire extinguisher were located. Grabbing the latest certification for the plane and himself, he handed it to Ben.

"Thanks," Ben said. "I know you're always up to date but at least, if someone asks, I can honestly say I saw the paperwork, as much of a pain in the butt it is."

Dean radioed for approval to taxi out from the charter terminal, received his runway takeoff instructions, and off they went on another journey.

"Seventh flight with you, right, Dean?" Ben asked.

"Sounds about right—seven...your luckiest flight," Dean answered with a huge smile.

Ben settled in for the two-hour flight and, after about fifteen minutes, grabbed the water bottle he always carried with him. Dean watched him drink and felt compelled to grab his own water. Ben told himself to relax. His fear of flying in small planes was long gone, but he still didn't like flying these "white knuckle airline" flights, though he knew he was in capable hands.

"Still around two-hours until we touch down, Dean?" Ben looked out the window and scanned the thunderheads, wondering if they might have to detour around a storm. When Dean didn't respond,

Ben looked over at him. "Hey! What's the matter with you? You're shaking. Are you feeling okay?"

Dean tried to speak but failed. His eyes were suddenly wide open and glazed as they rolled side to side. He turned toward Ben; his face was whiter than a ghost.

Ben was horrified by what he saw. As Dean began shaking and wheezing, small blobs of white foam dribbled out of the corners of his mouth and ran down his chin. His head slumped forward. And then there was silence.

Ben cursed as panic seized his chest. "What just happened?!" His heart pounded in his chest as he worked to remember the basic first aid training he'd undergone. This was beyond anything he'd ever expected to see, but he knew he had to try. He pushed Dean's head back. The man's glazed eyes stared into nothing. He forced himself to check for a pulse, his worst fears slamming him like a sledgehammer to the gut. A sickening horror settled over him.

A string of rapid-fire curses flew from his mouth. "He's dead. He's dead! What is going on?" Ben's breathing mirrored that of a couch potato being chased by a race car. Sweat poured from his body as he wracked his brain for a solution. What does one do when their pilot keels over dead?! *What am I going to do? I'm not a pilot! Okay, calm down… just calm down and think.*

His eyes roamed the cockpit, reading dials he didn't understand. He'd seen Dean switch the autopilot on, so at least he had that going for him. There was at least an hour and a half left until the plane reached Fresno. He knew how to use a radio… *I know we are on autopilot because I saw Dean switch it on. I know we have at least an hour and a half flight time before Fresno. I know how to use a radio. Damn it, get a hold of yourself and think!!!*

Chapter 31

Ben worked to regain control of his terror-stricken nerves. He took deep breaths and glanced over at Dean. With a trembling left hand, he closed Dean's lifeless eyes. He turned back to the front and stared at the control pane, thinking back on the many times he'd seen it under Dean's masterful command. He gathered his thoughts as he sat, his gaze wandering over the instrument panel, yoke, and the gadgets he didn't understand. Nausea teased his stomach, and he fought to keep down the contents in his stomach.

His eyes fell on the mic cord, dangling from the instrument panel. Grabbing the mic, he took a deep breath and, in a shaky voice, yelled, "Mayday, mayday, mayday! I need help immediately! This is a forest service contract flight in a twin-engine Cessna, on the way to Fresno. The pilot is dead and I'm in the co-pilot seat next to him. I am not a pilot. I repeat, I am *not* a pilot!! Can anyone hear me? Please respond. Hurry!!"

After what seemed like an eternity, a deep voice blasted over the speaker. "My name is John Wilson. I'm an FAA controller. I'm going to get you up on my radar. What's your name?"

"My name is Ben." His voice sounded distant and foreign in his ears.

"I want you to listen carefully, Ben. Everything is going to be okay. We are going to see you through this mess and make sure you land safe and sound, okay? Do you see the transponder on the instrument panel?"

"Yes, I know where it is."

"Good. Do you know how to set it?"

A hint of hope bloomed in his heart. "Yes. I've watched Dean do it a dozen times. What should I change it to?" He listened intently as John gave him the frequency, then adjusted the transponder.

"Okay, now that your radio is turned to the right frequency, we can communicate without interference and can follow you on radar," John assured. "Do you have access to all the controls and instrument panel? Is the pilot in your way?"

"No. I can get around him, but I think I have a set of controls— for a co-pilot, I guess?—in front of me. He always yelled at me not to touch anything. Now look." Ben breathed a shaky laugh.

John's voice came back over the speaker. "I've contacted Fresno Charter Services. They're sending Chuck Ames over. He's probably the number one trainer for this aircraft in the entire western United States. He knows this particular aircraft inside and out and will be on with you in about five minutes. He's inside the building, heading upstairs to the control tower now. Hang on, Ben. We've got you."

Ben breathed a sigh of relief but one look at Dean's lifeless body had his heart pounding like an oversized bass drum. His stomach lurched again, and he pressed a hand to his mouth as fought the urge to throw up. Tears stung his eyes as he stared at the control panel. Could he pull this off? Could *he* fly a plane? The enormity of his situation set in and panic flooded his nerves with ice. His thoughts began to race. *Will I ever get to see the twins again? Or hold Gianne and tell her how much I love her? Did I tell her before I left?*

He tried to calm himself by taking a couple of long, deep breaths. He looked over at Dean and cursed. "I wish I'd paid more attention to you when you were doing your thing, Dean. I can't believe I'm in your plane, you're dead, and I could be joining you soon."

"Okay, Ben," a hearty voice filled the cockpit. "This is Chuck Ames. I am a senior flight instructor for practically every Cessna aircraft ever made, as well as a dozen other manufacturers. You're in capable hands. I'm going to get you down safely. You are now about fifteen minutes out, so sometime in the next five to ten minutes I'll have you switch off the autopilot and walk you through what to do. We've cleared the runway and rerouted any other air traffic, so it's just you and me."

"Okay," Ben responded, fighting his tears. "I've been in one of these small planes a dozen times, but I need you to remember that I am definitely *not* a pilot! I'm so frigging scared right now. You hear me? I mean scared to the core!"

Ames calmly gave his answer. "I hear you, Ben. You're going to be okay. I totally understand. Believe it or not, this is not rocket science. With a few good moves, you'll be down here in no time, safe and sound. And, when you get here, I'll buy you a beer, okay?"

"Deal. Now let's get this thing on the ground." Though his nerves had calmed some, his shirt was drenched in sweat and his hands were shaking so much he wondered if he'd be able to grip the controls. His heart pounded in his temple, the beat resounding in his ears.

"Alright, Ben, you're about five minutes out. Do you know how to activate the landing gear switch?"

"Yes. I always wondered what would happen if the pilot forgot to hit it as we started our descent. I can't say that I care to find out."

Ames chuckled and then walked Ben through how to turn the autopilot off. He explained the controls as the plane began its descent. Ben worked to maintain focus and keep his mind off the fact that he had full control of the airplane. Ames gave detailed instructions on how to reduce the airspeed and keep the nose of the plan where it should be.

Ben was now only a few minutes out and had successfully reduced his air speed to 135.

"Go ahead and put the landing gear down. Let me know if the green light comes on in a few seconds," Ames directed.

"O-o-kay," Ben stammered. He flipped the switch to gear down and listened to the sudden thud as the landing gear opened. "It's down," he announced in a rushed tone. "My altitude is twenty-five-hundred feet, and my airspeed reads 125. I'm having trouble with this thing pitching up and down but can see the airport and runways in front of me. Where the heck do I go?"

"Ben, you're a natural. You sure you've never flown?" Ames praised him. "Keep doing what you're doing. Drop your air speed down to one hundred, like I told you, and get prepared to land on that far right runway you see. On the left, you'll see the taxiway. The runway is the longer one, and it's all clear. You'll see a bunch of fields before the runway begins. At the far end of the runway, there's nothing but smooth grass. If you come down early, or need more room at the end, it's smooth ground. You're doing great!!"

"Okay, here we go." Ben was now only five-hundred feet off the ground. His airspeed was at 95 and dropping fast, but he hung onto the yoke and listened for Ames' instructions, telling him when to kill the power. Down, down, down, down, he dropped. The left wing tilted slightly, he corrected, then the right wing went down. He tried to correct that, but Ames' voice sounded again.

"Cut your power. You're fifteen feet off the deck."

Ben saw the front of the runway and quickly did everything Ames instructed him to do as the plane bounced ten feet into the air. With all power cut, the next bounce was five feet and, finally, he was on the ground, racing along the runway at 85 mph without a clue as to what to do next. "Holy crap, Chuck! What do I? What do I do?!" he screamed, panic driving his words. The plane swerved to the left and right, but Ben still managed to keep it on the runway. He followed Ames' instructions on braking, although he got carried away and the plane tipped slightly to the right, the wingtip almost touching the bare ground. Then the airplane nosedived and pitched to the left after the wingtip almost scraped the ground. Miraculously, it righted itself and spun around close to forty-five degrees before screeching to a stop.

A slew of curses flew from Ben's mouth as relief washed through him. "Oh, wow! I'm on the ground!! You did it, Chuck, you did it! Thank you, thank you! You really saved my butt."

"Not at all, Ben," Ames answered. "That wasn't me. This was your landing; you did exactly what I told you to do and that's what got you here. Now, don't be alarmed. We've dispatched the fire engines and ambulance just to ensure you're okay. They should be pulling up in…about…thirty seconds. Are you hurt anywhere?"

"Other than a small bump on the side of my head, I'm fine. Received that when the plane lurched to the right." He glanced to his left and blinked back tears. "Dean, on the other hand…" He sniffed. "I have no idea what happened to him. It happened so quickly!"

Ben's fingers trembled as he tried to unstrap his seatbelt harness system. He finally managed to control his hands long enough to get the seatbelt buckle unhooked then slowly opened the door. Dean had shown him a million times how to get out in case of emergency, so he considered himself an expert on door opening. Ben jumped to the ground and stood still. He stared blankly at his surroundings, slightly dazed. His stomach lurched, and he gave into its persistence and hurled on the runway. Wiping his mouth with the back of his sleeve, his body shook as he walked away from the plane. Turning back, he stared at the damage from his landing. It wasn't extensive, but he knew plane repairs were not cheap. *I'm glad I don't have to pay that repair bill,* he thought. Turning back around, he took steps away from the plane, stopped in his tracks, covered his face, and burst into tears.

Loud sirens pierced the air right before an ambulance made its appearance, followed by a fire engine. With full sirens and lights, the emergency vehicles halted twenty feet from the Cessna.

"Hey," one of the medics shouted. "Are you all right? Anything hurt? Any bleeding? Bruises? Lacerations?"

Ben quickly wiped his eyes and forced a laugh. "No. Actually, considering everything that happened, I'm physically fine. Just shaken up and grateful. I'm alive and probably shouldn't be. The pilot's friggin' dead. But I'm fine." He dropped his gaze to the tarmac and felt the sting of tears all over again. He pictured Gianne and the twins and hoped the incident wasn't being covered on the news for them to see.

One of the paramedics approached him. "Look, after what you've been through, it's probably best if we check you out. Now hop up here and let us take a good look at you."

"Okay," Ben answered. "I have a splitting headache. Can you give me something for that?"

The two paramedics checked Ben's vitals and gave him a couple of strong ibuprofens. "You're in great shape, despite the incident. You've sustained no serious injuries, aside from that bump on the noggin. But you need to watch out for the possibility of internal injuries—you know, the emotional kind."

Ben looked up at them with a slight smile. "Yeah, the trauma is in here." He pointed to his heart and head.

Crewmembers from the fire engine checked out the plane for any signs of fuel or oil spills but found none and started to leave. The engine captain looked over at Ben and said, "Ben, right? Someone is coming over from the sheriff's office to talk to you about what happened to your pilot. He'll be here in a minute; he just left the charter terminal."

Before Ben could answer, he spotted the sheriff's Bronco heading toward him.

Sheriff Jennings stepped out of the vehicle and approached him. "Ben, is that you?"

Ben immediately put his finger to his lips in a warning to keep silent. "Yes, Sheriff, I'm Ben. I was on my way, as an infrared interpreter, to a fire near here."

Sheriff Jennings walked closer to Ben and whispered, "Sorry about that. I'll introduce myself as though this is the first time, so these yahoos can hear me. Then you can walk me through what happened, step by step." In a voice loud enough to be heard by the others, he went on, "I'm Steve Jennings, County Sheriff. That was a fine job getting this sucker on the ground—and with everything in as close to one piece as possible! Can you walk with me to the plane and tell me what happened?"

Ben followed him to the airplane as the paramedics were offloading Dean's body. Dean's skin was gray, and the telltale signs of foam still clung near the edges of his mouth.

"We'd been in the air for about, I don't know, maybe fifteen or twenty minutes. Everything was going on like normal. We were at

258

altitude; the plane was on autopilot, and Dean and I were talking. Suddenly, he started shaking. I looked over at him, and his eyes were kind of glazed looking. Then, there was some kind of foamy stuff at each corner of his mouth. I asked him if he was okay but before he could answer, his head slumped forward, and he was… Well, I didn't think he was dead. At first, I thought he might have had a bout of something—you know, a stomach attack or something. But I reached over and tried to find a pulse on his neck and there was nothing. I knew right away he was dead but didn't have a clue as to why!"

Jennings, in turn, asked, "Ben, can you think of anything unusual that happened in those fifteen or twenty minutes? Did he take any medicine or eat anything?"

"Nothing. No food, no pills, but wait…wait a minute!" His eyes grew huge at the memory. "He grabbed his water bottle. It's a stainless-steel dandy. He's had it with him on all our flights. He took a drink of water right before all this happened. Holy crap, do you think he was poisoned?"

Jennings frowned. "Highly unlikely. I've never heard of anything that could kill a person that fast. At least nothing you can find in this country. Let's go get your gear out of the luggage compartment. Do you know which one he used?"

Ben walked to the rear of the plane and pointed to where his stuff was stowed.

Sheriff Jennings opened the hatch and, with a puzzled look, asked Ben, "Why are there four suitcases in here? Which one is yours?"

"Mine is a red fire pack. I didn't bring a suitcase. That blue duffel bag has my equipment in it. I was the only passenger on this contract flight, so I have no clue about those other suitcases," Ben answered.

"Well, something's not right," the sheriff muttered. "If you were the only passenger on the flight, what would these suitcases be doing there?" He reached in, pulled out all four soft-sided suitcases, then laid them out on the ground. They were identical. No tags, same size, same color, no visible brand, and they all had a small padlock looped through the zipper pulls. They each seemed to weigh the same. Jennings rushed to his Bronco, pulled out a small set of bolt cutters, and snipped the padlocks. Once all four had been cut off, he looked at the first suitcase, poked it a couple of times, and then pulled the zippers open.

A stream of curses flew from his lips as the sheriff gaped at the bag's contents. "Would you look at that?" He opened all four cases and cursed again as he looked at Ben. "Can you believe this?"

Ben stared, taking in the approximately eighty pounds of packaged and processed marijuana, ready for sale on the streets. It looked as though they had been packed and ready for delivery. Each suitcase had around twenty-gallon freezer bags, each holding approximately a pound of the street-ready marijuana.

Still in shock from his earlier excitement, Ben's words were slow to come. Finally, he spoke. "What would these be doing in there? This is the weirdest day of my life. First, Dean keels over dead. For whatever reason, I'm the only one on the flight with him, though the plane could hold up to five more passengers. And now this! Do you think he was some kind of mule delivering weed all over the west for distribution? Or maybe he stole this stuff," Ben mused. He gasped, his eyes growing huge. "Do you think he was murdered?"

Jennings shook his head. "I have no clue, but this is a major drug find. I need to talk with Agents Jeffries and Lutz. This is their field of expertise. Don't discuss this with anyone else until I brief the agents. What I'm going to do now is call in and tell your dispatcher to replace you ASAP. I'll tell them you're being held overnight for observation. If anyone asks, you hit your head on the landing and are going to the hospital as a precaution. In the meantime, I'll get ahold of Lutz and Jeffries and see if they can get over here this evening. I'll get you checked into a hotel tonight."

"All right," Ben replied, "I'll give my wife a quick call and let her know I'm okay."

"I think she knows that already; you've been on the live newsfeed all over the West since you radioed your mayday message. You have several media stations waiting for you in the terminal. Only disclose how you survived that landing: who helped you land safely, how you're feeling now, etc. Once that's done, you get out of there. I'll wait for you. Oh, by the way, that was a dan fine landing, no matter what you think!"

As Jennings had warned, they walked into the charter terminal and were bombarded by the media. Half a dozen reporters shouted for attention, and the glare from the camera lights of the TV stations blinded them. Everyone blurted questions at the same time.

Ben, experienced in dealing with reporters, raised his hand and loudly stated, "I'm going to tell you what happened, take a couple of questions, and leave. I have a headache that I need to have examined." Without dwelling on Dean's untimely death or the surprise cargo, Ben gave a brief statement about what had happened, leaving out their after-landing discovery. He refused to answer questions concerning Dean's cause of death and quickly said he had time for one last question. After that, Sheriff Jennings ushered him off to the Fresno Almond Inn.

Chapter 32

The phone rang as Ben returned to his room after a leisurely breakfast. He snatched up the receiver and said, "Ben, here."

"Ben, this is Sheriff Jennings. How are you doing this morning?"

"Honestly, I'm still pretty numb. I didn't get a lot of sleep last night. I think everything's starting to sink in. I talked with Gianne and the twins and found out they saw the whole thing on TV. They weren't tuned in live, thank God, but they saw the news clips of the plane at the end and some video clips of the interaction on the way down. And, of course, they saw my interview. I think they're more traumatized by this than I am, at least for now," he mused.

"Okay," Jennings responded. "Well, I called to give you an update. So far, I know that the task force is not being activated. This, unfortunately, is part of some of our law enforcement agencies' normal workload. However, this is some serious stuff, Ben. You have a dead, federally approved contract pilot and a plane with a compartment full of drugs. This pilot could go in and out of any US charter terminal without anyone suspecting anything illegal. He was a perfect courier for God knows what, or for who. So, with that in mind, you and I, along with Jeffries and Lutz, are meeting at your hotel room in about an hour. They need to be brought up to speed on what's going on over here. Not for a task force assignment—this is just part of their normal jobs, alright?"

"Got it," Ben answered. "I'm guessing everything is all square regarding my overnight observation stay? You have a replacement for my IR fire assignment in place?"

"Affirmative. We have everything in hand. We'll meet, and then you'll be on a commercial flight back home. Are you okay flying right away?"

"I sure ain't walking," Ben laughed. "Yeah, I'm all right. I'll make sure I check the age of the cockpit crew."

About an hour and a half later, everyone was gathered in Ben's room. Jaws dropped as the men were caught up on the previous day's events.

'Yesterday was a huge surprise," Sam Jeffries spoke. "I have to tell say...I've met Schmidt several times at different drops, and he always seemed pleasant. There was never anything that would indicate any of this was going on."

"Nobody was more surprised than I was to see those drugs in the luggage compartment of that airplane. I flew with Dean at least half a dozen times. We've talked about family, laughed, and traded jokes. He told me about his wife, kids, and new grandkids. I don't think I will ever get over what I witnessed on that flight. And I have to tell you, the way he died had me wondering if I was next."

"I know what a shock this whole thing has been," Lutz interjected, "but this is a serious bunch of weed, ready for street sale. This very well could be part of the plantations cultivated on the Oso Negro Cartel site. We raided this very site and put an end to that particular portion of their lucrative enterprise. I'm not sure how Schmidt figures in all of this, but it is too coincidental. Ben, didn't you say Schmidt saw you get into the Learjet when you left on that task force assignment?"

"Yeah, but there's no way he could have ever known my interaction with the task force, let alone that I'm a member." He sat in silence for a moment, pondering Dean's sudden death. "How can someone pilot an airplane one minute and be dead the next? What *happened* to him? Was there something in his water bottle?"

"Here's the deal," Lutz answered. "Do not, I repeat, *do not* mention *anything* about the drugs we found. And don't mention anything at all about how he died. Ben, Steve, if anyone asks, you tell people he died of an apparent heart attack. Okay? As Steve mentioned, this is not a task force assignment. But this thing has been turned over to several agencies and could end up in our laps if more sites need an IR look."

Not satisfied with this answer, Ben blurted, "Okay, but you didn't answer my question. I still want to know what you think happened—unofficially. That was no heart attack. If he was poisoned, what kind of poison or chemical could have killed him so fast? And—

Jeffries quickly interrupted, "Look, there are several theories out there. Ricin is one, but it's a rather violent poison and, Ben, from what you described, it can be ruled out, at least for now. From your description, it doesn't sound like he died a violent death. However," he frowned, "it's always possible there are versions of Ricin we're unaware of. Another possibility to consider—and I know this sounds weird—is that it could be poison from plants, animals, insects, amphibians from a jungle or tropical environment. I've worked on diplomatic cases involving suspected assassination attempts or actual assassinations of foreign leaders and some of the things that turned up were amazing. One case appeared to be a poisonous substance that was a throwback to two-hundred-year-old poison darts used by warring jungle tribes. But this stuff is real. We've only recently learned about these little-known poisons. A drug cartel wanting to knock someone off has the cash to go anywhere in the world and search this stuff out, believing their poison purchase to be untraceable. Bottom line, just another reminder…, we cannot discuss this with colleagues, friends, or family unless authorized. Ben, you know you're one exception to this rule. Alright, let's get out of here. Decompress as much as possible back home, because it's highly possible we could be back here with the rest of the task force before long. Ben, your flight is scheduled for 1330 hours."

Chapter 33

Ben stared absently out the airplane window. There was no room for relief to set in as he flew home. His mind was filled with images of the past few days—images he was desperate to forget. The past forty-eight hours had been the most adrenaline-producing he'd experienced since leaving Vietnam. As the memories tormented his mind, he broke into a cold sweat as his hands began to tremble. He took deep breaths as he fought to regain control, relieved to see his hands still after several minutes.

Beside him, a little old lady studied his features. After a moment, she asked, "Are you alright, hon? You seem out of sorts."

Ben stared at her, his eyes empty. Forcing a smile, he answered. "Yeah, I'm alright. I think I probably put in too many long hours in a short time. I'll be fine, once I get home. Thank you for asking." He turned back toward the window and tried to catnap for the remaining ninety minutes of the flight. No matter how hard he tried, he couldn't shake the image of Dean's dead body. A chill ran down his spine as he remembered sitting in the co-pilot seat, panic seizing his mind.

Thank God, the flight ended quickly, and Ben drove home in a pickup one of the summer kids left for him at the airport. At last, he pulled into his driveway, ready to put the last two days behind him. Resolving to treat this trip like a normal dispatch, he unloaded his gear and hurried to the front door, eager to hug the twins and Gianne. Before he could reach the porch, Joe and Joy ran out, grabbed him as tight as possible around each leg, and clung to him as long as they could.

"Daddy, are you an airplane pilot? Did you really fly a plane all by yourself? Do you do that a lot at work? Do you?!" Joe excitedly asked. In his eyes, his father was a hero.

Ben looked down at the twins and smiled, leaning to kiss the tops of their heads. "Shh, no, I'm not an airplane pilot, and I had a lot of help getting that plane down on the ground after the pilot got sick. Gianne, you okay?" His gaze turned to his wife as she followed the twins out to the porch. Tears glistened in her eyes.

Sucking back a sob, she wanted to know what happened. "What was all that about, Ben? What in the world happened to your pilot? Heart attack? Oh my, what am I saying?" She pushed her hair away from her wet cheeks. "I don't care about all that. I only care that you are alive, safe, and here with us." Gianne grabbed Ben and hugged him so tight he was sure he would lose his breath. "The whole thing was live on TV. The twins begged me to allow them to watch you land the plane, but—" Her voice broke off as a fresh pool of tears formed. "I refused to let them. I made them go out and play. I was afraid for them to watch the horror of that moment since I had no way of knowing what would happen. I am so glad you are here. I cannot believe what I saw on TV."

Ben gave her a half smile. "It was even more unbelievable from where I was sitting. But now it's over. I'm okay—*we* are okay— and I have two days off. I can get rid of this headache, and we can all get back to normal and relax."

Plagued by a question burning her soul, Gianne swallowed hard and forced herself to voice it. "Ben, is there anything about this IR assignment you aren't telling me? The whole thing sounds crazy strange, especially considering that you've been to that same airport twice in less than a month. The TV reports from Fresno speculate that the pilot died under mysterious circumstances. What's going on with that?"

Ben's features paled. "The only thing I'm allowed to say is that Dean died of an apparent heart attack. And to me, it appeared that way. He was gone so quickly, it was—"

"Oh, honey, I'm sorry for asking crazy questions. You know I don't normally push you, but that was scary, and I was—still am—terrified. And after all that, I wonder if there's anything else we should be worried about. I still think of that black Suburban around the folks' house."

"No," Ben assured, "I don't think there's much to worry about. Right now, I just want to go to bed and try to calm down. Maybe I can forget how scared I was, too."

As they headed inside, Ben was thankful for the extra days off and relieved that the next week would only be a three-day workweek.

****

After his four-day weekend, Ben was glad to return to normalcy, especially in his mind. Back in his office's familiar and safe confines, he was completing a stack of routine paperwork when his phone rang, causing him to jump. "Good morning, this is Ben, how can I help you?"

"Ben, good morning. This is Phil Whitecloud. Do you remember me? We met shortly after you transferred here, at the annual Forest Spring Barbeque in March, at the Grange Hall. I'm the old Indian," he laughed.

"Phil, heck yeah, of course, I do! You were about the only one at the barbeque who came and talked to me and Gianne. I remember the warm and welcoming conversation we had. I really appreciated it. What can I do for you, Phil?"

"I'm not sure who to talk to, but I have something that's been gnawing at me for nineteen of my twenty years working on the Monument Pines National Forest, and I need to talk to someone about it before I retire. Do you have any free time in the next few days? Now, mind you, this would be a discussion that needs to stay between us."

"You bet. Actually, I have some time after lunch today, if that works for you."

"That would be great. I'm in the shop all day doing some maintenance checks on the grader and backhoe, so how about 1:30?"

"See you then." Ben hung and thought back to their first meeting. He remembered well his conversation with Phil at the March barbeque. He was Native American, one of the first to be hired full-time in the last twenty years. He'd been a heavy-duty, construction equipment operator until the company had gone bankrupt. He applied to the Forest Service and was hired as a temporary employee. When they found out how good he was, they made him a full-time employee at the age of forty-two.

Wow, Ben thought to himself, *now he's sixty-two and still working full-time as a heavy equipment operator. Just amazing. A good lesson for everyone to never give up.*

****

Phil knocked on Ben's door at exactly 1:30.

"Come on in, Phil, it's great to see you again. What can I help you with?" Ben greeted him.

"Well," Phil started, taking a seat, "this is going to take a while. Like I said on the phone, it's haunted me for nineteen years. It's about something I was involved in during my first few months on the job."

Ben gave Phil his undivided attention.

"You probably remember reading about the huge chemical spills from the Keystone Gold Mine, about fifty miles from here.

Those spills happened throughout the late 50s, and by spills, I mean some extensive spills that were covered up and never reported until some well waters were tested, and the results showed some really bad stuff. These spills all happened when I was still a temp, but stories of these chemicals continued during the long cleanup period for the next ten or fifteen years. There was cyanide, mercury, and who knows what other kinds of chemicals were used on those mine and milling sites—sites that had been active since gold was discovered in the 1860s. The spills of the late 50s were so bad that the government eventually came in and declared it a superfund site sometime around 1960. During the next fifteen years, they spent a hundred million dollars to clean things up. They moved twenty-one houses out of the area, filled the whole site in, bulldozed it level, and fenced it off. It's partially fenced off like it was originally, and you can still see the cleared-off area today."

He paused for a moment and then went on with his story. "Newspaper stories talked about an alarming number of stillborn babies and a tenfold increase in several types of cancer, as well as other illnesses and diseases that could never be explained. Investigative journalists laid the blame on the spills. News media from all over the world covered farm animals being born with five legs, or

275

two heads, or unexplained malignancies in newborn livestock. Now, I can't decipher the truth from rumors since this all stemmed from a bunch of hippie types, especially since this was near the beginning of the environmental movement, and everyone was going crazy over this story. But during the early part of the cleanup, I was ordered to do some things that have haunted me."

Confused, Ben interrupted. "What were you ordered to do? And why did you do it if it went against your conscience so badly?"

"Okay, look, Ben, reality check time." Phil leaned forward in his chair. "In 1962, I was one of only a small handful of Native Americans working for the USFS in the entire Western US. At that time, I could have been the only one in line for a career, and I wanted to make sure I had that chance for permanent employment. Get it?"

"Do I ever," Ben answered, thinking about his memorable first summer. "So, what happened?"

"I was working as the forest's backhoe operator," Phil continued. "I went wherever they wanted me to go, and did whatever I was told. One late afternoon, I got called into the Forest Engineer's office. He told me there would be some work to do at nighttime. I would get some overtime for night work, but I was not to tell anyone

276

about what we were doing. Since overtime was unheard of, I couldn't say no. He told me to haul the backhoe up to an area near Horton's Peak—it's a shallow basin area. I met some guy there, and I'm pretty darn sure he was from the mining company. Anyway, he told me to get my backhoe in there and dig about twenty holes, each five feet across and around six or seven feet deep. So, I did. It was good soil, so it only took me a couple of hours.

"Our engineer then came onsite and looked at my holes. There were around twenty, all dug tightly in a small area. I finished, and they told me to wait on the other side of the hill. I heard a heavy semi-truck coming up the mountain. It was carrying large, barrel-shaped containers, you know, like those fifty-five-gallon drums that gas, oil, and chemicals come in. Actually, they were bigger than the fifty-five-gallon drums we're all used to seeing, but these were shaped differently. The truck had a small forklift that could be off-loaded easily. They let it down and that little sucker, with a couple of straps connected to the forks, unloaded all twenty of these weird-shaped barrels into my holes. The forklift was reloaded and off they went. I noticed the mining company's logo on the side of the truck cab."

Ben was on the edge of his seat, listening to every word.

277

"After the semi left, I was ordered to carefully refill those twenty holes and ensure that everything was covered, and the area smoothed to look like no one had been there. The Forest Engineer came over to me and, quite bluntly, told me, 'Look, Tonto, if you want a chance to work permanently with us, you'll keep your mouth shut and never tell anyone what happened here tonight. If you blab one frigging word about any of this, I will make sure you never work anywhere—and I mean *anywhere*—whether that be with the federal government or anywhere else. You got that?' I let his threat scare me into silence. You're the first person I've ever told this story to. As an Indian, I knew darned good and well if anyone heard that story from me, I could kiss this job I love goodbye. But now, with my retirement finally on the horizon, I can't, in good conscience, leave without telling someone and getting some experts out to the site to see what has happened to those containers in the last twenty years. These are bad news chemicals, and if those barrels start deteriorating and leaking, who knows what the environmental effects will be."

Ben's eyes were huge. "That is some story! I don't blame you one bit for not saying anything. Look, here is what I think we should do. I'm in pretty good with the Forest Supervisor. Let me go give him the short story of what you just told me. We can get our Forest Engineer, and perhaps an EPA rep, out there to take a look. But listen, I will only tell Supervisor Wolden your story—and your name—with your permission. Everyone else, including the media and other employees, will only hear that we had an anonymous tip that led us to the site. Does that sound good?"

Phil thought for a minute and responded, "If you can trust the FS not to go ballistic and blame me, then yeah. Let's get this over with. You talk to the FS and let me know when, and I will take both of you to the exact site. It's been etched in my brain for all these years; I know exactly where it is."

Chapter 34

Two days later, Ben, Phil, and FS John Wolden hopped into a six-pack Ford and headed to Horton Peak. The trio was quiet for the ride, each pondering how bad this could be.

Ben was the first to break the silence. "Okay, listen, if this indiscretion is as bad as it seems, we must protect Phil as the source. When we get back to the office, I'll put together a communication plan for the media and elected officials. I'll also put out a separate message for you to send to employees, John. I fear this will blow up big time if we aren't the first to get this story out there. We've got to be the first to fess up."

"Agreed," John answered with a nod. "Draft something quickly and let me take a look tomorrow afternoon. Are you okay with everything, Phil?"

Phil thought for a minute before replying. "I don't want this coming back to me or my family, but I'm glad to see this whole thing coming out in the open. If this stuff is leaking into the soil, I'll finally have peace knowing the right people are working on stabilizing the area."

When they arrived at the site, they got out of the pickup truck and walked a hundred yards up a recently constructed logging road that, unbeknownst to anyone, was built way too close to the site.

John cursed. "I'm glad this area wasn't disturbed during road construction. What a catastrophe that could have been. Imagine a D9 running through the area, whacking metal drums of who knows what, busting them open, and knocking that mess all over the place."

They followed Phil as he walked to a clearing. He showed them the area, marking off— as best he could remember—where he'd started and stopped digging. The area covered over half an acre.

Leading them to the lower part of the area, where the last hole was thought to be, Phil shouted, "Look at this! This is what I've worried about for twenty long years. Look over here. See the partially exposed top of that barrel? You can barely see the edge of the barrel where the ground has eroded away. Look at that exposed edge; you can see some type of liquid around the lid. It looks to me like natural erosion—you know wind, rain, storms—has taken away quite a bit of the layer of dirt I put on top of the barrels. I had at least twelve inches over all these containers."

Ben went to the pickup and returned a few minutes later with a fire shovel. He gently dug around a couple of the containers until his shovel clanged against several of the metal lids. As he dug near the last one, he removed some soil around the top, near the edge of the lid. "Uh oh!" he exclaimed, drawing every eye to him. "Look at this shovel full of wet soil—that's gotta be chemicals. In fact, I'm leaving this shovel right here on the ground. I have no clue what kind of toxic crap I just dug into, but I'm not taking any of it back with us."

John stared at the shovel and set his jaw. "I think that might be really smart. Let's get the heck out of here and get ahold of our engineering folks to see who we have for chemical spill contacts at EPA and anyone else who will be involved in mitigating this site. Phil, I want to personally thank you for finally coming forward. I understand why you waited, but I'm glad we can correctly address this potential disaster now."

They headed back to town, leaving the shovel where it sat in the most soil. Phil returned to his equipment safety checks while Ben and John went to their offices.

Sitting at his desk, Ben began to carefully word a news release as part of his communications plan. He knew they needed to get this out right away. If anyone besides the three of them became aware of the site, the rumor mill would spread the word about dangerous chemical leaks endangering the world. He finished his draft news release and went to Sue to see if John had a minute.

"Yeah, go on in," she said.

Once inside the office, Ben showed John the draft news release. Agreeing that it needed to go out that afternoon, he approved it as he called the engineering folks to inform them and confirm their contacts. Ben returned to his office, completed the release, and, using his mailing list, faxed it out to the local and regional media. For the next two hours, he called the key political players at the local level first, leaving the agency, department, and congressional contacts to John.

It only took twenty-four hours before at least a dozen inquiries poured in from a wide variety of local region and statewide media. All the inquiries were low-key and positive toward the agency getting the story out on their terms. The fact that Ben had written the release before someone else had a chance to bust the story went a long way in toning down any negativity, The media had soaked up the planned response, which began that morning. Oddly enough, only one reporter—from the local newspaper—wanted to visit the site, and Ben agreed to take her the next day.

The following day, Ben escorted the reporter to the site, and she marveled at how quickly the mitigation measures were evolving. Barely two days since the news release there were already trucks, tarps, specialized containment barriers, and tanks being unloaded and left ready for use. It was impressive and made a great story, with lots of photo opportunities.

When asked, Ben reminded her that he didn't know who'd phoned in the tip. "Look, even if I *did* know who it was, I don't think it would be in that person's best interest for me to release his or her name, don't you agree?"

"Yeah, now that I think about it, it's probably for the best. Divulging his or her identity could endanger their life if whoever is responsible takes exception to their honesty. Listen, thanks for the tour. This will make a great story, especially with the photos they allowed me to take," she concluded.

Later that day, when Ben returned to his office, there was a message on his desk to call FBI Special Agent Sam Jeffries. Grabbing the phone, he sat behind his desk and dialed. "Hey, Sam, what's going on? Are we going to be activated for another assignment?" Ben asked.

"I think so," Sam replied. "I wanted to give you a heads-up. There's been a flurry of activity in the Southwest. It's mostly on National Forest, BLM, and Indian lands. It's a sophisticated pot-hunting operation. They're using heavy equipment, moving into remote areas late at night. They set up work lights, dig up the site, leave holes and crap all over the place. These idiots end up destroying more artifacts than they recover. Can IR pick up this type of work during the dead of night?"

"Heck yeah! What's great about the new IR imagery is its ability to pick up a heat signature as small as the size of a cigarette if conditions are right. All you need to do is make sure the USFS IR ship is available unless you can access another aircraft."

"Not an issue," Sam answered. "Even without the fire mapping IR ships, we can access whatever we need. Right now, it's quiet, so they probably are available. Don't be surprised if you get a fire order to New Mexico or Arizona, okay?"

"Got it, sounds interesting. Explain to me what the big deal is about this. Doesn't this kind of stuff go on all the time?"

"These pot-hunting sites are well-scoped and are primo. By that, I mean the thieves are recovering a lot of pottery in one piece or, if broken, easily restored. For your information, one of the larger, rarer pieces of recovered pottery was appraised for somewhere between ten to fifteen thousand dollars. There's something fishy going on. It seems someone has access to privileged information on the location of old sites, ruins, and encampments that have been used in Indian Country over the last fifteen centuries.

"That larger pot I mentioned was confiscated when the idiot tried to sell it to a tribal member who recognized its design and value. We don't think the seller was part of the operation. We think he was some poor fool who probably ripped off his pot-hunting employers and tried to fence it on his own. There is no honor among these dudes; they would screw each other in a heartbeat."

Ben thought about this, then said, "I had no idea their value was that high. It wouldn't take many pottery pieces to bring these thieves a small fortune. This should be a fascinating assignment and a learning experience for me."

Ben's excitement ramped up, and a chill shot through his spine as he thought over the toxic waste site he'd been involved in. He'd learned more about the dangers of those chemicals than he'd ever wanted to know. While he was glad everything had turned out like it had, he was eager for another adrenaline rush and couldn't wait to embark upon his assignment in the Southwest. After all, he'd never been there before.

And, sure enough, a few days later, he received his fire orders to fly to Albuquerque, New Mexico, where one of the task force members would pick him up. They already had an out-of-the-way place to use as a command post at a local cultural center. The task force would meet up with two local, highly regarded archaeologists who worked with several of the Pueblos and the Apache Nation.

Ben called Gianne as soon as he found out he was going. "Guess what?" Excitement laced his tone. "I've been ordered to go to New Mexico for detection flights and one large fire in southwest Arizona. Pretty exciting, don't you think? I've never been to the Southwest on a fire assignment."

Gianne, who was no stranger to fire seasons, asked, puzzled, "I don't get it. I thought the Southwest was in their monsoon season. Aren't they getting rain?"

Ben thought quickly before answering. "Weather between New Mexico and Arizona is really strange. The high country can get wet while much of the desert areas still sees fires. But yeah, you're right. It's the beginning of monsoon season there, but it's really scattered this year, and all the rain so far has been somewhat spotty."

When they'd disconnected the call, Ben let out a long breath. Gianne made it a point to stay tuned in to all things weather. She was savvy to anything that might affect potential fire assignments around the West. His white lie might have helped him to dodge a bullet this time, but he expected a fight next time.

****

When Ben hopped onboard the regional jet, he was filled with excitement. However, that excitement soon betrayed him, as his mind filled with thoughts of the last time he'd flown. It had only been weeks since Dean's death. The incident remained as fresh in his memories as if he'd landed the plane only yesterday. Taking a deep breath, he stowed his carry-on IR gear overhead and sat down. He remained completely still, nervous, and uncharacteristically quiet for the entire flight, blankly staring out the window as he waited for the plane to touch down.

When they'd landed, Sam Jeffries met Ben outside the passenger terminal exit, near the baggage claim, and they went to the cultural center for their first briefing. Upon arrival, Ben marveled at the displays as they were directed toward the meeting room in the back of the center. The cultural center also served as a rather large, public museum. There was pottery of every size, shape, and design, kachinas, various Native American clothing, large, framed arrowhead displays—some in the hundreds—bows, baby cradles, beadwork; it was amazing. He could not believe all the outstanding displays in the large museum room.

Approximately a dozen people, in various uniforms, attended the briefing—the FBI, several members of tribal law enforcement, and the two archaeologists. Leon, one of the archaeologists, led the discussion. Leon was a tall, rather striking individual with a long black ponytail, a turquoise pendant around his neck, and a beautiful, turquoise-banded watch on his wrist.

Ben knew he was staring but couldn't pull his eyes away. *This guy is such a cool-looking dude. He could be on the back of any of our coins.* He was brought back to the moment as Leon thanked the FBI, and other federal personnel, for their support, then walked to a map and pointed to the latest locations where heavy equipment had been brought in overnight and their sacred grounds vandalized by the pothunters.

Ben raised his hand. "Are there recent aerial photos of this area and areas you suspect will be hit next? It would give me a frame of reference for what the terrain and vegetation looked like before the intruders hit. If so, I'd like to take the photos and go out on the ground and compare the vandalized site to the photo. I do this to get a feel for what I am looking for. If we get some intelligence on where you all think they might hit in the future, we can order an infrared flight to cover any potential targets. The flight can cover a large area and be high enough not to scare them off. We can cover hundreds of square miles if we have to."

"Yes, we have all areas covered in up-to-date aerial photos," Leon answered. "If it's okay with Sam, we'll take you on-site tomorrow morning before it gets too hot."

"Not a problem," said Sam. "If you have room, I wouldn't mind seeing the site myself."

The briefing ended after an hour, and the next morning came fast. Sam and Ben met Leon and his archaeological trainee, Bear, in their hotel lobby at 7:00 AM, and they immediately headed out to the site, which was an hour away. During the drive, Ben had a lot of questions about pothunters and what type of network they could have for fencing so many easily identifiable items. He also inquired about the level of damage to the vandalized sites.

Leon explained, "These grave-robbing pothunters can somehow figure out where many of our people's ancient cultural sites are located. The sites could be old structural remnants from cliff-type dwellings, abandoned encampments, or even village sites that only a handful of our elders and I know about. Somehow, and I have no clue how, information is getting leaked to these guys and they can dig under the cover of darkness before we figure anything out. We know they scout out the sites using those new four-wheeled ATVs because we have seen the tire tracks on most of the recent sites that have been dug up."

"Leon, Bear, do you think someone may have figured out where the best pothunting sites are located by doing some good old-fashioned research?" Agent Jeffries asked. "Or, do you think someone, perhaps even a tribal member or scholar, is leaking the information to the pothunters?"

Leon thought for a minute, then sighed. His response was careful—intentional. "I hate to think about the possibility of one of our own leaking this stuff to these scavengers, but I have to admit that the location information for the violated sites is barely known to us archaeologists—and only to a few of our elders—let alone any tribal members. So, I guess what I am saying is, perhaps it is someone in the know, and I mean someone with access to the locations I just discussed. It seems to me that, unofficially, information is being leaked internally. From there, it goes to the pothunters. I have no evidence concerning who, where, or how, but sooner or later, the leakers will be discovered. And, when they are, they'll find out firsthand that our tribal prisons are not a nice place to spend their leisure time."

"I doubt anyone from the tribe knows these locations, but I do know it is quite possible to do academic research on these sites and map out their potential locations," Bear added, his tone subdued and monotone. "It would take a lot of digging through libraries, archives, and other public documents, but it could be done."

****

"Well, here we are," Leon announced. "This is as far as we can drive this rig. It's only a couple hundred yards through those pinyons and over that rise. I'll grab the radio. Let's all grab some water; it'll get warm in an hour or two."

The four of them walked a short distance, up a hilly area. As soon as they started down the other side, they saw how the pothunters had ravaged the five acres below them. There were holes dug all over the area, with mounds of dirt beside each one. Small pottery shards were mixed in with the dirt in several mounds.

Ben cursed. "I can't believe the extent of the damage to this area. There must be a dozen separate holes. Look at the broken pieces of pottery and all the small shards mixed into the mounds. Is this what all the pothunting sites look like?"

"Yes, but this is not as bad as a lot of them," Leon answered. "Sometimes they dig trenches far worse than this with heavy equipment, like dozers and backhoes. They find an area with surface shards and then start digging their trenches. They don't care what is destroyed, because if they find one pot intact in all their mess, they're in the money big time. Depending upon condition and design, a single

293

pot could be worth thousands. Sometimes, dependent upon the age, size, and uniqueness of the colors, tens of thousands."

Sam walked around the site and then turned to Leon. "Look at these four-wheeler tracks. These types of ATVs are pretty new on the market. Can you have your law enforcement folks come in here and make some tire casts? I have a sneaky feeling they may be a big help in the long run."

The four continued searching the site for anything the thieves might have discarded, hoping for some clue that might help the investigation.

A noise caught Ben's attention, and he motioned for the others to listen. "Is that one of those new-fangled ATVs? Sounds like a loud lawnmower or chainsaw—something with a small gas engine."

With furrowed brows, they headed back toward their rig, listening. As they got within fifty yards, a shot rang out, followed by another.

Bear studied the horizon. "Someone wants us to leave. Since our pickup is unmarked, they have no clue who we are. They might think we are rival pothunters, and they are trying to scare us off."

Ben's heart pounded as the thought of stray bullets teased his mind. "I've seen enough to help me get a feel for what to look for. We just need to figure out what area to have an IR flight cover, and when. I have no doubt IR will pick up the hot engines of any equipment since this country cools off so well at night. The fresh soil from any hole should also show on the imagery, mostly because of their shape and pattern. Fresh-turned soil is in the middle of nowhere. And besides that, I don't like the sound of bullets outdoors. Some idiot deer hunters almost shot me in the foot the first year I worked for the Forest Service. I don't need that happening again. Do you guys think that was intended for us, or just some yahoo out target shooting?"

Leon laughed. "No, this was not just somebody out here plinking. If it were, you would have heard everything from machine guns to shotguns going off until either the ammo or beer ran out. At this hour, it's probably what Bear stated."

After returning to the center and settling into their meeting room, everyone looked at a map showing the locations of the last six pothunting sites marked in red. All six were pretty much the same, around five to ten acres maximum, with lots of holes, and a couple with longer and deeper trenches, probably from a small dozer or backhoe.

"Look, these sites are all within a few miles of each other," Ben stated. "I've drawn a line around all six sites, going out twenty miles beyond them. We should order an Infrared flight between 11:00 PM and 3:00 AM, fly the outlined area, and see what happens. If we can get a flight, I'd prefer it be around midnight. A prime time for those idiots to leave town, do their dirty deed, get out, and be back in whatever town or village they came from."

Everyone agreed to the plan, and Sam called to see if any IR ships were available, either wildfire or military.

Twenty minutes later, Sam told the group, "Good news, we can get a flight tonight and tomorrow night around midnight. We're all set; let's get out of here and figure out if we want red or green for dinner tonight."

Chapter 35

The morning rolled around quickly. Once the group gathered again, they loudly discussed the previous night's dinner, playfully bantering whether the red or green chili was the best. This was an age-old argument for visitors and locals alike.

"All right," Ben interrupted their fun. We're set to fly over this area at quarter past midnight. They'll fly strips east to west, and given that this area isn't large, they're expected to be done within an hour and should be back at the airport by 1:30 AM. I'll pick up the imagery and start looking at it as soon as I get back."

"Sounds great," Sam responded. "Leon, Bear, and several members of the tribal police force will be the ground troops. I'll only be along as a liaison. Since we're flying Indian Country lands, as a sovereign nation, this is under their authority. Ours is a support role."

"If these guys are on the ground, I'll have their location radioed to you using the coding we discussed so no one picks up on our operation. Everyone has radio scanners these days. How does that sound?" Ben asked, satisfied when the group nodded in agreement.

The players were in place as Ben headed to the airport at midnight. The IR ship landed at 1:45 AM, and the technician on board relayed to Ben the location of some lights they'd spotted on the ground in the middle of nowhere. Ben grabbed the imagery and headed to the workroom at the cultural center—a quick ten-minute drive. He rushed into the workroom, turned on the light table, and started unrolling the imagery film. In less than ten minutes of searching, he'd found the pothunters. He noted small heat signatures indicating ATVs or, perhaps, generators. He also saw two larger heat signatures, which he quickly assumed, based on their MO, were either backhoes or a flatbed truck used for carrying the backhoes. Ben radioed the coded location to the team.

"Affirmative," Bear answered. "I will pass this on to everyone. Good work."

After Bear's voice had faded, static crinkled over the radio. For a moment, Ben thought someone was trying to call back, but it turned out to be nothing. The radios were old technology—nearing the end of their usefulness.

At the site, Sam followed the tribal officers, Leon, and Bear within a hundred yards of where Ben thought the clandestine pothunting was occurring.

As they approached, Leon cursed and called the team. "Look over there! They're gone! I can see where the backhoe has been digging. It's only been an hour since Ben called this in. How did they know they were about to get busted? I don't like this at all." He cursed again and kicked a mound of dirt.

The group spread out over the site, counting six dug holes and the beginning of a small trench.

"Crap, Leon." Sam frowned. "Look at this hole. The other five are four or five feet deep; this one is barely a foot. It looks to me like these guys were warned to leave while digging this hole and got out of here fast. I can't believe we couldn't see or hear a truck." He cursed and spat on the ground. "Someone warned these turkeys for sure."

With the night's operation a total bust, they loaded up and left the site, deciding to do a complete review the next morning and determine why the operation had failed.

The four met after breakfast the next day to privately discuss the failed mission before the tribal police arrived. Ben Sam, Leon, and Bear went over everything, trying to figure out how these guys had gotten word so quickly and almost instantly got out. They discussed the coding they'd used over the airwaves and whether anyone could have deciphered its meaning. As they were in the middle of the discussion, something hit Ben in the head like a sledgehammer and he cursed.

I know exactly how those pothunters got word so quickly and escaped before our guys could make arrests. He sat with his realization for a moment before looking at Leon. "Can you take another look at my mapping and photos over here on the light table? I need to have you help me double check something really quick. Perhaps it will help for next time."

As they hovered over the light table, well out of earshot of the others, Ben said, "Leon, please don't get me wrong with what I am about to say. I was wondering about something. It's only a guess, but it might explain a lot. I called in the location information using our code system, right?"

Leon nodded, confused.

"Your assistant, Bear, took it down to pass on. Correct?"

Another confused nod.

"Here's the thing: there was some static on the radio after I gave him the message. I couldn't figure it out, but I think it might have been Bear keying his mic rather quickly several times. I think he used his own code, warning those guys to get out of there *muy pronto*. It would be easy for those guys to have radios tuned in to the same frequency. I've used a radio enough to know what a keyed mic sounds like. I could be wrong, but—"

Leon cursed, his eyes growing wide. "I understand what you are saying. It would be easy to get this type of warning signal past us. We would never think anything of it. Someone could do that at any time during our operation." His face fell as his eyes drifted to Bear. "I hope we're both wrong. I have a new plan for tomorrow. We will go through the same rollout as last night. The only difference will be that I will tell Bear there are no IR ships available, so we will have our next flight the evening after tomorrow."

The meeting broke up and Leon asked Sam to call him later and discuss another issue he wanted advice on.

Leon was alone when Sam called. "Sam, this is hard to admit, but I think we have a mole in our group. I'm pretty sure it's Bear. I've only known him for a few months. He came highly recommended by one of our northern Pueblos. Ben and I have set up a plan. Tomorrow night we will proceed as before but Bear will not be involved this time.

I told him no IR ships are available tomorrow night, and that we will have to wait one more night."

Sam cursed. "Good thinking. It's got to be difficult admitting a stoolie could be one of your own. Let me know if there is anything I can do. I'll have our folks run him through the system and see if anything turns up from a criminal standpoint. I'm guessing you had to inform your officers why he won't be there tonight?"

"I quickly made up an excuse that he had something personal to deal with and would not be available. So, we are a go. Ben has another potential area laid out for tonight's flight. He'll meet the ship around midnight. He's pretty confident the pothunters will be within the flight's outlined boundaries. The three of us, along with four or five tribal police officers of the highest caliber, will be tonight's team.

****

Excitement rushed through Ben's veins as he picked up the infrared imagery at the airport and quickly rushed back to the workroom. He immediately set to work at the light table. He knew tonight's success was riding on his idea of where the flight should go. The onboard IR technician hadn't seen much on the imagery as it passed out of the imagery developer, making Ben's job a bit more difficult than the night before. Refusing to give in to defeat, he searched until he finally found heat signatures in the southwest corner of their search area. Based off the intensity of the heat signatures, he was convinced the heat sources were from heavy equipment engines.

He radioed Leon and gave him the coordinates of the pothunters, using their coding system. This time, however, they were on a different channel, and there was no static from anyone keying their mic. *Maybe we can catch them in the act this time. What a feather that would be for this technology*, Ben thought.

Leon, Sam, and five of the best-trained tribal officers headed out to the site known as Luna Wells. To archaeologists such as Leon, Luna Wells was a well-known site. Although no one had seen water there in over two-hundred years, at one time, the ancient ones camped, lived, and planted crops there. It was an area he had hoped would never be vandalized. Remote and hilly, the topography offered many escape routes. Their approach would be from three different directions, on foot. All three approaches had cover in the pinyon and mesquite. Once they were within fifty yeards, they'd split up and try to catch the pothunters red-handed. Sam and Leon would cover the fourth quadrant together, in case the criminals decided to take that escape route.

As they approached the site, two of the tribal officers came upon the unsuspecting criminals and caught them in the act of digging and sorting a few pieces of pottery that hadn't been completely ruined by their dig.

"Drop your weapons and get on the ground!" one of the officers shouted.

Three out of six dropped to the ground while a fourth ran toward Leon and Sam. The other two grabbed a rifle and pistol and opened fire on two of the officers. Shots rang out as the officers returned fire, dropping one of the pothunters instantly and wounding the second with a round to the leg and one to the upper body.

"Don't fire! Stop! Don't shoot! Please don't shoot!" one of the criminals yelled. "We're done firing—our guns are on the ground. I think he's dead!" He cursed. "Oh, man, he's dead! We didn't want this to happen!" The perp screamed hysterically.

Tribal police quickly secured the scene, checked out the victim who was lying motionless on the ground, and yelled to Leon, "This one's dead, but you'd better come and take a look!"

Shock exploded through Leon as he walked over and gaped at the dead man. "That's Bear!" He cursed. "What went wrong with him? He's educated, has his four-year degree, and was working on his masters to boot. What does that say about me and the way I hire? He's only been here for six months, but I'm beginning to think he was the one who brought these pothunters to our lands. Before he arrived, this kind of activity never happened. I cannot believe this! What really scares me was his willingness to use lethal force and shoot it out with us. I just absolutely cannot believe what just went down!" Leon lowered his head and muttered something in his Native tongue and silently wept.

Sam, equally shocked, shook his head. "Well, on this side of things, it's clear that this entire pothunting crime spree could only be possible with an inside man. There's no way anyone would have ever suspected that Bear would be the one. I honestly think this was his operation, and his alone, from the get-go. Perhaps, Leon, there is a silver lining. From now on, you will only be dealing with the occasional tourist picking up things that should be left alone. And their intent would be one of ignorance and not malice."

Leon radioed Ben, excitement lacing his tone. "No code needed, Ben. This pothunting mess is over. We have everyone in custody who we think was involved. One pothunter dead, one wounded, and all of us without a scratch. Our people owe you a debt of gratitude for picking this site up so quickly. If not, they would have been out of here in another hour. Great job! I'm going to brief His Honor, the Tribal Chair, tomorrow, and I will mention that this never would have been successful without you. Again, Ben, thank you, from all of us!"

It was 4:30 AM by the time everyone finished giving statements during the debriefing. The meeting room buzzed with excitement over the recent developments, though the men wore exhaustion on their faces as they sat around the table. Leaning back in his chair, Leon summed up the debriefing. "I want to thank the tribal officers for putting their lives on the line to help protect this part of our people's heritage. You are the reason the ground operation was successful. I know how hard it was to see one of our own lying on the ground. I can't prove it one hundred percent, but I think Bear was the leader of this operation, and you all will be honored for your effort in due time. Sam, thank you for getting that IR ship. I don't know what strings you had to pull, and I don't know whose ship that was but thank you and the FBI for being here and supporting this mission."

He turned in his chair, angling his head to the side. "Ben, what can I say? The one thing you and I have in common is science. Your deeds this week will be spoken on the winds of time for eternity; thank you on behalf of my people."

With that, everyone was off to their homes and hotels and a much-needed night's sleep.

As Ben waited for sleep, he stared at the ceiling in his hotel room, allowing his thoughts to roam. *I cannot believe what we just did. What I just did. I wish I could tell someone. I can tell John Wolden, of course... But, man, what a rush to be part of this and see it to the end. The one big thing I will never understand is why Bear screwed his own people over. It's just hard to believe.*

Chapter 36

Home, at last, Ben was glad to be back in the real world. Like clockwork, the moment he pulled into the driveway Joe and Joy raced out the front door and latched onto his legs.

"Did you put out the fire, Daddy, did you, did you?" they asked, their faces beaming with pride.

"No, kids, I didn't, but I did help," was Ben's same old reply.

Gianne met them in the living room. "Well, how was it in Albuquerque? Isn't that where you always met the IR plane?" She gave Ben a look he couldn't read. "Funny, I didn't see anything on the news. Were all the fires rained out with the monsoons?"

"Pretty much," he answered, working to keep his tone level. "Only three days' worth of flights. All that dry air around Arizona and New Mexico got chased out. They say it will rain all over the Southwest, starting tomorrow or the day after. That pretty well wrapped up our fire detection mission." Ben had to stay one step ahead of Gianne. He knew she would start to figure things out sooner or later if she grew more curious about his assignments, and he had no idea how he would answer her if that happened.

****

Fall was approaching. News coverage was filled with fire news regarding part of the southeastern areas of the States that were bracing for a potential late fire season. These areas hadn't seen anywhere near their normal rainfall, and Ben eagerly anticipated an assignment. So far this summer, he'd only had a few wildfire assignments, along with a couple of his covert ones. Those harrowing moments during his amateur pilot days still haunted him. The thought of his favorite pilot, lying dead next to him, interrupted his nights way too often. He still wondered what had killed him so quickly.

Ben tossed his pen onto his desk and let his gaze roam his office. He'd been writing down some thoughts regarding the pothunting mission, his heart still refusing to settle on their discovery about Bear. His supervisor had been on a special assignment in Washington D.C. and had been unavailable to him for some time. He knew John was back in town now and determined to seek him out to discuss the assignment.

After being admitted by John's secretary, Ben entered his office and sat with him. He went over what had happened during his pothunting assignment, including who the leader of the operation was.

309

He shared his surprise with John and explained that he couldn't make sense of Bear, an archaeological trainee working on his master's degree, giving up a promising career to lead a bunch of criminal pothunters.

John looked at Ben, his brows raised. "Well, you know what they say. The reason behind the criminal element in any society is either sex, money, or drugs. I'm betting money in this case."

Ben half-heartedly laughed. "I suppose so; it was a complete shock to me that Bear would go to that extreme and then take on his own tribal police in a shoot-out. That was such a crazy assignment, resulting in a serious ending. What good is money if you're dead? He's about as dead as can be!"

John agreed, then reminded Ben about another set of briefing papers that he needed ASAP. "If you can get those to me by Wednesday, you can go ahead and make yourself available for a fall fire assignment—a real one this time."

Ben looked forward to another "real" fire assignment, but none came for another week. No fires, no task force assignment, only regular work. He filled his time at home with Gianne and the twins and with teaching his conservation education classes. Summer was almost over, and the local fire season was nearing its end.

By mid-September, Ben thought the fire season was over for him. Then, one day, Larry Capps, the fire management officer, strolled into his office and stated, "Guess what, IR guru? They're looking for some help out in Kentucky and a couple of the surrounding states. I understand the infrared ship left the fire center two days ago and headed to Atlanta. Last I heard, they'll be based out of there and fly wherever needed. There are lots of good, small airports where they can land and drop off the IR. Their fall fire season is starting at least a month early, due to the extended drought across a substantial chunk of the Southeast." He paused before adding, "But remember, their drought is a lot different than what we're used to. I'm not sure yet if this is a go for you, but we'll see. It looks promising."

The thought of an actual fire assignment brought a smile to Ben's face. If he could get one that lasted the full two weeks, there would be enough vacation money to take Gianne and the twins on a trip down the Oregon coast and into the California redwoods next summer—something they'd always wanted to do.

That evening, Ben discussed the fire assignment possibility with Gianne.

"I'll be okay," she assured him. "And the twins will be fine. Some of your assignments have been rather short. I'm sure we can get along for two weeks. I guess it doesn't really matter, with the twins starting their second week of school—we'll have a busy schedule. What kind of an assignment this time? You've been on some rather weird ones—shorter than usual."

Ben read the look in her eyes and swallowed. She knew something was up—he saw it all over her face. "Well, the IR ship left last Saturday and is already in Atlanta with a full crew. I think it will be a lot of all-night detection work. This is their fall leaf fire season. I hope to be able to fly with them occasionally, but we'll have to see what happens and where I report—if they even order me up."

The office was a welcome friend for Ben after his discussion with Gianne. He'd been working on some congressional briefing papers regarding a natural resource issue for John for well over six weeks now. They'd been up and down the chain of command, from their region to the Washington office. At last, it was time for Ben to sit down with John and discuss the final draft.

"These look really good, Ben, just what I needed," John praised. "The final brief on that chemical container contamination cleanup was the right length for the congressional folks. It will be great to get them off my back on this one. They finally figured out they couldn't blame the agency or us. That must have hurt." He laughed.

With a grin on his face, Ben returned to his cubbyhole office, but Larry Capps rushed in before he could grab another cup of coffee.

"Okay, Ben, dispatch has your orders. They just came in for Kentucky. You'll be working out of the Oak Creek Ranger Station in the John Finley National Forest. There's a lighted, paved airstrip adjacent to their compound that can accommodate a King or Queen Air. You can head down to dispatch for your orders and flight instructions, then you should be all ready to go; you can grab them anytime. You'll be flying out with me and a bunch of miscellaneous, overhead personnel tomorrow morning around 09:00. I'll be heading to the Atlanta coordination center as an operations mentor. You're going to love the aircraft!"

Ben cursed and laughed. "I don't really care what we fly in, as long as the pilot is healthy."

"Oh, yeah," Capps replied. "They're both healthy. You'll see."

****

After a long kiss goodbye from Gianne and a healthy hug from the twins, Ben was off to the airport to fly out for, possibly, his last fire assignment for the season. He could hardly wait to work in this part of the country and view imagery of an area where he had never before been. As he parked and unloaded his small gear bag and trusty red bag, he looked for the typical twin-engine plane. Although he thought it odd, Larry didn't mention where they would catch a commercial cross-country flight. Ben glanced around, furrowing his brows. Sitting near the taxiway was a large, private, business-type jet. It was larger than the one he'd had fun riding earlier that year.

Larry sauntered up to Ben. "Well, what do you think? That is one fine-looking ride, isn't it? It'll take us straight through to Atlanta. From there, you'll fly a short, one-hour flight to John Finely National Forest. Pretty nice, eh?"

Ben sighed and walked to the jet. The pilots helped him get his gear stowed and then showed him where to sit once onboard. This model of business jet held nine passengers plus two pilots. There would only be five on this flight, so Ben could settle in and enjoy the luxury.

The flight was smooth and uneventful. They climbed to 38,000 feet—well above the thunderstorms across the Rockies and the larger storms above the Mississippi River. Ben marveled at the huge thunderstorm cloud formations below him as white lightning flashed an eerie brightness throughout the dark, moonlit, black cloud formations. It was truly an amazing flight.

Not long after their jet landed, Ben boarded the final, one-hour leg of his journey on a tiny prop-driven plane. He only had enough time for a quick bite to eat. He was grateful that this flight was also fairly smooth, though the landing had him bouncing and his knuckles were white when they neared the ranger station.

As the pilot unloaded his stuff, Rich Gracer, the Oak Creek District Ranger rushed up and greeted Ben. "Hey! Welcome to the South, or at least our part of it. Follow me; I'll show you where you're going to bunk. We have some rental campers plugged in and set up as temporary housing, so you won't be sleeping out with the snakes, gators, and who knows what all else," he said with a chuckle.

"Great, thank you for that," Ben answered. "I'm not a huge fan of cottonmouths or any creepy crawlies you have out here. By the way, do you know the IR flight schedule? And the reason you need it?"

"I do; the fire control officer and I ordered the flights," Rich responded. "We've been experiencing a series of arson fires throughout our district and the forest. We can't catch the perpetrator. We're hoping you can help us out. The fires are getting larger, and some have threatened many of our isolated cabins, summer homes, and outbuildings. We've lucked out with occasional light rain that helped keep the fires small, but who knows how long that will last. This area has a lot of localized microclimates that lead to fires growing large in some areas and going nowhere in others.

"Since it's so late in the day, and you've had a long haul to get here, we won't have a flight until tomorrow night, sometime after 11:00. Given our vegetation and local temperatures, that should be the start of good times for you to pick up any heat. Tomorrow, you should familiarize yourself with our vegetation and the latest aerial photos and look at our district maps to get a feel for the lay of the land. There will be several people around if you have questions on anything."

They arrived at Ben's quarters, and Rich informed him, "Since we have you and six others overhead, plus two fire crews here on the compound, we've contracted a local mobile kitchen for everyone's meals."

Ben was happy to have his own camp trailer. It was wired with AC, plumbed for sewer and water, and had a small cook stove, fridge, and a welcoming bed. *This is a lot nicer than some of the motels I've had to stay in*, he thought to himself, *especially with a mobile kitchen next door*. Contentedly, he settled in for the night. He'd had plenty to eat at the Atlanta charter terminal while waiting for his last flight, and food was far from his mind as sleep overcame him.

****

After spending his first day getting used to the maps. the road and trail system and looking at a bunch of aerial and ground photos, he was ready for the flight. He had a fairly good idea of some of the vegetation types. It was after 10:30, and he was glad the runway was only a couple hundred yards away from the compound. Easy access to the plane had not always been something he could count on. It was close to 11:15 PM before Ben spotted the King Air IR ship coming in. Once it landed, he quickly retrieved the IR imagery.

"I didn't see much on this film, but I'm not sure what to look for in this part of the country," the technician told him as he handed him the imagery. "It's good you have the time to give it a once over. We didn't cover much ground but doubled back and covered it twice."

"Thanks. This should be interesting. I'm looking forward to seeing if I can spot anything. This is a strange climate, with strange vegetation."

Ben took the imagery to a light and quickly went to work—his trained eyes scanned every inch of the IR and maps. The edges of the imagery on the runs still had target detection markers showing heat anomalies. As he scanned the south side of the flight lines, he picked up a strange pattern along a back road. He could clearly see the main access road leading into one area. He also noted, what looked to be, some Jeep-type roads branching off and ending within a quarter of a mile. At the end of two roads were three or four teardrop shapes. They were close together, and all points of the teardrops in each group were located close to the same place on both spur roads. "Hmmm," Ben mused aloud. "That's the weirdest pattern I've ever seen. It shows just enough heat to make me wonder."

Nothing else in the imagery stood out. He determined to talk to either Rich or his fire people about what he'd noticed. He grabbed a piece of typing paper and quickly sketched a crude map of what he saw. His map showed the county road, Forest Road 286, and a couple of unnamed side roads. He thought this would be easier than dragging a bunch of photos out.

The next morning, Ben described to District Ranger Rich Gracer what he had seen on the IR imagery and had him look at the sketch he'd made, using the district's map.

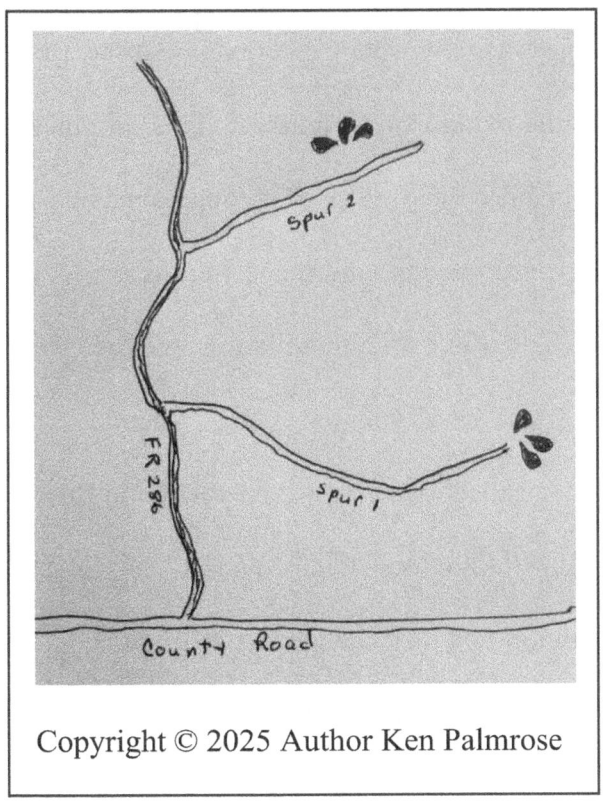

"Those teardrop shapes on the two spur roads don't seem like huge amounts of heat, but they indicate that something is burning," Ben explained. "I've never seen anything like that pattern on an IR photo. I couldn't find the names of those two roads, but I noticed quite a few Jeep-track type roads that on aerial photos and the IR that aren't on the map."

Rich shook his head. "We have a lot of these unofficial roads that locals seem to create in the dead of night. They've never made it onto any maps, as far as names or numbers go. I'm going to tell you something. This is exactly what I'd hoped you'd see. Believe it or not, you're seeing the pattern of an arsonist. This criminal will go up a forest service main road, find one of those unnamed roads or Jeep tracks, drive toward the end, and try to start as many fires as he—or she—can." Rich paused a minute, thinking, and then went on. "Those teardrop shapes are what you see when someone drives out there, stops their rig, wanders away from the road, and throws something akin to a small, Molotov cocktail. You can tell—the pointed area is the start of ignition and then the arson fire spreads out. If conditions are ripe, we have more than we can handle. This person goes into the forest, tries to set some fires, and then works their way back out to a county road or state highway, throwing that flammable stuff off as many backwoods roads as possible. Then they hit whichever main road is convenient for their escape and quickly disappears without a trace. They know the area, they know the back roads as well as the main roads, and they know how to get out of there fast."

"I'm going to ask you the same thing I ask everyone when I'm on an assignment in an unfamiliar area," Ben said. "You know different vegetation, topography, soils, and climate. If it's all right with you, I'd like to go out there as soon as we're finished here. I want to take these aerial photos, the district map, and that imagery with the arson indicators and see what it looks like on the ground. This will give me a good idea of what's going on vegetation-wise. It will allow me to see local topography of that site and understand why those starts stayed so small, and perhaps even get some clues on where fires could quickly grow out of control."

Ranger Gracer nodded. "That's a good idea. But listen—I want to provide you with some local protocol information and advice, in case you encounter some of our locals. They're not dangerous, but you do have to remember that this is moonshine country, and we have some entrepreneurs growing pot who are new to this part of the state.

Our soil and growing conditions are great for them. They like to hide deep in the forest or in some way back holler. Whatever you do, do not get out of your pick-up if you drive near someone's farm or shack. You stay in that truck unless they motion for you to get out. That's the way things have been around here for the last century or more, and folks aren't interested in change. It's one of those local courtesies we all abide by."

"Works for me," Ben answered. "I have no desire to upset any of the locals around here. I'm just here to see if I can get some clues about how these arsonists think and to see what the area looks like. If it's all right with you, I'll be on my way. It's only about an hour from the compound to that site, so I should get there by about 10:00. I'll have a radio and will give you my location on the admin channel when I arrive. Should be a safe, sound, and informative day."

Chapter 37

Ben grabbed his portable light table, stereoscope, and the maps and photos and loaded everything into one of the available rental pickups, including a nice sack lunch from the mobile kitchen. He was glad not to have a regular Forest Service "green rig" this time. This old blue Ford would do fine, even if the government plates did give him away. He took off down the state highway that led to the county road on his sketched map. The scene drive relaxed him as he took in the diverse plants. When he came to an intersection, he turned north onto Forest Road 286 and found the Spur 1 side road. He drove to where he'd seen the first teardrop-shaped burned areas. As he neared the site, he was surprised that the teardrops were much larger on the ground than they'd appeared on the imagery—up to two hundred feet long and seventy-five to one hundred feet wide. Ben perused the site before heading up to the section he'd mapped as "Spur 2," an old logging road recently used by locals.

He drove quite a way, looking for Spur 2, but somehow missed the turn-off and ended up several hundred yards farther north. Cursing, he turned onto another Jeep Road and drove about a quarter of a mile, the distance he suspected the arson indicators were on Spur

2. As he came over a rise, the road dead-ended, and he found himself in someone's driveway. There was a large, modern-looking cabin in front of him. Behind it stood a much smaller, older log cabin, outbuildings, and a fenced-in pasture.

Ben drove closer and started to turn around but froze when at the site of a rather imposing young man holding a rifle. *Where did he come from?* Remembering what the local district ranger had advised, he stopped the truck, opened the door, and gestured to ask if it was okay to get out and talk.

Narrowing his eyes, the man lowered the rifle and waved him over. He was a rather large man, six feet plus, wearing what Ben thought was typical "holler wear" bib overalls and a rather bold flannel shirt. He appeared rather unkempt—maybe even unwashed. As Ben stepped closer, he caught sight of his boots. *He's wearing a better pair of white boots than I own. I guess this Bubba has some kind of taste or money.*

"Sorry for the bother," Ben called out as he approached the. "I took the wrong turn. Seems like I should be way south of here."

"What are you doing out here?" The man eyed him suspiciously, tightening his grip on the gun. "You some kind of government agent sent out here to spy on us law-abiding locals?" His gaze wandered to Ben's truck. "That pickup ain't yours. It's a fed truck, and that only means one of three things. You're either a snoop, revenuer, or a Forest Service pig out looking to give us a raft of mess we don't deserve. Now which is it?" he asked as he raised his rifle back up and pointed it at Ben.

"Hey, man, easy." Ben held up his hands. "I'm just out here checking out reports of arsonists trying to start a bunch of forest fires. These fires won't do you any good if you're seeking to be left alone. If we get a big one, you'll have more firefighters and people out here than you can imagine. I just needed to check out the two roads below your place, but I missed the last turn," Ben explained. "If it's okay with you, I'll just head back to my truck and leave you in peace. I hope you have a great day and thank you for understanding." Without waiting for a response, Ben headed back toward his truck.

He made it three steps before something slammed into the back of his head. Stumbling forward, blood ran down his ears and neck as he dropped to the ground and his world faded to black.

The sun had already begun its descent into the Western sky before Ben's eyes slit open. Face down on a floor made from rough-cut lumber, he worked to get his bearings through the unrelenting throbbing in his head. Blood was caked over the back of his head and down his shoulders. No matter how hard he tried, he couldn't force himself to focus. Through the fog, he wondered how long he'd been out. For the next few minutes, he lay motionless on the floor, working to remember what had happened. At last, he tried to gather his faculties and sit up, but quickly realized his hands were fastened too tight to move, though they were in front of him. *Crap, zip ties, who in this forsaken Hell Holler would even know what a zip tie is? No one I know even knows what the heck these things are.*

Ben rolled to his back and managed to sit up, though the pounding in his head made him second-guess his choice. Scooting back until his back touched a wall, his eyes roamed the room as he wondered where he was. Based on the size of the room, he felt it safe to assume that he was in the small log cabin he'd seen behind the main house. To the left was a small kitchen area with an old-fashioned farm sink. Connected, was a room with a cot covered by a green Army blanket. *What the heck,* he thought, *a wool blanket in this hot dump*? Leaning forward, he attempted to stand, but the pain in his head refused him the right.

Moaning, Ben slowly scooted his butt toward the sink and reached up and grabbed it. The zip ties seemed to tighten around his wrists as he gripped the rounded edge. Taking a deep breath, he slowly pulled himself onto his shaky feet. A wave of nausea washed through him as he looked at the large log walls. At the end of the main room was a small window. The glass had been broken into jagged pieces yet clung to the frame. There were bars outside the window that looked to be hand-made from old rebar. Between the bars and broken glass was a screen to keep critters out. Slowly, he walked to the door.

As he neared the door, his heart sank, and he cursed. The hinges were outside the door—and the wood was as thick as a four-by-four. It looked like someone with a small sawmill had made it out of heavy, rough-cut lumber. The door seemed stout enough to withstand a tank ramming it. Ben forced himself to think through the cloud of pain. He had to figure out how to get out of this place. So far, the window was out, and the door was practically impenetrable. He stared blankly, amazed at his lack of luck. How could one person experience the same level of trouble twice in four months? He looked up at the ceiling and groaned. It was also solid and well-built from local timber—no doubt oak. Ben's eyes drifted to the kitchen table and chair situated in the corner. He shuffled over and sat down, shaking his head in disbelief. Scanning the room, he noted the small, homemade kitchen cabinets above the sink, then stared at the small bedroom next to the main room. He spotted a small door inside the bedroom and assumed it might be a small closet-sized bathroom.

Ben sat for an hour, pondering his plight. Suddenly, the sound of a rattling chain caused his head to snap up. His eyes were fixed on the door as it opened and "Bubba" sauntered in.

"What's the deal?" Ben stammered. "Why'd you do this? I told you—I wandered onto your place by accident. I don't care who you are or what you do around here. It's none of my business, so you can let me go. I have no interest in whatever your business is."

Ben's local holler-Bubba gruffly answered, "Listen, you piece of crap, until I figure just exactly what you've been up to, you'll be my guest here in my corner of the world for some time. You can yell, whine, and scream all you want, but no one will hear you. And even if they could, no one would care to help you. So, I'm going to ask you one more time. What's your reason for snooping and sneaking around my place—no fooling, just a straight answer!!"

"I have nothing else to say except what I told you before you bashed my head in. That's still the why and the where of it! Look, I need some first aid help. I need something to put on my head; it's still bleeding. And I need some water."

"Bubba" glared like Medusa before walking to Ben and punching him square in the mouth.

"Listen, you squirrelly hunk of pig crap. Until you tell me what I want to know, you're in for a lot more of that. You want first aid? Get off your butt and look around. There's water over there in that sink. All you gotta do is pump the danged handle. There's a toilet of sorts next to the bedroom. While in there, you just might find some towels and soap to clean yourself up. Now shut your mouth and think about why you're here. If you want out of here alive and in one piece, you'd better give me some better answers."

****

After "Bubba" left him alone, Ben sat on the chair with blood dripping from his mouth and down his chin. His fears heightened after his captor made his expectations clear, tears flowed down his cheeks until the tiny rivers of salt stung his bleeding lip. His mind flashed back to his airplane misadventure, and he cursed as he fought to hold back his tears. *I have no friggin' clue what is going on here.* He gathered himself, took a few deep breaths, stopped the needless crying, and stood. He walked to one of the old kitchen cabinets next to the sink and looked inside. His goal was harder to obtain with his hands still bound, but determination pushed him to reach up and grab a cloth off the top of a pile. At the sink, Ben grabbed the water pump handle and slowly but surely got fresh water to flow. Next, he wet the cloth and wiped his mouth, grimacing in pain. Slowly, he stretched his arms over his head and gently tried to clean away the dried blood. His bound hands made the task difficult, but he knew if he didn't clean it well, he'd be in serious trouble, so he forced himself to scrub. Pain shot through his head and he jerked the cloth away as tears sprung into his eyes. "Come on, Ben," he coaxed himself. "You can do this…" His head throbbed and he dropped the cloth into the sink. He *had* to clean the wound. Taking a deep breah, got rinsed the cloth out with fresh water and slowly washed away as much dried blood as possible. It took a while, but when the job was finished, most of Ben's dizziness had gone away. He now felt in control, aware of his surroundings and was grateful to be thinking more clearly.

It was late in the day, and getting darker outside, when Ben walked to the small window and looked out across the meadow. He'd seen the same meadow from his truck and remembered thinking what a neat picture it would make. At the far end, he spotted another small cabin, similar to the one that now served as his prison. He looked closer and noticed some smoke coming from the chimney in the middle of the cabin's roof. *Odd to see smoke coming out of a chimney this time of year,* he thought. It was still warm outside, although comfortable inside his thick, log prison walls. On the far-left corner, he could barely make out an antenna—a strange sight to behold in the boondocks. He watched the distant cabin for a while longer and noticed a light switch on. He thought he saw someone standing outside, but wasn't sure if what he was seeing was real or a result of his head getting bashed in.

Ben left the window and moved to the kitchen to search for the three small cabinets for food. He found some crackers and an old tin of corned beef. He was starving, but this would have to do. He glanced down at his left wrist to check the time and stared in surprise. "That dirty scumbag stole my Seiko! I've had that watch since I left Vietnam!" He glared at the door as though looking at "Bubba," himself. He guessed it must be getting close to seven or eight in the evening. With a resigned sigh, he grabbed the opener key on the side of the corned beef can and began to slowly pull. After three attempts, he secured the key into the slot at the end of the zipper strip and started turning the key. He wound the strip all the way around the can. His mouth was on fire and his head still bled. The effort had sent him into a fresh dizzy spell, and he had to stop for a moment to breathe. At last, he was able to double thumb the corned beef lid off the top of the can.

He grabbed some of the meat and a few crackers and sat at the small table and ate as much as he could before he felt like barfing, which didn't take long at all. But what little he ate made him feel a whole lot better. He walked to the sink and pumped some more water, this time drinking it straight from the tap and cooling off his fattened, throbbing lip. He spit some blood into the sink and wandered over to the crappy-looking bedroom. The small, army style cot was about all that could fit in there with the closet-sized toilet area at one end. He hid the corned beef can lid beneath the mattress. The edges of the lid were pretty sharp, and he thought he might be able to cut through the zip ties. *Although*, he thought to himself, *what's my plan after that? This place is a fortress.*

It was now dark outside and the throbbing in Ben's head was driving him mad. Surprisingly, it was growing chilly in the cabin. Restless, he walked to the cubbyhole bedroom and lowered himself onto the cot. He lay back and stared at the ceiling. The bleeding on his head had finally stopped and his swollen lip had quit throbbing. He slipped off into a troubled sleep filled with nightmares of "Bubba" finishing him off. He tried to turn himself over in the old cot, but couldn't move easily to his side, so he remained there the whole night, on his back. Ben's mind wandered in and out of an almost bizarre, dreamy state, as he watched the ceiling above blinking off and on in his struggle for a sanity-reaching mind. The sky was still dark, the air surprisingly very cool—downright cold, in Ben's opinion. He forced himself off the cot and wandered to the window.

Ben stared out the window, focusing on the smaller cabin at the far end of the meadow. The light was still on, and he was sure he could see movement inside. *Odd,* he thought, *what is going on around here? I just don't get why someone would knowingly grab a federal employee, knock him out, lock him up, then hold him in a Bubba-style, log cabin prison. It makes no sense.* Needing to wet his wounds, he walked to the water pump and got the water flowing. He rinsed his head and swirled some cold water around in his sore mouth. He felt

much better and was relieved when to find no more bleeding from his

mouth. He was getting hungry again but decided the opened corned

beef might be the greater evil. Instead, he took some crackers out and

drank some water from a crappy, old, coffee-stained cup he found in

the back of one of the cabinets.

Chapter 38

John Wolden sat at his desk and sipped his morning coffee. It was only 7:00 AM, but he was always at the office early and often stayed until 7:00 PM. When the phone rang, interrupting his calm, he frowned. Lifting the receiver, he was met with the excited voice of Rich Gracer, DR in Kentucky.

"John, this is Rich Gracer. I've got some bad news for you. Yesterday, your boy Ben went out to do some field work before his next flight. He was intending on doing some on-site checking on an arson case we've been working on. He saw an interesting arson site on the IR imagery and went to look on the ground to see it."

"Sounds about right," John answered. "He loves to compare what he sees on the ground with what he sees on the photos or IR imagery. What's the problem?"

"Well," Gracer replied, his excitement building, "he went out yesterday, late morning, and we haven't heard or seen hide nor hair of him since. He has a radio with him, but he's not answering. He checked in on arrival, but that was around noon, our time. He knows our admin radio procedures, so this is not good at all. He isn't some kind of scatterbrain, is he?"

"Absolutely not!" John defended. "If he hasn't radioed in or come back, something is wrong. He knows maps and photos. Ben knows how to find his way back from anywhere. I've seen him do it under pressure on a lot of assignments. What do you think happened? This is your territory, not mine." John's voice belied his frustration. He couldn't divulge how he knew Ben was unflappable in tricky situations, but he was starting to worry. "I think I need to call in some outside help. Perhaps another agency, like the FBI. Someone who's used to figuring this type of stuff out. Kidnapping, vehicle, theft, or worse, happens a lot to federal employees these days, so federal law enforcement might be needed. Listen, Rich, if he doesn't show up in the next few hours, call me back and I'll get the ball rolling. Meanwhile, you do all you can with your local law enforcement folks and any others you can count on."

Rich laughed at this. "Well, since we're all feds, there won't be many law-abiding folks around here willing to bust their collective tails to help, even though I do have good relationships with local officials. But I'll talk on the QT with a couple deputies I know at the sheriff's office. There are a few of them I trust, and I'll fill them in. Believe it or not, our local USFS officers, as poorly trained as they are, have been called in on several local missing person cases in this county. They'll have some ideas."

"Great," John replied. "Listen, when do you think I should go over to Ben's house and let his wife know what's happening? I fear that if she doesn't hear from Ben in the next twelve hours, she'll know something's up. Ben told me he always calls home as soon as he gets to any assignment and, most nights, right before he goes to whatever airport he's flying out of. What do you think?"

Ranger Gracer answered, "Let's wait two more hours. Go ahead and call your contacts at the FBI, or whomever you think should be in on this. I'll call those I trust at the sheriff's office and call you back in two hours."

****

Two hours later, John and Ranger Gracer discussed the current situation. Ben had been missing for over twenty-four hours. Even the local guys were getting worried.

"I'm not going to lie, John, it doesn't look good," Rich told him over the phone. "One of the deputies told me they have some moonshiners who would do almost anything to protect their investment. They've also got scattered pot farmers—not a lot, but enough. My guy advised that some could be more dangerous, since they're from other parts of the country. He didn't think any of the locals would kidnap a fed, but he did say there's a whole new drug-making issue around this part of the country. There are isolated, small lab setups that are manufacturing a synthetic, crystal-looking, heroin-style drug. He wasn't sure what they call it, but the first two he'd ever heard of were in a small rural area fifty miles east of here. Whatever that stuff is, it's extremely potent and highly profitable. It requires dangerous chemicals to manufacture, along with someone with the brains of a chemist. And, in the end, the product sells in the city for a large sum of money to a ready-made clientele."

John cursed. "This is not good. If Ben stumbled on something like that, he could be in real danger. I'm definitely going to give my FBI contact an update, and I think I'm going to have to pay a visit to Ben's wife and kids. I'll be careful not to needlessly panic about her, but I gotta tell you, I am definitely worried. I'll only tell her we think he went out into an unfamiliar forest setting to do some groundwork and probably had an engine problem or some other issue with his rental pickup. I'll give you a call after I talk with my FBI contact and after I talk to Gianne. I want to make sure we're all on the same page, because she is a bright, strong young lady and will figure out who you are, if she hasn't already, and probably call you direct."

****

"Hey, Sam, this is John Wolden. We have an issue going on with a missing federal employee. You think this might be of interest to you and your folks?"

"Yes, of course. Who's the missing person, and what can you tell me about the situation?" Sam queried.

John spent the next ten minutes telling Sam everything he knew. When he told him who was missing, Sam was cursed.

"*Ben*? *Really?* If there's one thing about that young man, he doesn't do dumb things like getting lost, farting around the country looking at trees and grass, and angering the locals. This sounds serious."

"I have got to go talk with Ben's wife. You know how good Ben was about calling her as soon as he got to a new assignment. Even if he had to answer in riddles about his work, he always called. I'll go over right now, then call the local ranger and let him know I've called Gianne and updated him on what was said so everyone's on the same page."

"You do that. I'll go talk to our task force commander and let him know what's up. Tonight, I'll fly into Atlanta on a redeye and meet up with some of my local counterparts. Then I'll drive to Ben's assignment site. Hopefully, they'll have an agent or two with local knowledge they can spare for some help. I'll call you from Atlanta and you can give me all the updated info before we head out."

"Sounds good," John agreed. "I'll make sure I'm back in the office by 5:30 in the morning and have all the info ready."

John hung up and headed to Ben's house, gearing himself up for what he hoped wouldn't be a dramatic conversation. He sat down with Gianne and, without giving too many details, calmly explained that everyone thought Ben's rental pickup had broken down and that he'd had to spend the night in the woods. "I just wanted to make sure you were in the know, just in case something came through the rumor mill that was less than factual," John explained.

She appeared to take the news well. After all, it had only been a little over twenty-four hours since he'd left, and she knew Ben was capable of handling himself in the forest. Gianne thanked him for coming and sent him on his way with some freshly baked cookies for his troubles.

John left her with a promise that he would call her first thing in the morning, but Gianne was not satisfied. Alarm bells were already ringing and, despite her assuring words for John, she was concerned. Once he'd gone, she walked to the phone table and looked through Ben's scratch pad, searching for a contact number for the location he'd flown to. After searching for some time, she tossed the pad onto the table and breathed a curse under her breath before snatching up the phone and calling her friend, Brenda, who worked in dispatch. She had met Brenda at their spring potluck. They'd gotten along well and, over the last several months, had enjoyed lunch together on several occasions. They both had kids the same age and in the same classes.

"Brenda, this is Gianne. Can you tell me exactly where Ben was sent on this latest IR assignment? He gave me a contact number, but I seem to have lost it."

"Sure, I've got it right here." Brenda's voice was cheerful as she the sound of shuffling papers crossed the line. "Just hang on a minute... Got it! His orders say he was to report to the Oak Creek Ranger District office on the John Finley National Forest. The district ranger's name is Rich Gracer and is listed as the contact. It's pretty late there, so I doubt anyone is around," Brenda offered. "If I were you, I would call around seven tomorrow morning; that would be their local time, okay?"

"Thanks, Brenda. I need to be careful what kind of note paper I throw out. Talk to you later." Gianne ended the call and went to tuck the twins into bed. She read them a quick bedtime story, then went to bed soon after so she could get up early and figure out why Ben hadn't checked in with anyone.

****

Ben had been in bed for about three hours. As he fought for a peaceful sleep, his head began to throb again, causing him to sweat profusely. Though he hadn't thought much of Vietnam in the past year, the war now plagued his dreams and he found himself back at his old compound with his Vietnam sidekicks, Phil, and Greg.

Greg cursed. "Look how high the Saigon River is from the monsoon rains. It's pounding down a few miles upstream from us and is practically up to the top of our dock now."

Ben, in his sleepily dazed and disjointed dream, remembered how high the water had risen after fifteen to twenty inches of monsoon rain poured like a gigantic shower head down from the clouds. A monsoon shower could be like one huge waterfall raining down all around them. It had flooded a dock, and water was now running up onto the compound. *That was amazing,* he remembered to himself. There were dead animals floating down the river in the swollen river current, everything from oxen to a wide variety of other local livestock. By the time they got hung up on the dock, they were big, bloated hulks of whatever they used to be. This also included an occasional VC soldier and perhaps a civilian or two. Hard to say when they are bloated up like a water balloon. The Battalion's local Vietnamese counterparts were assigned the unenviable task of prying them off and away from the short pier and dock or throwing rocks and home-made spears, to pop the bloat and sink them out of sight in the swift current.

God, that was gross, he thought to himself as his weird dream continued.

After about an hour of the currents dislodging a bloated cow, an enlarged human body was spotted swiftly floating downstream, right-on target to hit the middle of the dock. With a waterlogged thud, the body was hung up on the dock. It was the bloated corpse of a white man, not a soldier, but a civilian, judging by his clothes. The two

343

soldiers standing in two-feet-deep water that had overrun the small

dock tried to snag the body and push it out into the rushing current.

Ben cursed, shocked as recognition hit. He yelled at the

soldiers as he proceeded to slosh his way over to the body where he

began punching at it as hard as he could with a long willow spear,

trying to sink it. He rammed and rammed the body to no avail.

"What are you doing?" Greg yelled from the riverbank.

"I know this prick!" Ben yelled back. "He tried to kill me. This

is Bubba, from Kentucky, and..."

Ben's mind slowly released him from his completely off-the-wall dream. He woke in a sweat and realized there was blood caked to the side of his face. As he came to his senses, he was shocked to see the devilishly smiling face of "Bubba." Not the bloated "Bubba" from his dream, but the one holding him prisoner.

"You sure are a squirrely fed piece of crap, aren't you?" The man sneered down at him. "Do you always talk in your sleep and move around like a two-year-old who lost his bottle?"

"What do you want now?" Ben groaned as he worked to sit upright. "Who a*re* you?" he demanded, feeling it was high time he got some answers. "You're not some local, redneck 'good old boy,' and

I'd bet anything you're not from around here. I want my watch back. It's of no value to anyone but me—if you sell it, you won't get anything." A wave of dizziness washed over him and he moaned, leaning his head back against the wall.

"Listen, buttercup, I didn't steal your stupid watch, so shut that crap-talk up. Why would I have any need for some piece of junk Timex when I have this golden beauty?" He rolled up his sleeve and showed Ben, what appeared to be, a genuine Rolex.

"Whatever. Tell me who you are and where you're from. Why are you here? Why did you kidnap a federal employee and risk federal prison time?"

"What makes you think I'm not a local? This is my place. Been in my family for at least five generations," "Bubba" halfway blared.

Ben stared at the hulk of a man and, in a decidedly calmer manner, answered, "For one thing, that watch. For another thing," he held out his tied wrists, "there's no one in the next thirty redneck hollers that even knows what a zip tie is, let alone how to use these things. The only reason I know about them is because my cousin is an electrician. And look at those boots you've got on; you're wearing a better pair of Whites than most loggers or firefighters wear. And what's with those stupid bib overalls you're wearing? They look like they came from some manservant's ironing board. Seriously, who are you. and what do I call you besides 'Bubba?'"

"Just call me 'boss,' and keep your mouth shut. There's some fruit, water, and a sandwich in that sack. Don't try to call out to anyone passing by. Don't do anything to draw attention to yourself. If you do what you're told, you just might get out of this alive. Don't do anything to anger me or I won't stop at smacking you around, I'll be cutting you up for hog food—got it?" he snorted.

And with that, he stormed out of the cabin, latching the door behind him. Ben's heart sank as he listened to him chaining the door.

After he'd gone, Ben got to his feet and looked out the barred window, staring aimlessly at the countryside across the meadow. In the daylight, he could clearly see the small cabin to the left. To the right, he spotted a gently rolling hillside scattered with oaks. He thought he caught a glimpse of movement on the hillside across the meadow, but couldn't be sure, due to the blinding sun. An idea came to him, and he remembered the corned beef lid. Walking to the bed, he pulled it from beneath the pillow. He grabbed the sharp edges of the lid carefully between his tied hands, washed it off, and then went

346

back to the window. Hope swelled in his soul as he flashed the lid against the bright, morning sunlight, hoping it would reflect like a mirror. He flashed it three shorts, three longs, three shorts—an SOS signal, just in case he *had* seen someone on the hillside. He remembered seeing several trails on the aerial photos and hoped he'd caught a brief glimpse of someone hiking on one of the hillside trails. He continued to flash the signal every couple of minutes for the next hour, not stopping until he figured anyone who'd been passing by had seen it and ignored it. They were probably long gone by now. At last, the dizziness returned, and he gave up, going back to his cot and working on staying calm. As he closed his eyes, he worked to push down his fear. The headaches and dizziness weren't going away. What would become of him if he had no medical treatment?

Chapter 39

FBI Agent Jeffries and fellow task force member DEA Agent Lutz were sent to find out what happened to Ben. They quietly sat in Rich Gracer's office; the Oak Creek ranger they hoped would be able to provide some answers. It was late in the day by the time Rich finished explaining what he knew. They now knew Ben's departure time, the vehicle he'd been driving, what his assignment was, and his reason for being in the area from where he'd disappeared.

"His plans were to drive west on the county road that leads up to our Forest Road 286, then head north and check out these two spur roads where our suspected arsonist attempted to torch off part of the forest. This is a copy of the sketch map he drew; it's what he used to get there. It's now been a day and a half since we've heard from him. He took a radio, so I'm guessing the worst; he either had a bad accident or an encounter with one of our more notorious locals. He could have accidentally stumbled onto somebody's still. Who knows?"

A shrill ring interrupted their conversation and Rich glanced at his phone. "I'd better answer this," he stated. "Afternoon, this is Ranger Gracer, what can I do for you? Uh huh…Oh really? And when did you see it? What, exactly, do you think you saw, and where did you see it?... Thank you very much for the call; you've been a great help!"

When he hung up, he looked at the agents and cursed as a grin spread across his face. "You'll never believe it. That call was from someone who was hiking out at the north end of Road 286, on the trail above Middle Oak Creek. She said she spotted something through the oak trees that struck her as odd. Said it looked like someone flashing an old-fashioned SOS sign. She told me she saw it several times, maybe three or four, in less than a ten-minute span while she was hiking. That might be Ben. If it is, then he's in some kind of distress. Maybe he did wreck his pickup. At least we have a place to start now. You guys can grab your gear and ride with me."

Pete glanced at Sam. "I think we should take some Kevlar and extra ammunition. You know me, I always suspect the worst and want to be prepared if I'm right. Do you have an extra vest for Ranger Rich?"

Gracer looked at them in surprise. "Do you really think we need to go to these extremes? Sounds like a lot—being armed and dressed in bulletproof vests just for the possibility of a truck accident…"

Lutz gave him a long look. "With all the problems you've been having with marijuana and moonshine, and now these new labs that are making synthetic drugs, you bet your butt we do."

And with that, the three headed down the county road and turned north up FR286. They turned right onto the first spur road and found the arson site with ease, but there was no sign of Ben. They headed north again, turning down the second spur road, but still to no avail.

Frustrated, Gracer cursed and slammed his hand against the dashboard. "Where could he have gone?" Thinking a moment, he narrowed his eyes. "Drive toward the end of the road. Let's see if he went looking around for more arson sites."

The three drove another quarter mile before spotting a long, obscured, narrow road off to the left that Ben could have taken.

"Let's see where that road leads," Sam suggested.

They slowly drove down the road, unaware they were following the path Ben had taken.

"What's this?" Gracer asked, staring at the cabin with furrowed brows. "Check it out. There's a smaller cabin about fifty feet down that path. Seems an accurate distance to meet the description that caller gave us."

"Let's go see what these people know," Sam said.

They opened the doors but, the moment their shoes hit the dirt, a shot rang out, the bullet bouncing off the dirt inches from the right front tire.

"What do you want?" An angry voice called. "This is private property—no one invited you out here. Get out of here, unless you wanna feel the next round in your flesh."

"FBI!" yelled Sam. "Put your gun down or face arrest. NOW!"

"Bubba" fired another shot from his hiding place behind some oak trees. His next rounds went through the front of the truck and above the motor before glancing off the motor and striking Ranger Gracer on the right shoulder.

"I've been hit!" Gracer cried out, cursing as pain seared his shoulder.

The men struggled out the driver's side door, dragging each other as quickly as possible out of the truck. They laid on the ground, out of the line of fire.

"Bet you're glad you had that vest on." Lutz gave Gracer a look as he fought to catch his breath.

Gracer cursed. "Hurts like a mule kick. And I mean a danged strong one."

"At least you're not dead," Lutz quipped.

"Bubba" raised his rifle again and aimed at the pickup, but Sam was faster. He fired off three rounds, chasing their assailant farther from this new perch near the edge of the front porch.

"Pete, you stay here and cover me. I'm going to fire off a couple more rounds and see if I can get closer to that cabin door." Firing off three more shots, Sam raced for the safety of the oaks, situated on the opposite side of the cabin from "Bubba." He and Pete had a clear view of the front porch. With his gun reloaded and ready, Sam crouched as low as possible and snuck up next to the large, timbered front door. He thought about slamming his way in, but was unsure if anyone might be inside.

Pete, with pistol in hand, slowly headed down the Jeep Road to the cabin, but something on the ground glinted in the sunlight and caught his attention. Reaching down, he grabbed it as his eyes grew large. Hurrying toward Sam, he held up his find. "Check this out," he said as he approached the cabin. "I found this watch in a tire track back there. It's a Seiko. Does that ring any bells?"

Sam laughed. "That's gotta be Ben's. He's proud of that stupid watch. He bought it while he was in Vietnam, out of some exchange catalog. He loves that watch. He'd never give it up. Now we know he's here somewhere—or at least he *was*."

Gracer watched as Pete and Sam stepped onto the main cabin's porch.

"Look down the meadow, toward that cabin," Pete whispered. "See that? There's a guy near the front door. Who knows how many are down there. We'd better deal with him before searching this cabin for Ben."

After the shootout, "Bubba" had run down a narrow path, between some oak trees, and headed toward Ben's prison. Panic shot through him as he heard the men approaching from behind. His meaty fingers worked to release the chain from the door so he could gain entry but froze at the command shouted at his back.

"Stop right there! Do not move! Get away from that door now! This is your last warning!"

Deciding to ignore the warning, "Bubba" moved the chain through the holders as fast as he could. When he'd reached the last holder, two shots rang out, landing just above the top of his head. He dropped the end of the chain and took off into the woods, running toward the distant cabin with the chimney smoke. He ran as fast as he could, falling twice as he ran through the thick oak stand. Bleeding from scratches covering both arms, he finally made it inside.

"We'll deal with him later," Sam shouted to his crew. "Let's find out what he's keeping chained in that cabin!" They raced for the door, with Gracer standing guard in case the gunman returned.

"Ben!" Pete shouted. "Ben, are you in there? Are you all right? It's Pete, Sam, and Ranger Rich. We're coming in, okay?"

Sam slowly pushed the heavy door open, aiming his gun in front of him. To his horror, he saw Ben lying motionless on the cot. Rushing forward, Sam's heart sank at the sight of blood caked on

Ben's head. "Ben." He gently shook him, but got no response. "Ben! Hey, buddy, can you hear me? Can you answer me?"

Ben slowly opened his eyes and blinked in confusion as he focused on Sam. "Sam?" he weakly called out. "What are you doing in my dream? I didn't know you were here in Vietnam. How did you find us? Where's Greg? Did you see that fat body hung up on the dock? It was huge! I tried to get it out of there, but I couldn't." He began to weep as he pressed a hand to his eyes.

"Did you find him?" Gracer called over his shoulder.

"Got him!" Pete called back, joining Sam at Ben's bedside. "Get help"

"I've got a radio back in the truck. I'll call for a medivac! We've got a fully equipped helicopter on standby. If it's not available, I'll have an ambulance on its way ASAP. Do you guys want some backup from the local sheriff's office?" Gracer poked his head inside the cabin door, wincing at the sight of Ben. "He does not look good… The sheriff's got some good, trustworthy deputies. I can get them here before you attempt to approach that cabin."

"Yes!" Sam and Pete said together.

"Get them in here with some EMT help for Ben. When they get here, be sure they take a look at your shoulder. We'll stay here and figure out a strategy. Tell the sheriff his team is gonna need Kevlar and let him know we could use some tear gas canisters or grenades if he has them. Based on that nutcase firing a round into your vest, this isn't going to be easy. Those idiots have no problem taking on the cops or feds in a shootout situation."

Gracer nodded and disappeared back outside.

As the fog cleared from Ben's brain, he studied his rescuers. "Sam is that you?" he slurred, his tongue feeling thick and foreign. "How did you guys find me?"

"A hiker said she saw something that looked like a signal coming from this general direction. She said she saw it several times before their party disappeared into an oak thicket. As soon as she got near a phone, she called to let Gracer know that she was worried it was a distress signal," Pete answered.

Ben's mind fought to process the memory. "I had a tin lid… I flashed an S.O.S. I thought I saw someone…"

"You did, buddy," Sam assured. "You did."

****

There were only a couple hours of daylight left in the meadow by the time the sheriff and his deputies arrived at the cabin. Once Ben and Gracer were loaded into the ambulances, the team set to work.

"The idiot who grabbed Ben has no problem shooting anyone who gets within his sights," Sam briefed the team. "He knows we're the feds, and prison doesn't seem to be a deterrent for him. We don't know how many potential shooters are down there. I'm thinking a good tactical position would be for the sheriff and his deputies to go down to that thick oak stand that's parallel to the target cabin. When you're in a position that offers a field of fire, key your mic three times. We're all on the same FS tactical channel now, and they shouldn't have a clue which frequency we're using. Sam and I are going to go way over to the other side of the meadow, near where Ben saw the hikers, and make our way down toward the cabin, opposite your position. Looking across the meadow, it's not all that far to the tree line, and we should be able to get in place within thirty minutes. We'll key our mic twice when we're ready. You respond once, then we'll advance on the cabin. If you have good cover, identify yourselves and demand their surrender. That will give us time to move closer. If, for any reason, they start firing, launch those tear gas canisters through any window or convenient opening. Got it?"

Everyone nodded and the groups dispersed. The sheriff and his deputies crept through the woods on the left side of the cabin while Pete and Sam crossed the meadow and paralleled the sheriff's men on the right side, hidden amongst the oaks. From where Pete and Sam positioned themselves, they could make out two men on their side of the cabin. A peaceful trail of smoke drifted from the chimney—a stark contrast to the tension in the men's muscles. Glancing at each other, they nodded and keyed their mic twice.

A deputy responded, and the sheriff and his team crept closer to the cabin. As they drew nearer, they noticed a large man, holding an AK47 type rifle and looking around the area.

Sam and Pete aimed their weapons at the cabin and waited.

"This is the sheriff. Drop your rifle. You are surrounded—I repeat, we have you surrounded. Drop your rifle quickly, and you'll make it out of here alive," the sheriff called out.

In response, "Bubba" turned toward the commander and opened fire, spraying the woods with as many rounds as his clip would hold. When he stopped to reload, it was the sheriff's turn to open fire.

The deputies followed suit and soon, bullets were flying past the team from automatic weapons coming from inside the cabin. Overwhelmed by four pistols firing at close range, "Bubba" ran into the cabin and slammed the door.

Pete and Sam yelled at the two men rushing outside, closest to them. Both of them opened fire. Sam grabbed his radio. "Hit these guys with a tear gas grenade!!" he yelled to the sheriff.

One of the deputies threw a tear gas grenade, following up with two more in quick succession. The grenades exploded almost simultaneously inside the cabin. In a split second, the cabin exploded in a huge ball of fire and the structure was instantly consumed in a bright orange ball of flame, reaching fifty feet high. It was as if a napalm bomb straight out Vietnam had hit the cabin dead center. Everyone grimaced as screams split the air.

Pete looked at Sam, a portrait of shock on his features. "There had to be a chemical lab in there for that grenade to explode the cabin. Amazing!" He shook his head, sadness gripping his soul.

The team regrouped a safe distance from the cabin and watched the bright blue-orange flames.

"Ain't nobody coming out of that alive," Sam stated.

"I've never seen anything like it" the sheriff said. "I can't believe a couple of tear gas grenades is all it took to turn that cabin into a fireball. I hate drug runners, but that's no way to die. I don't care who you are."

They stood there for another thirty minutes, watching as the cabin was reduced to rubble. Finally, the sheriff spoke. "Sam, Pete, you guys can go back to the hospital to see how your boy's doing and check on Ranger Gracer. I don't think we're going to have any more problems around here. The only thing to do now is to wait for the flames to die down so we can figure out all the particulars."

Pete and Sam debriefed the sheriff on safety precautions for poking through the aftermath. Once they felt the sheriff had a good grasp on the dos and don'ts, they headed to the only hospital within fifty miles in any direction. At the hospital, they found Ranger Gracer.

"Rich, are you alright?" Pete asked. "How's Ben doing?"

"They life-flighted Ben from Atlanta to Portland to some university hospital to take a look and see if his head trauma is more serious than we thought. Hopefully, they'll find out it was only a run of the mill concussion. I phoned his wife and filled her in on what happened, without getting into the nitty gritty of Ben's injury and kidnapping. I told her he'd been held against his will and had suffered a head injury during that time. I didn't mention either of you, as I wasn't sure that was appropriate. After I called her, I talked with his forest supervisor, John Wolden. He's going to meet Gianne at the hospital there in Portland. No one is sure how serious that blow to the head was, but he shouldn't be that disoriented after this much time."

"Thanks for the update. That's great news. Sounds like he's on his way to capable hands. I'm glad to see you're doing alright after your Kevlar test."

"Well, I have a cracked bone in the old sternum, but it's not a major break. I should heal just fine. I won't be taking any fire line assignments for a while."

With the knowledge that Ben was in good hands, Sam and Pete got on the next "puddle jumper" flight to Atlanta, then went on to San Francisco and home.

****

Early the next morning, John Wolden arrived at the University Hospital in Portland where he was shown the way to Ben's room. When he walked in, he was pleased to find Ben sitting up in bed, talking to Gianne.

"The doctor says I'm going to be fine. It's a mild concussion that shouldn't result in any problems down the road. I'll be out of here in two days." Glancing at his concerned wife, he smiled. "It's going to be fine, Gianne."

Gianne, refusing to be consoled, glared at him through tear-filled eyes. "Ben, you scared the crap out of me. The twins knew something was wrong just by watching me on the phone. You need to come clean with me about what's really going on when you're out of town. You go on fire assignments that last for only two or three days, and I *know* most fire assignments can go up to two full weeks. You nearly died while trying to land a plane with a dead pilot and, finally, you get kidnapped and beaten up by some drug lab guy! Something's not right, and I want answers!!"

When Ben only stared, lips pressed tight, she breathed a frustrated yell and turned to start in on John. "What do *you* know about all this? He talks to you more than he talks to me, and that makes me think you also know something isn't right!!"

John's eyes went from Ben to Gianne, and he swallowed hard beneath their stares. "Just...give me a minute. Let me see if I can get you some answers." Ignoring the quizzical look on Ben's face, he

362

rushed out of the room and walked past the nurse's station where he found a pay phone booth. He called the one person he, Sam, and Pete were allowed to use if they had a question about the operation of the task force.

"Look," John stated when that person answered. "Ben's wife is smart. She knows something is up and wants some answers about what Ben is involved in. What do you think about telling her, in general terms, about Ben's involvement with the task force without revealing names, places, or actual operations...Okay, good, that should work out fine for everyone. I'll be careful what I say."

When John re-entered Ben's room and, he looked at Gianne. "Okay, Gianne, you cannot repeat anything I am about to tell you. Ben told me about the guys at his folks' house in the black Suburban hanging around. Well, they were double-checking Ben's activities since his Top-Secret clearance was issued for his Vietnam tour back in the late 60s. After his up-to-date background check, he's had that clearance reinstated and has been assigned to a special task force. Now, before you ask me anything, his assignment is not one that puts him or you and the twins in any danger. He's not involved in tactical operations. He's assigned to use his skills as an imagery interpreter to help us find criminal activity on public lands. Once he finds it, then a skilled group of law-enforcement experts from a wide variety of agencies goes to work. The airplane pilot dying was purely coincidence, as was Ben wandering down the driveway into some drug runner's lab set up. So that's why some of his assignments were only for a few days, rather than the normal two weeks."

Gianne rubbed her hands over her eyes and took a moment to process this. "Who's in charge of this task force? And exactly how do you fit in?"

John set his jaw. "Like I said earlier, Gianne, I can only say so much. I cannot say anything about the task force itself. I've told you all I'm allowed to say about Ben's involvement. As far as my participation, before my Forest Service career, I participated in a lot of top-level military intelligence assignments, and those in charge knew I could be trusted. I became Ben's only outside contact, which is why we see a lot of each other compared to my other staff officers and employees. He could call me anytime from anywhere to discuss task force activities. Listen, Gianne, I meant it when I said nothing, he does on these assignments is inherently dangerous. Outside of that, fire assignments themselves can be, and are, dangerous at times. I'll leave you two to discuss this. I'm taking our favorite white-knuckle flight back home in a couple hours. Ben, you have anything to add?"

Ben shook his head. "That about sums up what I've been wishing I could come clean and tell Gianne. I'm glad she heard it from you. Hey, I'll for sure be cleared for office work in two days, so I'll be back on the job then."

"Good," John concluded. "We have a situation going on right now that could bring a lot of public scrutiny to the forest. Perhaps even regional and national news media. We have a serious issue with a rancher not paying his grazing fees for the third year in a row. Next week, we're going to confiscate his cattle due to trespass and give their operation one final notice to pay the late fees plus any interest or penalties. If he doesn't comply, we'll auction off his cattle to pay his bill and honor the permit."

"Which rancher are we dealing with?" Ben asked.

"The Rolldys' permit. The big allotment up on that nice grazing area near Green Mountain. To make matters worse, this family has been part of the local leadership of the sagebrush rebellion since the early 70s, and that rebellion has never been over for them. They're in a continual fight against federal management. They've been involved with ranchers all over the west. They despise federal control but don't mind feeding themselves at the public trough. We'll talk more about it when you're feeling up to it and the doctor releases you for work. I'm going to need a detailed communication plan for this one, so rest up!" With that said, John left the two alone. He knew Gianne had a million more questions, none of which he would be able to answer.

"Gianne, you now know everything I couldn't tell you before." Ben watched his wife, concern etched onto his features. "Are we okay? I would never keep anything from you unless I was sworn to secrecy for law enforcement reasons."

Gianne met his eyes. "Yeah, but don't ever wander down some redneck's driveway when he's guarding a drug lab. A drug lab, seriously? What were they making?"

"I'm really not sure. Some stuff that takes a lot of dangerous chemicals and is so new to this country, there've only been a few labs discovered so far. But it's said to be the next heroin, only more dangerous. I'm glad they're out of business, but it sounds like many more will pop ups around the country."

A few days later, Ben walked into his office and smiled to himself. He was glad to be back at work, cleared by his doctors and ready to go. He only had a small bandage on his head, but the larger, bald area around it caused quite a stir from his colleagues during morning coffee. As Ben caught up on some of the phone calls and messages left on his desk, John rushed in and sat down, his eyes filled with anger.

"We've got a real bad situation going on and I need to fill you in. I'll get some of the staff who are involved, and we can sit down this afternoon and discuss it. This one has potential to go Regional, if not National, across TV and newspapers. All I'll say now is that I have the Regional Office involved as well as several staff areas inside the beltway. It's that serious," John concluded.

Once John had left, Ben calmly sat and pondered the strange "meeting." *What in blue blazes is going on now?* Around 1:30 PM, John rushed to Ben's office and told him to come down to the conference room immediately. Ben quicky obeyed. As he pushed open the conference room doors, he was met by John, along with Range Staff Officer George Winegart, and the Forest Law Enforcement officer, Jim Will.

"Let's get this started," John stated. "Close the door! George, explain what has happened over the past several days and what you think will happen next."

George Winegart gave a curt nod and began. "I think you've all heard of the Double R Ranch. John may have mentioned earlier that this is the third year in a row they've refused to pay their grazing fees. Well, yesterday, we confiscated one hundred eleven heads of their livestock grazing on the Double R allotment, where they have the grazing permit. We informed Rod Rolldy, the range permittee, what we've done because of his refusal to pay his fees and, as warned, we've confiscated his cattle since they're now trespassing. I told him we have the cattle at the fairgrounds and that they will be sold off within the next two weeks if their fees are still unpaid. Now, Ben, since you're fairly new here, I'm not sure you understand the seriousness of this situation. Rod Rolldy and his son, Adam, along with his daughter, Sara, are part of the leadership of the Sagebrush Rebellion Resurgence group. They don't think we, as a federal agency, have the authority to charge them to graze on their lands; they consider these lands to be locally owned. Now before any of you dismiss this as a disgruntled ranching family—Jim, you know this family. What can you add?"

"I grew up with the Rolldy family," Jim answered. "My family still has the ranch south of them. What I've been told confirms that Rod Rolldy is still one of the National Sagebrush Rebellion leaders, working with his counterparts in Arizona, New Mexico, and Nevada. George asked me to give Rolldy a call, so I talked to him early this morning. He was absolutely beside himself and, with his typical foul mouth, informed me that he and his group would be coming to take his property back from us. He also said it was up to us but warned that it could get ugly. It wouldn't be out of character for him to encourage violence against our employees or anyone else who's crossed him. I've personally seen him shoot a neighbor's steer he found near his ranch house. It had wandered through a break in the fence. I think that's a prime example of what he's capable of doing—to anybody who crosses him. I've got to be honest about this whole thing. I mostly do campfire and firewood violations, so this isn't something I'm trained to tackle. John has been in contact with someone he knows in the FBI. FBI Agent Sam Jeffries will be flying in from his office in the bay area, and I will provide him any logistical support I can. John, you may want to explain."

"Sam and his office have been informed of the potential for violence and the fact that a violation of federal law may be occurring or about to occur. They were also worried about the threats to employees. He is scheduled to arrive within the hour, and we will reconvene around 3:30," John concluded.

Chapter 40

Sam was escorted into John's conference room shortly before 4:00 that afternoon. Ben, along with Range Staff George Winegart, LEO Jim Will, and the local sheriff, Jim Cox, took a seat and waited for John.

Rushing in after the others, John wasted no time. "First things first. Are you all acquainted? Good! Before I get into the details of why this situation has us so worried, let me tell you what some of our field folks just reported seeing around the Rolldy ranch late yesterday. They spotted approximately twelve to fifteen pickup trucks parked around the ranch house. The license plates were from four western states. Who knows what that means, but it has me worried. A lot. Now, let me tell you where we are today. We've confiscated a good amount of Rancher Rolldy's cattle that have been in trespass for the last three grazing seasons. Since the Rolldy Ranch has neglected to pay their permit fees for three years, we will auction them off over in Pendleton and use the proceeds to pay his overdue bill, including interest and upkeep. I can tell you he is not a happy camper, to say the least. He's angrier than a bull and has called me three times in the last twelve hours, threatening me, my family, our employees, and anyone involved in 'stealing' his livestock."

Just as Ben was about to ask John a question, Jim Will was handed a note by John's administrative assistant. Jim read the note carefully, his brow furrowing tighter with each word read. He cursed and tossed the note onto the table, drawing the attention of all in the room. "A large group of armed men have taken over the old Indian Creek Guard Station. Using their trucks, they've blocked off the only access road and have set up inside. One of our range techs tried to get in and was punched and kicked a couple times and told to get out. The guy told him he can have his precious guard station back when the stolen cattle are back on the range. He then fired a warning shot into the air, right behind the tech as he fled the scene."

Sam looked at John, his mouth set in a frown. "I'm beginning to get the picture. Do you think these cowboy terrorists are capable of any kind of serious business or are they dragging this out long enough to get the media in here and gain some sympathy about 'big brother' getting over on the little guy?"

"No way." John adamantly shook his head. "You're underestimating them. Based on the things I've read and seen; these

372

guys are capable of anything. Rancher Rolldy and his family are part of a group that would just as soon fight us feds than to compromise and settle an issue. They will not back down without a fight. The outside help from their buddies makes this an even worse situation."

"I think you guys are blowing this way out of proportion," Sheriff Cox responded. "I've known the Rolldy family since I was a small child. I grew up with Rod, and my kids went to school with his kids. He's known for blowing smoke. He wouldn't do anything violent. Let me go out there and talk to him. I'll go in my pickup, without my uniform. I'll leave my holster and gun in the truck and try to have a neighborly talk with him to see if this can be fixed."

John and Sam exchanged a look and shook their heads in dismay.

John leaned forward on the table and locked eyes with the sheriff. "There could be as many as fifteen outsiders involved— maybe more. I don't think these outsiders drove all this way to chat it out with the local sheriff, do you?"

The sheriff waved a hand in dismissal. "I'm telling you. I know Rod. He won't harm me."

John slammed a hand on the table and leaned back. "Fine. But don't say I didn't warn you! You'd better know what the heck you're doing, with a fool's plan like this one."

Sheriff Cox only smiled and stood. "I'll call you boys after I talk to Rolldy. I'll get him calm. You'll see."

"Freakin' idiot," John grumbled as he watched him leave. "Gonna get his fool head blown off."

****

Sheriff Cox headed home and changed out of his uniform before hopping in his truck and heading toward the Indian Creek Guard Station.

He drove down the road, keeping his eyes peeled for trouble. When he was about five minutes away from the guard station on County Road 66, he was stopped by two pickup trucks blocking the road.

Cox got out of his truck and was greeted by two strangers with loaded rifles pointed at him. "Hey, there," he called out.

"Who are you, and where do you think you're going?" one stranger demanded.

Knowing better than announcing his identity, he offered a lie. "Friend of Rod's. I thought I'd drop by to see how he's doing—maybe enjoying a beer together. I heard he was out here chasing some of his cattle and figured we could share a six-pack. We've been friends our whole lives. Who are you guys? Is Rod okay?" His brows knit as he feigned concern.

"You'd best get back in your truck and get out of here," the taller stranger advised. "We're helping secure this area, and you aren't part of the security. So, hop back into that worthless piece of crap you're driving and get outta here."

Sheriff Cox nodded and turned back. When he opened the door of his pickup, one of the gunmen spotted his gun and holster hanging from his gun rack.

"Don't move, you piece of crap," the guy yelled. "You just stay right there!"

Before the sheriff could respond, the second gunman opened fire, hitting him three times in the upper body.

Sheriff Cox dropped to the ground as a pool of blood painted its portrait around his lifeless body.

"What were you thinking?" the older man shouted in a panic as he faced the younger. "Can that freakin' pee brain of yours comprehend that you just shot that man for no reason? We're going to have every lawman for a hundred miles on our tails!"

Rod heard the shots ring out from where he was setting up camp in the guard station. As soon as he heard the gunfire, he rushed out and gaped in horror at Sheriff Cox's body before turning on the men. "What did you two village idiots do? We're here as a protest! A protest against the government stealing an innocent, ranching family's livelihood! You stupid pricks killed our county sheriff! He *also* just happens to be one of my oldest friends! He was probably coming here to try to help me." He looked around and cursed. "Look down the road. See that Volkswagen Beetle down there? I know who that is, and now you have a witness. This mess will be all over the world after an hour's worth of phone calls.

****

John, Ben, and Sam were still in John's office when the phone call came through from the county dispatcher. John put the call on speaker, and they listened as she relayed the bad news.

"Sheriff Cox was stopped at a roadblock about an eighth of a mile from the Indian Creek Guard Station," she explained. "He was stopped by two armed men, who appeared from behind their pickups that were blocking traffic. One of the perps talked to Sheriff Cox for a minute before the other opened fire as he attempted to get back into his pickup. He reportedly died on the scene a few moments ago, according to a passerby. The woman who stopped is a nurse and found the sheriff next to his pickup. There was no one else in the area when she found him."

The dispatcher paused for a moment as she gathered herself. "She thinks she saw Rancher Rolldy and two men retreat into a building at the guard station. It looks like those three, along with as many as ten others, are now barricaded inside and have the driveway blocked with their trucks. When one of Sheriff Cox's deputies arrived on the scene, Rolldy and his idiot followers threatened to burn down the station and its three historic buildings."

Sam shouted a curse into the air and threw his notebook across the room. "I'm gonna get on the phone, call back east, and get some people out of bed and out of the night clubs. We need to get something going down here. We are not going to go up there and be target practice for a bunch of vigilante, cowboy terrorists. I'll call my San Francisco office first and let them go up through the chain of command and see what kind of response we can get at the federal level. The local departments are going to be devastated by the loss of Sheriff Cox and the circumstances surrounding the shooting."

Chapter 41

By 10:00 PM, the tension in the conference room could be cut with a knife. They still hadn't heard from DC, and anxiously awaited word. They'd been told that the FBI regional leaders had informed everyone within the beltway what was going on, all the way to the White House. When a shrill ring split the air, the men leapt to attention. All eyes were on John as he answered.

"Yes, this is John Wolden, Forest Supervisor. I've got the whole team here, including your FBI Agent-in-charge, Sam Jeffries. What's the plan? You understand that these guys are now holding my guard station hostage, right?" As he listened, his jaw clenched tighter. Five minutes later, without getting a word in edgewise, John slammed the receiver down and cursed.

The team watched him intently, each on the edge of their seats as they awaited the news.

John stared blankly at the wall. "We're on our own."

A collective grunt of disapproval rippled around the room.

John leaned forward on the table and leveled Sam with a look "The bonehead on the other end of that call wants you to call him in twenty minutes. I don't see what good it will do, though, since he made it clear that they have zero understanding of the seriousness of this situation. They're the pro-environment protection administration for cryin' out loud! The no-nonsense platform they've preached against criminal activity and eco-terrorism is starting to sound like pure political bull. Here's the number." He tossed a piece of paper at Sam. "When you talk to them, see if you can propel them into action. Otherwise, we could be seeing part of my forest—the *public's* forest—being held hostage for quite a while. Who knows what these idiots will do out there. I wonder how those beltway-wonders feel about regional and national news coverage over their lack of response. I guarantee I'll personally make friggin' sure the media is up to speed!"

After Sam's call was over, he placed his hands behind his head and stared at the ceiling, arching his back as he stretched. "I think we all need to go home, get some sleep, and meet back here at 0600 tomorrow morning. It's time to come up with a new plan. I'll call and find out who the acting sheriff is, then contact the local State Police office and some other law enforcement folks around the region."

Nodding in agreement, the men abandoned the table and each resigned themselves to closing the day without answers.

****

Morning rolled around before Ben was ready. As he dressed for the day, he explained to Gianne what was going on, ensuring she knew he would be nowhere near the crime scene. "I'll be in the office, planning the communications approach to the hostage takeover." Feeling her eyes on him, he turned and smiled. "I swear I won't be anywhere near the confrontation. My job is to go out there and herd the media around—media that is going to overrun this town as soon as word gets out. I want nothing to do the line of fire. This group is hellbent on making themselves martyrs for their cause and that, coupled with their fear, is ripe pickings for a disaster."

Feeling like he'd eased her fears, Ben gave Gianne a kiss and left for work. As he entered his cubbyhole, he stopped by John's office.

"I've been thinking about this all night," he told him. "That guard station gets its power from right-of-way lines across the forest, and the water source for the guard station is part of our forest-supplied water system. I've been told the guard station's water is fed by a spring box a quarter mile up the slope. Why not cut the power and send someone up to the spring box to shut the water off?"

John nodded, thinking. After a minute, he said, "I made a couple of phone calls to some guys I served with years ago. Now," he pointed at Ben, "don't you dare repeat this to anyone, but these are two of the best and most experienced snipers in my old unit. Interestingly, they came back to Oregon and are part of a State Police SWAT unit. I've explained to the State Police commander that we've been pretty much abandoned by our federal level people in DC. He authorized them to provide whatever assistance we need. He also knows my background and connection to the two. They're on their way here and should get into town about 1:00 this afternoon. Since we're on our own, Sam was able to convince his higher-ups to give him permission to act as liaison and provide tactical advice and coordination. We've got to be careful not to divulge our earlier task force planning and operations—especially to the media. That's why Sam will remain somewhat hidden."

"So, what's the plan with these two sharpshooters?"

"We'll place them in hidden, strategic locations and give those idiots a choice to come out peacefully and quickly. If they don't, the power and water will be cut off and any refusal or adverse reaction will be met with the appropriate response. The guys from my old unit are the best shots in the world from inside a thousand meters. They'll start picking these guys off one by one. Not kill shots—just wounding hits. The idea is to pick off two to four of these idiots and wound them as quickly as possible. We'll execute this right before dusk. Hopefully, with some of their crew wounded and the water and power outage, they'll surrender. We have the rest of the afternoon to discuss this plan and solidify the details. We'll refer to the snipers as S1 and S2. There's no need for anyone to know anything about their background, my connection to them, or what agency they're from. The only thing we'll tell the media, if asked, is their type of expertise was provided upon request."

As nighttime fell, John briefed the acting sheriff, Deputy Sims. He'd been a close friend of Sheriff Cox and was the consummate professional and well-trained. He and three deputies met up with S1 and S2. The two sniper shot experts showed Sims where they would deploy. During the afternoon hours, they'd had a chance to sneak around and find two well-hidden areas to deploy. These areas were wide open, yet unseen and protected. Radio communications were in place between all involved, and John was set to monitor from his post in town.

****

"The targets have all been advised to surrender," Deputy Sims quietly radioed. "Let 'er rip."

Out of sight, S1 and S2 scanned the guard station compound for targets. They were within thirty-five yards of each other and had a clear view of the buildings less than three-hundred yards from their positions. S1 motioned that he had one in sight. S2 gave him a thumbs up and signaled that he had another target near the far-right side of the main guard station building. With a silent command, they both sighted in on their targets and, with one last hand signal, they fired.

A man patrolling the front porch of the guard station dropped like a rock while grabbing his left shoulder. Everyone within a mile heard him screaming in agony. His screams were soon joined by his counterpart as he took a bullet above the knee. Two cowboy terrorists bolted outside, pointing their rifles in all directions as they raced toward the screams. In the fading light, S2 held up a finger, showing he had one more in his sights. He fired off another round, hitting one of the two who'd rushed out to help.

Panic surged through the uninjured man, and he screamed into the night air. "What is going on? What are you doing? Why are you shooting us? This is our land, our range! This station belongs to those who live here. Why?" Before he could shout another word, he dropped to the ground, bleeding from a clean shot through his upper left shoulder.

Deputy Sims grabbed his radio and keyed the mic. "Alright, cut the power to these pricks. Whoever's stationed at the spring-box, cut the water, NOW! We have three bleeding murderers in there— let's see how long they last!"

"Alright, everybody, our work here is done," S1 spoke into his mic. "We're gonna self-extract and get the heck out of here before anyone figures out what happened. You all know the drill—no talking to the press about us. We'll clean up our trail before it gets darker. John, Deputy Sims, it's all yours now. Good luck. We're both really sorry for the loss of Sheriff Cox. We know what he's done for your community."

"10-4. Thanks for the help," John responded.

At the guard station, Deputy Sims and his men listened to the confused shouts of the cowboys.

"Someone get some flashlights!"

"Where are those lanterns we found?"

385

"Everybody get your tails busy; we have three guys who've been shot and are starting to lose a lot of blood!"

Sims and his men had managed to get within 15 yards of the guard shack as darkness fell upon the scene. He motioned for two of his men to cover the sides of the compound. Taking a deep breath, he yelled, "You have five minutes to throw down every weapon in your possession and walk out here, hands held high. If you do not comply, we will start picking the rest of you off one-by-one. Rolldy, you piece of crap, are you in there? Get your butt out here and leave your guns inside!"

"He's been hit, and he's bleeding pretty bad in the leg—maybe an artery. We need an ambulance now!" a shaky voice responded.

"You all get your butts out here, no weapons, and hands up high. Then I'll call for the two ambulances on standby, but not a moment before. Got it?"

Within two minutes, Rolldy's remaining eight cohorts shuffled outside with their hands in the air, squinting against the spotlight Sims shone on them. Ashen and almost in tears, no one said a word as the deputies cuffed them and sat them on the ground. Once the criminals had been detained, the deputies set to work rendering first aid to the wounded while Sims called for the ambulances.

Sims looked down at Rolldy. His features were pale—his face pinched with pain as a deputy wrapped the wound to stop the bleeding. "I've known you my whole life," Sims shook his head. "So did Sheriff Cox! What on earth were you thinking? The sagebrush rebellion is in everyone's rearview mirror, Rolldy. I'll be calling in outside help and will see to it that every last one of you is charged with murder—at the very least, accessory to murder! You cheap coward. You couldn't pay your freaking grazing fees like every other rancher in this county? I hope you rot in jail for the rest of your miserable life. And let me tell you something, you sorry waste of air." He leaned closer to Rolldy, his face inches from the wounded man's. "If our investigation finds that *any* of your like-minded kids were involved, I'll charge them so fast your head will spin."

Rolldy glared up at Sims, tears pooling in his eyes. "Leave my family out of this, or you'll end up like your boss. Do you understand? I have an army out there, and all I have to do is order them up!"

Sims shook his head in disbelief. "You are a dumber than you look, you know that? You're just an ignorant, peckerhead, drugstore, cowboy rancher. Do you understand that you just threatened me in front of everyone? Go ahead and order them up, whoever 'they' are." He breathed a laugh. "You'd best remember what just happened here. You see that those other two yahoos over there were almost killed because of your stupidity, right? Go ahead and try. After the crap you just pulled, those two idiots who followed you will tell everyone what went down here. They'll warn everyone they know against even *considering* following the likes of you."

As sirens sounded in the distance, announcing the approaching ambulances, Sims stood and kicked Rolldy. When the man cried out, Sims tightened his jaw and glanced at the other wounded. "Just think When you're medically cleared, you'll be transferred to a federal holding facility. Won't that be fun? The media already has your names as the instigators of this land-ransom endeavor. Who knows what you and your band of idiots thought you were going to gain with this rebellion. You committed murder and almost got three other men killed, at the worst. At the best, all three of you can recover behind bars and enjoy a federally funded recovery."

On that note, Sims spun on his heel in disgust, leaving them to the EMTs. Before leaving the scene, he let everyone know he'd like to hold a debriefing as soon as everyone involved returned to town.

Upon hearing about the briefing, John radioed Sims. "Let's do it in my office. How about we sleep on this whole affair and get together around nine tomorrow morning? You and I, Sam, and Ben, along with any of your folks you want involved. That way, we can decide how each of us should approach the news media and know-it-all politicians. There will be dozens here in the morning, and I'm sure most will want to go to the scene."

Chapter 42

The next morning found the team back at John's conference room with coffee in hand.

Deputy Sims wasted no time. "My idea for today is to have you forest folks take the lead on a tour of the historic guard station. I will be there if there are questions about the shooting incidents. I won't be going into detail about the good work of S1 and S2. We won't say anything, other than the fact that law enforcement sharpshooters were involved. John, can you have Ben talk about the guard station and compound buildings? Have him explain their history. I know there's still blood all over the ground, but he can defer questions concerning gunplay to me. You guys have plenty to say about the destruction those idiots caused."

Ben looked at John and nodded his agreement. "I've already thought about it and have a list of talking points I want to cover. John has concurred, and if you're escorting the media to the scene, I'll get out on-site in the next hour and get ready for them. I'll focus on the damage caused from a historical and cultural angle rather than the shooting. I won't talk about the trespass grazing, but rather the uncalled-for destruction of one of the oldest remaining guard stations in the nation."

****

It was close to 11:00 when Ben surveyed the damage to the two historic buildings at the station. One was a cabin, where several fire guards lived throughout their fire season, and the other building was an intact remote office from the 1930s or earlier.

Ben walked around to the front of the station and was surprised to see Deputy Sims and his team had escorted nearly twenty-five members of the media on site. Once the crowd was ready, Ben began. "I'm going to give you a brief rundown on the absolute sickening destruction that was done to this site. This guard station was built sometime in the late 1920's. Much of it is exactly as it was back then. Someone with an eye for history made sure original details have been maintained for around sixty years to date. I'll let you take a look inside from the doors, but you won't be allowed to enter. Know that you're going to quite a bit of damage. While some involved only small items, other damage is quite extensive. The antique handpump and farmhouse style sink have been smashed to pieces. The original hand-crank phone that was on the wall toward the back has been ripped down and smashed. You will notice there were a couple of old glass doorknobs. It looks like someone hammered them to pieces. Old photos, pictures and calendars that were used by numerous district rangers and preserved on the back wall were torn down, and it looks like they burned them in the old wood stove. Several beautiful, old oak, wooden desk chairs were broken up, and I'm pretty sure used for heat in the stove."

Glancing at the faces in the crowd, he knew he had their attention. "Before I open the door, I want you to look around to the south edge of the cabin; that would be to your left. There's a small graveyard that has been preserved over the decades. Our historians think it probably dates back somewhere between 1920 and 1930. No one knows exactly who is buried there, but there were four hand-cut, stone grave markers that have now been shoved over and, from the looks of them, busted up with a hammer. That's pretty much all I have to say. This is a sad day for the forest and for all those who worked to maintain the culture and history of this guard station. Those who have worked hard to keep this site as close to its historical originality as possible. I will now answer questions about this Forest Service site and what happened here."

Ben answered a half-dozen questions before taking a deep breath and walking away from the media. He looked at John and sighed. "What a waste. And for what? A bunch of stupid cattle. You know as well as I do the Rolldys could afford to pay the grazing fees a hundred times over! If you're alright with it, I'm going to go home and take the rest of the day off. " John nodded and Ben left as fast as he could. He headed down the mountain toward home, thinking on how stupid these events were and how disappointed he was for the lack of help from the administration.

Several months later….

Ben looked his bedroom window, pondering on how grateful he was to see the first signs of Spring in Goldville. It wouldn't be long now—the summer crews would soon be arriving in the Monument Pines National Forest. He was glad to say goodbye to fall and winter. Both had been hard seasons in his life. There was still quite a bit of snow remaining in the high country, but as the days of early April passed, a lot of the snowpack melted away. The murder trials for the "sagebrush terrorists," as Ben now called them, had gone as well as a murder trial could go. Although murder convictions were not found for all five of the major players, the gun that was used in the murder of Sheriff Cox was traced to a well-known rebellion rancher from Nevada. He was found guilty of second-degree murder. Rolldy and the others who'd been wounded received ten-year sentences while the other terrorists had received five to ten for their roles as accomplices to murder, as well as for breaking and entering a federal facility, damage to historic and cultural sites, and several other criminal counts. Ben smiled to himself as he thought over how justice ahd been served.

"Gianne," he yelled as he entered the kitchen. "I'm heading to work now. Everything okay? Is it my turn to pick up the twins today or yours? I can be there at 3:30."

"No, I've got 'em covered," she called. "I'm heading for a hair appointment around eleven o'clock and will have plenty of time to pick them up. You have a good day."

Ben headed to the office and spent the better part of the day doing the things he loved the most—he had another fun-filled conservation class in the morning and some communications planning work with the fire staff in the afternoon. The day flew by, and he looked up at the clock in disbelief as he realized it was already around 4:15—almost time to head home.

John rushed into Ben's office, fighting to keep the concern off his face. "The front desk just got a call for you. It was the school. They said the twins were still waiting for their mom to pick them up, and the school secretary was getting worried. She knows Gianne is always on time."

Confused, Ben's thoughts raced. *Strange…that's not like her at all. I wonder if her van broke down again.* "I'll go pick them up and see what happened," he answered. "We've been having some minor, but irritating, starter issues with that van. She may have stopped somewhere and couldn't get it going."

"Okay, let me know if there's anything I can do or if anyone needs a lift or tow," John offered.

Ben headed to the school, grabbed the twins—who were quite upset—and headed to the house. Relief flooded Ben when he pulled into the driveway and saw that the van was in the garage. *Oh, good! She probably figured out how to get it started. I wonder why she didn't call me right away…*

"You two go grab a snack and start your homework. I'll go check on your mom and see what happened to the van," Ben told the kids. He looked in the garage but saw no sign of Gianne. Checking the backyard, his eyes roamed. She wasn't tending to her prized flowerbeds, nor was she working in the small vegetable garden patch she'd recently weeded. Frowning, he told himself she was probably inside the house. Pushing down his worry, he rushed back into the house and searched every room before he remembered the front door was unlocked when he and the kids came home. His eyes dropped to the entryway as a confusion knit his brow. "Where's our rug that was on the living room floor?"

Panic choked him as he envisioned someone breaking into the house with Gianne there. Quickly, he searched the house to see if anything was missing. There was a tremor in his voice when he called John and explained that there was no sign of Gianne. John told him he would call Sheriff Sims. Sims was now the official sheriff after the special election held in March, and since his office was the lead law enforcement agency for the county municipality, including Goldville, he was the best contact.

After John discussed the situation with Sims, the sheriff sent deputies over to question the neighbors, hoping to find someone who had seen something earlier that day.

Ben was feeling more panicked by the minute. Taking a deep breath, he called his folks in Sisu Bay. "Listen," he said, "something isn't right here. Gianne didn't pick up the kids this afternoon." His voice caught in his throat. "It appears someone has been in our house. Can you guys come over and help with the twins while we get this figured out?"

"Is she alright?" his mom asked, tears already forming. "Oh, I'm sorry; that was dumb. Of course, we'll be there as soon as we can. It shouldn't take us more than three hours to get there. We'll throw some clothes in a suitcase and be on our way. Expect us around nine or nine-thirty at the latest, okay?"

Ben struggled to keep it together. "Okay," he answered shakily. "I can't really say much to the twins except their mom seems to be gone somewhere and we're trying to figure it out." He hung up the phone just as one of the deputies knocked on the door. It had only taken five minutes for them to gain some rather startling information from the Clanceys, next door.

"Your neighbors claimed to have seen a white van with a carpet cleaning logo on the side in your driveway around one o'clock. A man and woman dressed in white coveralls came to the door. About fifteen minutes later, they carried a carpet out to the van. Mr. Clancey didn't think much about it, as he assumed you were getting a rug repaired or cleaned. But then he mentioned the carpet cleaning signs were magnetic, which he could tell quite easily."

Ben cursed as his chest tightened. "I noticed that carpet missing after I came back into the living room. It's about 10 by 12, and stupid me walked right by it at first. I know this sounds a little crazy, but do you think those two kidnapped Gianne by carrying her out in our carpet? It would look completely normal to anyone around the neighborhood."

The deputy frowned. "It's too early to speculate, but I have to be honest with you—it looks that way. Clancey though it is unusual that it took two people to haul out what was essentially a run-of-the-mill living room rug. He told us he'd seen that rug in your house and didn't think it was a very heavy item."

Ben nodded. "Yeah, the Clanceys have been over here numerous times, and he is right. We bought a really cheap rug to keep the twins from having to play on a cold floor during the winter."

Chapter 43

Gianne's eyes were heavy as she tried to force them open. Her vision was blurred, and she couldn't shake the feeling that she'd been drugged. She searched her mind for any clue as to what had happened. She remembered taking a drink from her Coke bottle. There'd been voices—faint and far away—and then darkness. Cold darkness. She

blinked a few times, willing her eyes to adjust. As her senses slowly

returned, dread filled her bones when she realized she was lying on

the floor with her hands tightly bound. She rolled onto her back and

forced herself into a sitting position, moaning and closing her eyes

tight when her head started to spin. The room faded in and out until,

finally, her vision stabilized and returned to normal. Her mind was a

jumbled mess as she tried to piece together how she'd gotten here and

who had done this to her. Her eyes scanned the room for clues that

might help her understand.

This is someone's ski cabin, she thought. The front entry was

bordered by beautifully hand-carved wooden benches, and there were

a couple sets of downhill skis and snowshoes hanging near the entry

door. At the far end of the room was a blue and white tiled European

wood stove at and a door that led to a bedroom. She spotted another

door and guessed that to be the bathroom. A fire extinguisher hung

near the bedroom door, not far from the tiled stove. On the other side

of the ski chalet's main room was a modern, well-stocked kitchen.

Expensive, copper-clad pots and pans hung above an island with a

sink situated in the middle. *I must be somewhere up in the mountains,* she thought. *I'll bet this is one of the new places near the Pine Mountain ski area. How did I get here and why am I here?*

Thoughts of a crazed pervert having his way with her caused her to lower her head and tremble. A sob caught in her throat as she tried to stretch her wrists and loosen the ropes to no avail. The ropes were immovable, and stretching only made things worse. From where she sat, she could barely see over the ledge of a side window. There was snow on the trees. Now she was confident that she was in the mountains. The door opened, causing her heart to leap into her throat as her pulse pounded. She watched as a tall, skinny man entered the living room. Her body went cold as she took in the cowboy hat and black, Lone Ranger Halloween mask situation over his eyes.

"What is this all about?" Gianne shouted. "Why am I here, and who are you? We aren't rich; we don't owe money to anyone, so why me?"

"Just shut up and do what I tell you. You and your kind have screwed up my town for too long. Bunch of feds and their stinking ilk—you know-it-alls who don't give a crap about those of us who settled this place..." His voice trailed off, as though realizing he'd said more than he should.

Gianne narrowed her eyes, her bravado returning. "Look, you ignorant toad, untie my hands and let me go, and we'll pretend you made a mistake. I'll go back home to my family and won't say a word about this to anyone."

Snarling, her kidnapper strode toward her and kicked her in the ribcage, cursing above her screams. "Shut up! Don't talk, don't move, don't make fun of me, and don't you *ever* try to tell me what to do! I could easily kill you and throw you down some gorge where no one will ever find you. You'll become nothing but a distant memory." He snickered.

Gianne doubled over in pain. Tears wet her cheeks, and she grimaced, sure he'd broken a rib. She lowered her head between her legs and bit her lip until it bled to stop herself from saying what she was thinking. Then, as courage swelled in her soul, she looked up at her assailant, staring directly into his mask-hidden eyes, and smiled.

****

Sheriff Sims sat in John Wolden's office with FBI Agent Sam Jeffries and debriefed them on what he and his deputies had discovered about Gianne's disappearance. It was morning, and by now, kidnapping was the only conceivable scenario for what had happened. There was a reported sighting of a white van matching the description Clancey had given, only this one lacked the carpet business signs. It was reported to have been heading out highway 26, in the direction of the ski resort.

"I'm not sure about this sighting, but a one-ton white van is an unusual rig to be seen in this area," Sims said. "Most of the vans I've seen like this have been business vans. The fact that this one has no reported markings makes me believe the perps took the magnetic signs off and that the van could be the one reported turning onto Highway 26. Sam, John, what do you guys think?"

Ben walked in at that moment, having overheard part of their conversation. His features were pale, and it was obvious he'd been up all night. "I think you guys are on the right track," he spoke, his voice trembling. "It's too late for spring skiing, and most of the resort chalets are empty. It makes sense for a kidnapper to go there. There may still be snow on the slopes, but the main roads are bare. The side roads, however, are still covered in snow. All they'd have to do is stay on those surfaces, and no one would be able to track their location."

Sam nodded in agreement. "I have an idea. Ben, tell me what you think about this. Here's another chance for an IR pay off. What if we fly an infrared flight, high enough to avoid detection? Can you spot chalets that are being used or occupied, or vehicles, or—"

"It would be an easy task, with snow still on the ground," Ben interrupted. Excitement swirled with hope as he caught onto Sam's idea. "I can tell you instantly which chalets are being used and can identify any vehicle with a warm engine. Let's get a flight. The heat signatures will show day or night under these conditions. We'll have to do some IR detective work."

The flight was ordered, and its mission was completed at 9:20 that night. The imagery was delivered to Ben at his office an hour later. He rushed into the engineering room, clicked on a light table, and rolled out the film. He quickly found the ski runs, and directly below them, spotted the driveways to each of the ski chalets and A-frames. He searched the entire roll of imagery before shoving his chair back, irritation gnawing his soul. *I can't see anything out of the ordinary!* he thought, feeling defeated. Deciding to look again, he grabbed the film and slowly scanned each corner, crossing every area.

"Anything of use showing up?" John asked as he and Sam entered the room.

"Nothing so far," Ben admitted. "I've gone through the film once already. I'm going over it again now. It's good quality, there isn't much of it. Oh…wait a minute. I see something I missed on the edge of this image. Come over here and look at this. See that roofline? It's the last ski chalet cabin on the far west side of the lower ski run. See, right there!" He pointed to a tiny white blur next to the chalet. "There isn't much showing out of the ordinary from the roofs because no one is up around that cabin—there's no one firing up their furnaces and fireplaces. But right there," he pointed to an engine's tiny heat signature, "I'll bet you this is a truck or car motor that hasn't completely cooled off yet. Springtime or not, it's still in the twenties up there. You need to send the deputies to that ski cabin right there. Don't waste another minute," Ben urged.

****

It was 10:30 at night before Gianne realized she could no longer resist using the bathroom. Her ribs screamed in pain, but she forced herself to call out. "Hey. Hey! Where are you, cowboy? I need to use the bathroom. You've had me here for a day and half the night. I gotta go, and I gotta go now!!"

Her gaze flew to the door as she listened to the approaching footsteps.

"You must think I'm a fool. Why should I let you up for anything?" the kidnapper's voice sounded from outside.

"Listen, small brains, I'm thirsty, I'm hungry, and I gotta pee. I gotta pee right now, and you aren't going to like what else I have to do!"

Gianne watched as her idiot captor sauntered into the cabin, still decked out in his costume. The Long Ranger sneered as he walked past her and into the bathroom. After ensuring he'd checked it thoroughly, he walked back to her. "Here's the deal, sweet cheeks. There's no way out of that bathroom, so don't try any funny business. There aren't any guns or knives for you to grab, or anything else sharp. Get your sorry butt up on your own, go back there, and do your thing."

Gianne looked at him in shock. "My hands are tied, and I have a broken rib! How is that supposed to work, you moron?"

Getting madder by the moment, he rushed toward her, startling her. "That's your friggin' problem. That's the deal. If you can get your wimpy butt up and go to the bathroom, good for you. Otherwise, tough luck. If you foul this place up, I'll throw your sorry, stinking bum out in the snow!" With that, he went into the kitchen and sat on a bar stool.

Biting back the pain, Gianne scooted to the opposite edge of the kitchen island. Through sweat, tears, and much effort, she managed to get to her feet. Her legs were shaky, and she willed them to hold her. Staring at the creep, she stuck out her tongue and headed to the bathroom, stumbling past the wood stove and through the bathroom door. Switching the light switch on with her nose, she proceeded to close the door.

"Leave the door open," he yelled. "You got nothing I want to see anyway. Get it done and get back out here!"

In tears, Gianne managed to perch herself up on the toilet and, in a rush of relief, peed what she was sure would be a gallon. When she'd finished, she sat there thinking about what she should do next. She looked around the beautifully tiled bathroom and something clicked in her mind. She instantly knew what to do.

She pulled off a huge wad of toilet paper, then grabbed a washcloth from the sink and shoved everything into the toilet. Slowly, she got off the seat, wrestled with her zipper, and flushed the toilet. She held the lever down and watched as the whole mess got stuck.

With a smile, she watched the water fill the bowl, then flushed it again. The toilet backed up, and water ran onto the floor.

"Hey, dufus," she yelled. "Something's wrong here. That toilet is plugged, and water is running everywhere. You'd better come have a look; in case you need to use it yourself." Gianne stepped out of the bathroom and walked toward the tile wood stove. Turning her back toward her captor, she shielded her next move with her body. She quickly lifted the fire extinguisher from its mount. As her kidnapper rushed into the bathroom, she pulled the pin on the extinguisher and turned toward the bathroom door.

She watched as the anger transformed his face. Turning from the overflowing toilet, he rushed toward her. "You dumb cow! You plugged that up on purpose—"

Before he could finish the sentence, Gianne pulled the pin and pressed the discharge lever, spraying the contents into his eyes. While the cowboy shouted every cuss word known to man, she cradled the canister like a softball bat and hit him on the side of the head with a loud *thwack!* He moaned and stumbled back. As he started to fall, she hit him again, swinging hard. He slumped to the ground and blood seeped from his ears and nose.

Surveying the cabinets in the kitchen, Gianne ran to the island and pulled drawers out as fast as she could until she found a large pair of kitchen shears in the third one. She grabbed them, pointed the shears toward her stomach, and ordered her stiff fingers to cut the tight cords binding her wrists together. After what seemed like hours, she was finally free. Glancing toward the door, she grabbed one of the ski parkas hanging by the skis and ran out into the night.

Chapter 44

Adrenaline burst through Gianne as she raced out the chalet's front door. Spotting the van, she darted toward it, hopping inside and searching for the keys. Cursing when she found nothing, she fought back her panic. *I'm not going back inside to look for them,* she thought. She wrapped herself tightly in the parka, climbed out of the van, and ran down the driveway as fast as she could. As she ran, her thoughts plagued her. What if someone else was involved? Could her captor have lifted her and carried her off by himself? Determination rode her adrenaline as she continued to run. The safest thing she could think of doing was to put as much distance as possible between herself and the idiot she'd knocked cold.

As she approached the long driveway's end, she saw headlights approaching. *Oh no, who could that be?* She jumped off the road and hid behind a tall, stone house marker that displayed the neighbors' name and house number. As the Jeep approached the driveway, it slowed down, creeping toward her. Panic seized her as fear draped its cold shawl around her shoulders. As soon as the vehicle passed, Gianne realized she couldn't afford to pass up the chance at getting help. "Stop!" she screamed, showing herself. "Help, please! Stop!" She ran toward the Jeep, waving her arms. Relief flooded her as she recognized the Jeep as one from the county sheriff's office.

The deputy slammed on the brakes, opened the door, and stepped out. When Gianne fell toward him, he caught her, stabilizing her against his chest.

"I'm so glad to see you!" she blurted. Her panic shoved a torrent of tears past her eyelids. "I've never been so scared in my life. There's a guy up there. He *kidnapped me!* I have no clue who he is. He wears a cowboy hat and a Halloween mask—I never saw his face completely. He kicked me," her hand went to her ribs as the deputy's eyes grew large. "I think he broke a rib. I hit him as hard as I could— twice—with a fire extinguisher, and then I ran like mad. I think he might be dead." Gianne gathered herself and stood by the deputy's Jeep as the tears streamed down her face. "I just want to go home," she sobbed. "I want to see Ben and the twins. I cannot believe this happened to me! Why did that guy do this?"

Keeping his eye on her, the deputy radioed back to Sheriff Sims that Gianne was with him, and that she was okay. He explained everything she'd told him, relaying her desire for her husband.

Ben, listening to the radio transmission in John's office, was flooded with relief to know his wife had been found. That relief was soon replaced by fury. A fury that burned within his soul. Hot tears

411

stung his eyes as he narrowed his eyes at John. "How much can one family take? Why would anyone kidnap my wife and cart her off to the mountains?" His eyes went cold. "I'm gonna kill him."

"Ben, go to the hospital and be with your wife," John said sternly. "She needs you right now. Let me handle that guy." When Ben opened his mouth to argue, John pointed at him. "Don't make me send an escort with you!"

Glaring, Ben obeyed. By the time he arrived at Goldville Memorial, Gianne was already being seen by the doctor. A nurse walked him into her room and his jaw tensed when his wife saw him and burst into tears.

"He kidnapped me!" she sobbed. "Why did he do that? Who was he? Ben! Why did this happen?!"

Before Ben could answer, his parents rushed in with the twins, who immediately ran to Gianne. "Mommy, Mommy, are you okay? You were on the news. We were so scared. Mommy, are you alright?"

Working to hide her tears, Gianne put on a smile. "I am now; just ready to go home. The doctor said I'm fine—it's just a bruised rib. You both can make me breakfast tomorrow, okay? No school in the morning, how's that?" She offered a half smile, hoping they couldn't read her terror behind it.

****

When morning dawned, Gianne woke in a panic, thinking she was still living her nightmare. It took Ben thirty minutes of soothing her for her to realize she was safely by his side. She'd hardly slept at all. Her ribs had made it impossible to find a comfortable position, and her mind had played back her kidnapping on a non-stop reel of terror.

When he felt she was calm, Ben rose to make coffee. He brought in two cups and handed her one before settling in beside her. "Well, guess what? You'll never believe the reason this nightmare happened. The guy who kidnapped you was Adam Rolldy. Can you believe that? He's been hidden from public view for the last six months—ever since his dad was sent to prison. They say he's been on drugs, lost thirty-five pounds, and that few would recognize him. He's not been well—mentally or physically—since his father went to the slammer. He and his sister drugged you and carried you out in our rug."

Gianne took a sip of coffee then asked him to tell her what else he knew.

"For some reason, they were ticked off that I referred to their murdering old man as a cowboy terrorist, and they considered me partially to blame for his being in jail. Kidnapping you would somehow make everything even-steven in their books. But it's over now. There's nothing else to worry about. They were the only ones involved. You're safe."

Gianne could not stop the tears from sliding down her face as she laughed. "I just keep asking myself, over and over—how can this much happen to two people in less than a year and a half? Aren't we lucky? I think we should write a book." She laughed. "No one would believe us."

Chapter 45

For as long as Ben and Gianne had been married, their happy place had been sitting on either the front or back porch of Ben's family home at Sisu Bay. Ben looked at Gianne and smiled. "Well, hon, can you believe we made it this far? The twins are starting college and look at us! We're not exactly where I thought we would be after twenty-six years of marriage, but I'm happy. Sitting here on my folks' back porch, enjoying another Sisu Bay sunrise over the Coast Range... These sunrises still make everything worthwhile, especially being here and seeing the folks so healthy."

Gianne looked around the porch and laughed. "Remember way back when I said we should write a book? I was only joking. I had no idea you would really end up writing an award-winning novel. First the book, then the movie. I still can't believe it! And wow, look where we are now!"

"The best thing now is my early retirement. I don't hold any grudges about being let go after twenty-five years of service. The budget cuts had to happen—I know that. I'm grateful for the retirement pay. It may be a reduced paycheck, but now I'm free to really enjoy my teaching position at the college. Teaching has always been my Walter Mitty, other-life, dream come truem and I couldn't be happier. That stupid book that I—well, we—wrote, along with the movie rights, have paid us enough to let us do whatever we want. We can travel, afford the twins' college, and I am especially happy seeing you enjoying the things you have been doing these past years."

Gianne thought for a while and smiled. "Yeah, you know, after my cowboy kidnapping adventure, I was really impressed with the sheriff's response and professionalism. The smartest thing I ever did afterward, was to ask Sheriff Sims if they needed any help. What a stroke of luck, as now, ten years later, I still enjoy being the Sheriff Department's administrative assistant. Nice pay, nice reward, and nice people to work with."

Ben smiled. "You know, after all that has happened, from being safe during Vietnam, to surviving that first year or two with the Forest Service, to everything that happened to you and me—I'm proud of what I—I mean, WE—have accomplished. I no longer mind letting people know I'm proud of being a Vietnam Vet. I don't really think about my time there. Probably because so much has happened to us and more important things have crept into the cranium." He chuckled.

"You know," Gianne commented, "I'm glad your decades-old piloting fiasco was cleared up. I never did peg Dean Schmidt as a drug runner. Never felt right that everyone had labeled him as one."

"Exactly," Ben agreed. "I was glad to learn the truth. I could never believe he was involved in anything criminal. Those drug runners threatening his family explains why he did what he did. I'm so glad the DEA and FBI figured it out and cleared his name. It meant the world to his family to know he was always as they thought he was—a good father and grandfather."

Ben and Gianne sat for a while longer, enjoying their morning coffee, their favorite Norwegian coffee cake, and the rest of another spectacular orange and gold sunrise. Like usual, they would be joined by Ben's folks when the rest of the breakfast preparations were done.

Out of nowhere, Gianne sat upright in her chair and pointed. "L-look at that b-black Bronco coming down the street. Doesn't that bring back some bad memories?"

Ben laughed. "Yeah. It's funny now, looking back, but at least it's not a Suburban."

The Bronco quickly approached and veered closer, nearing the front gate and walkway. Suddenly, a rear passenger window opened, and a voice shouted, "Tongo gringo, el cartel nunca olvida!" Out of that same back window, an Uzi was thrust through the opening and opened fire, sending a hail of bullets onto the Hautanan's porch.

The gunman sprayed bullets back and forth across the porch and wall.

Ben's mother ran to the back door, screaming. "Ben! Gianne! What was that? Who was that? Are you okay?" She rushed onto the porch and gasped in horror at the sight of her children lying face down in a pool of their own blood.

****

John Holden looked over at his wife and smiled as they enjoyed their morning coffee, watching the same beautiful Sisu Bay sunrise. Something on the street caught their eyes and they glanced up to see a black Bronco nearing their mailbox...

The End.

About the Author

For many years during my 36-year Forest Service career, I was a writer/editor and later a contributing editor for an extensive Arizona wildfire story titled "The Monster Reared His Ugly Head." I wrote numerous news and web stories, special feature articles and additionally I continue learning to be an accomplished photographer having travelled to over 25 countries around the world.

When I started my first novel, my goal was to write a screenplay. I decided quickly I may not have the patience to write a screenplay. But now I think I do, and I hope to adapt this new, rewritten novel, A Forest of Fear as a screenplay.

As a 75-year-old first time published author from Meridian, Idaho I was thrilled to have my very first novel published and now I have more to write. And so, I recently completed my second novel, a revision of the first which is now doubled in length. Two years later, I had a unique collection of my first ever free-verse poetry published along with some photos I have taken during my travels.

I was born and raised in Clatsop County Oregon in the Seaside-Astoria area graduating from Seaside High School and later from Clatsop Community College with an Assoc. degree in Forestry Technology. I was drafted into the Army and then trained as an imagery interpreter at Ft. Holabird, MD Military Intelligence School. I then served in Vietnam for parts of 1967 and 1968 including during the infamous Tet offensive.

www.ingramcontent.com/pod-product-compliance
Lightning Source LLC
Chambersburg PA
CBHW051057030726
47504CB00006B/1672